HIDDEN IN THE DARK

BOOKS BY H.K. CHRISTIE

VAL COSTA SERIES

Gone by Dawn

Don't Make a Sound

THRILLERS

A Permanent Mark

The Neighbor Two Doors Down

MARTINA MONROE SERIES

Crashing Down

What She Left

If She Ran

All She Wanted

Why She Lied

Secrets She Kept

What She Found

How She Fell

Her Last Words

Who She Was

How She Escaped

Lies She Told

Echoes of Her

SELENA BAILEY SERIES

Not Like Her

One In Five

On The Rise

Go With Grace

Flawless

H.K. CHRISTIE

HIDDEN IN THE DARK

bookouture

Published by Bookouture in 2024

An imprint of Storyfire Ltd.
Carmelite House
50 Victoria Embankment
London EC4Y oDZ

www.bookouture.com

The authorised representative in the EEA is Hachette Ireland
8 Castlecourt Centre
Dublin 15 D15 XTP3
Ireland
(email: info@hbgi.ie)

ISBN: 978-1-83525-916-0
eBook ISBN: 978-1-83525-915-3

For Barbara

ONE

STEPHANIE

Peering over from the open-concept kitchen, I watched my two boys—my husband and my son—playing video games in the living room as if their lives depended on it. Seeing the two of them together warmed my soul. I turned back to the stove and placed the lid back on the pot of rice, turning the heat down to low. I called out to the boys, "Dinner is almost ready."

Michael said, "Mom, just a few more minutes, okay?"

I couldn't help but smile. At twelve, he was the quintessential boy—loved getting dirty, playing sports and video games, and didn't like cleaning his room or doing his homework. But we were working on that. Not that he wasn't a smart kid. He just preferred to be active rather than sit still reading a book or working out math problems. Mike assured me that he had been exactly the same when he was a kid, so I shouldn't worry too much about him.

"Okay, just a few more," I said, giving in. "But we need to eat pretty soon because you have to get ready for the tournament."

In addition to sports, he took karate. It was Mike who had really pushed for it, insisting that his son needed to know how to defend himself. We enrolled him in karate lessons when he was five years old. Tonight he had a big tournament, and he needed to eat early to have enough time to digest and avoid having an upset stomach while competing.

Ready to plate each of our dinners, I stopped. It felt like there was something missing—flowers. I could pick a bunch from the backyard. Spring was in full bloom, and it would be nice to have a colorful centerpiece while we enjoyed dinner together as a family. With Michael involved in so many activities, we rarely had time to sit down together and have a nice dinner without rushing.

Hurrying toward the backyard, I grabbed my clippers and headed over to the patch of daisies I'd planted. After a few snips, I bundled the red, yellow, and pink blooms and admired the yard. There were planters of spring flowers and succulents along with a lawn we'd put in so Michael would have a place to play. The massive pines towered our property line. It was magical. When Mike was trying to convince me to leave the city and move up here, I was reluctant at first, but when I saw the forest and lakes I was sold. We moved here right after we got married. No regrets.

Inside the kitchen, I arranged the flowers somewhat haphazardly in a jelly jar, placing them in the center of the dining table before plating our dinners and setting them on the table.

Everything looked perfect. I turned toward the living room, where Mike and Michael each occupied a sofa, completely absorbed in the video game. I called out, "Okay, boys, dinner's ready. It's going to get cold if you don't hurry up, and, Michael, you don't want an upset stomach during the tournament."

Michael started to object, but Mike said, "C'mon, Michael. You need to eat."

He frowned but paused the game. They made their way over to the table and sat down.

"Chicken, rice, broccoli?" Michael stared at me as if I was offering him doggie kibble.

"Your sensei said your dinner needed to be protein-rich with carbohydrates and vegetables so you don't have anything weighing you down," I said, knowing he wouldn't disobey his sensei.

I could tell by Michael's attitude that the teenage years, including the teenage attitude, weren't too far away. Mike sat next to me and gave me a kiss on the cheek. "It looks great," he said.

"Thanks." I always tried to eat a healthy diet and live a healthy lifestyle as I wanted to be around for as long as possible, and I wanted the same for Mike. He didn't always agree with that approach, though. Pizza was his favorite food, and he insisted we have it at least once a week. Still, I tried, simply wanting to keep my family together for as long as I could, although I knew that Michael wouldn't live in this house forever —he'd be off to college or whatever else he ended up doing, maybe going into pro sports, and I'd no longer have any control over his lifestyle.

As we began to eat, Michael said, "So they said that there are some real tough competitors coming."

"Really? Where are they coming from?" I asked.

"All the surrounding counties. It's a big deal."

I raised my eyebrows, concerned he may have the jitters. "Are you nervous?"

He shook his head. "Nah. What's the worst that can happen?"

It was a good way of looking at things.

A knock on the front door followed by the ring of the bell took me by surprise. We didn't get many random visitors; perhaps it was a salesperson. That is, if door-to-door salespeople still existed. I pushed my chair back to get up, but Mike said, "I'll get it."

He stood up and went to answer the door. I heard the door creak open, followed by a voice I had never heard before. Moments later, Mike walked slowly back into the dining room, stricken with panic. What I saw next sent a wave of terror through me as my heart raced with fear for both my son and my husband.

TWO

VAL

The fierce determination in my mother's eyes told me that today was the day. As her physical therapist gently lifted her hands, Mom scrunched up her face and mustered all her strength to lift herself from her wheelchair in a jerky motion. She placed her hands on the walker for the first time since her stroke eight months earlier. With my hand on my chest, I watched what seemed like a miracle. Although I knew it wasn't a divine act, the effort spoke volumes. Mom had endured relentless physical therapy sessions and countless doctor appointments. I knew she had been in pain, and what she had just accomplished might not seem miraculous to others, but I knew it had taken every ounce of strength within her.

"I knew you could do it," I said, my voice filled with emotion.

She glanced over at me and smiled.

Her physical therapist added, "That's right, Elizabeth. I knew you could do it, too. I've never met a more determined person in my life."

Mom chuckled at that, her spirit undimmed by the struggle.

"Enough of that. How do I get myself walking again? Standing is one thing, but I can't just stand around all day."

Her physical therapist and I exchanged a smile. Mom found it extremely difficult being wheelchair-bound and having to depend on other people. She was a former sheriff and single mother—asking for help wasn't her specialty. As a tough and independent woman, recovering from her stroke hadn't been easy, not just physically but mentally as well. She was usually optimistic but I'd witnessed her bad days where she seemed to be frustrated with the whole world. Not that she'd ever complained directly. But I knew firsthand what it was like to feel mentally ready when your body wasn't.

"Okay, Elizabeth, take your time," her therapist said encouragingly.

I stood by, watching as my mother took her first step. Pride swelled within me. It almost reminded me of when my son Harrison had taken his first step. His father and I had clapped, awed at the sight of our little boy, previously so dependent, walking on his own. This seemed nearly as monumental. After Mom's stroke, the doctors weren't sure if she would ever walk again. But I knew if anyone could overcome such an obstacle it was Mom. However, observing it now was something else entirely.

Realizing I had to share this moment, I quickly texted Harrison.

Grandma took her first steps today!

Harrison texted back right away.

Awesome! Tell Grandma I think she's incredible and that I love her. Love you too, Mom.

My heart was full. So much had changed in the last nine

months. Before then, like my mother, I had once believed I was unstoppable. But when my life was almost cut short, I understood the frustration of knowing I wasn't invincible after all. I'd been knocked down before, but when I had a hunch late at night about the Bear, a serial killer my team and I had been hunting, and chose to investigate on my own, I learned how quickly my sense of self could be shattered. My instincts were correct about the Bear's whereabouts but not about how he'd be hiding in the shadows, still as a cat, and got the drop on me. Thankfully, the team found me before I became another one of his kills, but not without leaving a mark—mentally and physically. It was then my world took a drastic turn. Forced to stay home, due to my injuries and mandated leave from the FBI, I had decided to retire when Mom had her stroke and needed someone to take care of her.

Life back in Red Rose County had been anything but dull. Between taking care of Mom and helping solve a few murders with the Red Rose County Sheriff's department, I hadn't missed my career in the FBI or the East Coast where I had spent most of my adult life.

The last case I worked on with the Red Rose County Sheriff's department had been the murder of a beloved school teacher, Claire Nelson, a complicated case. Mom's girlfriends had stepped in to help so that I could devote more time to the investigation. But life had been quiet since we closed the case seven months earlier.

With extra time on my hands, I had devoted most of my energy to trying to locate the Bear, which consisted mostly of me pestering Kieran, my old boss in the FBI, and trying to determine the identity of the anonymous "admirer" that had sent me notes after I had helped solve the Scarlett Douglas missing person case and the Claire Nelson murder. I had plenty of theories but no proof. The admirer could be the Bear, someone local, or an overzealous person who had followed my investigations and wanted to be an investigator themselves. But considering each note was signed with the letter "S", matching the one the Bear had carved into my chest, I was pretty sure I knew the identity of my admirer. However, there were still some aspects of the notes which remained unsolved, so I couldn't be one hundred percent sure.

Kieran and I had kept in touch, and he'd told me I was welcome to come back to the FBI, but I had no intention of doing that. The time I was spending with my mom was more necessary than I realized; it was something I hadn't known I needed or wanted, but now I understood it was where I belonged.

I didn't know how many years I had left with my mother, but I didn't want to spend them chasing serial killers across the country—a pursuit I surprisingly didn't miss. *Not really.*

My only son was away at school, his first year at MIT, so I'd found myself thinking there wasn't much left for me in DC and I decided to put my house on the market. There was no doubt about it, my life had changed, and here I was back in Red Rose County.

Turning my attention back to the room, I noticed my mother had taken a few more steps. "I told Harrison you took steps. He says, 'awesome. You're incredible and he loves you.'"

She stopped in her tracks and looked up, grinning. "Tell him thank you and I love him right back."

"I will."

As much as my move back to Red Rose County felt right, there were still so many unknowns. I was only forty-six and retired from the FBI, but I couldn't possibly stay retired forever. I had too much energy and life left in me. I hadn't worked in seven months, except on my own personal investigation into the Bear. The FBI's trail on him had gone cold. It appeared that his pattern, to kill four people in a state and then leave, had ended. But it was also incomplete, because I had got away from him in

Nevada, leaving only three victims. I knew he wasn't going to give up that easily and thought maybe he'd find a new victim to complete the pattern, but if he had, that fourth victim had never been found. It was like he'd disappeared into thin air, but nobody vanishes without a trace.

My gut instinct told me he was holed up somewhere, just waiting to attack because that was who he was. A tiger didn't change its stripes so easily. If my experience had taught me anything, it was that he was planning something new, something different, yet to be seen. Unpredictability was a terrible trait in a serial killer, but unfortunately that meant there wasn't much I could do to find him. Knowing he could find me kept me on edge. The only physical description I had of the Bear was that he had piercing blue eyes that I'd seen outlined by his black ski mask. Since my captivity, every man I'd met or passed on the sidewalk with blue eyes made my heart race as I frantically assessed their height and build to determine if it was him. None of them were. That didn't stop those eyes from haunting my frequent nightmares.

With no signs of the Bear and no more messages from the admirer, my life seemed to be on the right track again—my son was happy and healthy, and my mother was making real progress in physical therapy and walking again. I decided it was time to try and enjoy the peace and quiet for as long as I could. Because I knew better than most how your whole life could be turned upside down in a flash.

THREE

VAL

The last of the dinner dishes were done, so I turned around and said, "Mom, what do you say we have dessert to celebrate you taking your first steps today?"

"Oh, honey, I don't need a celebration."

Julie, Mom's friend and frequent visitor, chimed in, "Are you sure? Today was a big deal!"

My mom shook her head. "Nonsense. I know it was an accomplishment that I was able to take eight steps today. I'm sure tomorrow there'll be more, and more the day after that. I don't need to fill myself with ice cream every time I make any progress."

Julie shrugged. "If it was me, I'd be having ice cream to mark every milestone. Life is too short. You never know when it's gonna be your last day."

Mom said, "That's *cheerful*."

"It's true though, isn't it?" Julie chuckled, and we joined in.

"Can I at least offer anybody some wine?" I asked as I took a mental note to stock up on ice cream at the grocery store. Julie had the right idea; life could be short or long but nobody knew which way it would go, so why not enjoy everything we could while we still could? Plus, I liked ice cream and I knew Mom did too.

"I suppose I could have a glass, just half a pour. That could be our celebration—of many, many more," my mother said, upbeat.

Julie said, "Me too. But make it a full glass."

"Me three," Diane said. She was another of Mom's friends who loved to keep us all company.

"Coming right up." I turned back to the kitchen and grabbed a bottle of red I'd opened the day before and filled four glasses—only half a glass for Mom, as instructed. We were celebrating, even if Mom didn't think it was that big of a deal. It was significant that she was one step closer to getting her old life back.

It made me wonder if I needed to reevaluate my own life. I was super fit and ready to get out there. But where was there? I was helping Mom with the gardening, which was surprisingly good exercise. Mom did what she could from her wheelchair, like sowing seeds in pots, watering plants and of course telling me what to do. But I needed to be more active.

With the wine handed out, I sat down at the dining table and asked, "What are you all chatting about?"

"Diane and I were talking about going to a club in the next town over," Julie said.

"Like a nightclub?" I asked with surprise.

"No. Not really. It's like a seniors' club. Maybe see if there are any new friends we can make. Elizabeth, do you want to come with us?" Julie asked.

"Are you seriously looking for men?" Mom asked.

"Men. Women. Friends. They do dances at the community center in Redmond."

"I'm not really in dancing shape—not yet, anyway," she said, sadly. It broke my heart just a little. I hoped her dancing days would return soon. Mom was never one to stand still for long, until the stroke.

"Oh, Elizabeth, I know you can move in that chair and you'll be dancing in no time."

They chuckled and continued to discuss their plans.

I never tired of watching my mom with her two close friends, Julie and Diane. They had originally met when they joined the Red Hat Society, a group of women who wanted to live life to the fullest, and they had become lifelong friends. They'd helped so much with Mom's recovery that they were almost permanent fixtures around here—I was surprised they hadn't organized a room so that they could stay over. They were a lot of fun and good to have around, as they really lifted Mom's spirits. I enjoyed hanging out with them as well as my own friends.

Lucy, a researcher I'd met working at the sheriff's department, had been pretty busy since she and Jonathan became an official couple, Sally, the county's medical examiner, and I hung out quite a bit. When she wasn't busy working, that is. I was starting to feel like I needed something new to occupy my time. A hobby? A job?

Mom was gradually becoming less dependent on me, and without an active case to work on, I was beginning to wonder what else I was going to do here in Red Rose County. Not that I thought I should go back to the FBI—I mean, sure, I'd given it some thought, but I really believed I needed to stay here with Mom at least for the foreseeable future.

There were plenty of jobs at the sheriff's department, but I wasn't sure that was quite right for me, not yet anyway. Who knows, maybe I'd discover a whole new career. I could do private investigations or security. Or maybe I'd discover a new talent.

My cell phone buzzed. It was Brady. He was a childhood friend that had moved back to our hometown a few years earlier, following his divorce. We'd been close in high school but drifted apart over the years until I'd moved home to Red Rose County and worked cases with him at the sheriff's department. Everyone assumed that we'd be dating by now, but he hadn't made a move, and neither had I. But I was beginning to feel that spark every time we were together. Not that we'd gone on a date. More like a friend hang. Hiking. Dinner and drinks out with some of the gang from the sheriff's department. With a flutter in my belly, I answered, "Hi Brady."

"Are you busy?"

My curiosity was piqued. "Nope. What's up?"

"Can I stop by? There's something I want to talk to you about."

My heart rate sped up, and I tried to play it cool. Mom and her friends looked at me suspiciously. "Sure, you can come by. We're just chatting over a little wine."

"Okay, I'll be there in ten."

"See you then."

What could he want to talk about? Was it personal? Was he going to declare his feelings for me? Was I even ready for that?

"Who was that?" Mom asked.

"It was Brady. He's going to stop by. He said there's something he wants to talk to me about."

Julie's eyes grew wide and she pursed her lips. "Ooh, Val. He's going to declare his undying love for you. I just know it!"

I felt my cheeks flush. "Oh, I doubt that." He wouldn't, would he? Not right here in the house in front of Mom and her friends.

Mom said, "I don't know, Val. He does drop by an awful lot to check on me, even though he spends most of the time looking at you."

Diane said, "I've seen it too."

Mom clasped her hands together. "Finally!"

Stunned by their statements, I didn't know what to say. Yes, they'd been pushing me to ask him out for months, but it didn't feel quite right yet. Was now the right time? This was all silly. He could be stopping by for any number of reasons. "I'm not so..."

Mom tipped her head at me. "We know you like him too, Val."

I felt sixteen again. "We're just friends."

The ladies looked at each other before collapsing in a fit of giggles.

A knock on the door silenced them. I shook my head and made my way over to the door. Glancing at the screen to make sure it was Brady, I opened the door.

"Hey," he said, a little flushed. He was in his sheriff's deputy uniform, clearly having come here straight from the station. His five-o'clock shadow was sexy with his mussed hair.

"Hey. C'mon in."

He stepped inside. "Sounds like there's a party going on."

"Mom, Julie, and Diane. There's wine."

With a charming smile, he said, "Sounds fun. I'm jealous. I should probably say hi to them before we get to talking."

Nodding, with butterflies in my belly, we walked quietly into the kitchen and I caught a whiff of his sandalwood cologne. Wanting more, I attempted to play it cool in front of the ladies.

"Hi, Brady!" Mom exclaimed.

They were all smiles and knowing glances.

"Ladies, good to see you. I hate to interrupt your night, but I was hoping to steal Val away from you for a bit."

"No problem. Steal Val away anytime," Julie said with a grin.

To save Brady from their innuendo, I said, "Okay, we're going to talk in the other room. Try and behave while I'm gone."

They responded with laughter.

Looking at Brady, I said, "Let's go into the living room."

He followed behind. Out of earshot of the matchmakers, I said, "What's up?"

"There's been a double murder."

No declaration of love then. With a little disappointment and a spike of adrenaline, I said, "What do you know so far?"

"Patrol discovered three victims in their home. Two dead. One on the way to the hospital with what appears to be a gunshot wound to the head."

"Where?"

"Rosedale. About five minutes from here."

That was a little too close to home. "Who are the victims? Who's at the scene?"

"Responding officer and paramedics. CSI is on the way. I'm on my way there. The sheriff wanted me to be the lead, but after a discussion, I was hoping you'd join me. The sheriff is all for it and said he's got the budget for a contract for you. Same terms as the Nelson case. What do you say?"

Was this what I needed right now? I still hadn't caught the Bear and was no closer to finding out the identity of my admirer. And the media loved to explain that an ex-FBI agent was helping on the case, gaining me unwanted attention. Was it wise to put myself in the spotlight?

"I'm in."

His dazzling grin appeared. "Awesome. I'm happy for you to take the lead."

I liked to be in charge, but Brady was no slouch. He had skills. "I'll lead, but let's work it together."

"I'll be second."

Filled with purpose, I said, "Let me tell Mom and then we can head out."

Back in the kitchen, the ladies watched us with eager anticipation. "Brady's asked me to help out on a new case. It's a big one. I need to go to the scene, so I could be out all night."

Slightly deflated, Julie said, "I brought my overnight bag."

Diane said, "I've always got one. We'll stay with Elizabeth."

Mom said, "It's settled. You two go and do what you do best."

"Okay, I'll see you later." I could barely contain my excitement at having a new case to work on, with Brady, and not being grilled about my non-existent love life.

"Bye, ladies. Have a good night."

"Bye, Brady," Mom cooed.

"Go get the bad guys!" Diane sang out.

That was exactly what we intended to do.

FOUR

THE SECRET ADMIRER

I'd been watching Valerie's home for the last half hour. I'd parked my car down the street, far enough away to avoid attracting any attention or showing up on her state-of-the-art security system, about which I knew every detail. I was more than familiar with its every camera and motion sensor by now. The neighborhood, cloaked in the dim twilight, was a perfect cover. Tall pines, thick brush, and tall grasses provided plenty of hiding places for someone like me, someone who didn't want to be seen. Not yet anyhow. I relished the thought of being so close, enjoying the thrill of anticipation and the fantasy of when Valerie and I could be together again.

I'd been away, taking care of things that couldn't be ignored. But I was free now. Free to be with Valerie. Savoring the scene before me, I could see Valerie's silhouette through the window in the kitchen.

Valerie was inside, likely with her dear mother, Elizabeth. Perhaps those two old women who visited were there too. It wouldn't be easy to creep inside with a house full of women, but from what I had observed, they were older and less of a threat. Especially Elizabeth, confined to her wheelchair—once a formidable sheriff, now just another obstacle I could easily over-come if necessary. Valerie, strong and exquisite like her mother, was worth taking a few risks for. But taking unnecessary risks was foolish. I could be patient.

The thought of getting a glimpse of her set my pulse racing. Maybe I could throw a small stone at the window, just enough to draw her out to the front porch, in order for me to see her reaction, to see that luminous skin, those flowing brown locks, that striking physique. But as I crouched deeper into the shad-ows, my plan was interrupted.

A Red Rose County sheriff's SUV pulled up in front of the Costa residence. My heart sank. It was Deputy Brady Tanner, the annoying sidekick who always seemed to be too close to her for my liking. Had they gotten closer since I had left town? Romantic? It gnawed at me, the thought of him being near her when I couldn't be.

What was he doing here? It was getting late. Too late for a casual visit. I watched as he hurried to the front door, the door opened, and he entered without hesitation. My mind raced. I didn't need another pair of eyes scanning the area, especially not law enforcement. I quickly retreated, slipping back to my car. Once inside, I removed my cap and mask, feeling the cool air on my flushed face. Disappointment and frustration mingled, but I knew I would get my chance to see all of her. Maybe in the daylight, where she could be on full display. Until then, I would bide my time, waiting for the perfect moment to see my dear Valerie again.

FIVE

VAL

Brady drove down the tree-lined street with modest homes and large yards until the flashing lights from the patrol vehicles marked the spot. There were at least a dozen vehicles in front of the property, half of which were department issue. Brady parked in front of the one-story ranch-style home surrounded by towering redwoods. He turned to me, and said, "Are you ready for this?"

I thought I was ready. Did I not seem ready? Could he tell the nightmares had persisted? The dark circles under my eyes must have been a giveaway. I said, "Let's do it." And with that I climbed out of the SUV into the crisp spring air. It was a gorgeous night. Pity it had been spoiled by a murder. We approached the scene, trekking across the green lawn, toward the front of the house. Crime scene tape barricaded the front door, where a sheriff's deputy stood guard alongside a few others I knew from previous cases—including the sheriff, Allan, and Baker. On the drive over, Brady and I had discussed the preliminary plan for the case and who we'd like on the team. Baker and Allan were included in our top picks since we'd worked with them on the Nelson murder investigation. However, our plan was a guesstimate, seeing as we weren't exactly sure what we were walking into yet.

The sheriff said, "Thanks so much for coming, Val."

Despite the sheriff's multiple full-time job offers, I didn't feel ready to commit. But a paid contract for the duration of the case was just right. "No problem, Kingston. Glad to help." With a wave to the guys, I said, "Hey, fellas. What do we have in there?"

Allan said, "Kingston and I just got here. We were waiting for the two of you to go in, to avoid too much traffic in the crime scene."

"Who called it in? Who was the responding officer?" I asked.

Baker said, "I was the responding officer."

"When did you get here?"

"About thirty minutes ago. I responded to a request for a welfare check. The child had a karate tournament tonight. When he didn't show up, one of the moms on the team called the mother, the father, and the kid's cell phone but got nothing. So, she called one of the neighbors—a parent of one of their kids' friends—and asked them to pop over and see if they were still home. When the neighbor saw the front door open, she called out their names. No reply. Says she got a spooky vibe and decided to call us to do a welfare check."

"Where's the neighbor now?"

"Next door. We took her statement and sent her home." Glancing at the home, I thought it was far enough away for the neighbor not to have heard anything even if they were home when the crime was being committed.

"What did you find inside?" I asked.

"Two deceased. One with a gunshot wound, with a pulse. Paramedics left about fifteen minutes ago. I did a sweep but there's nobody else in the home. Other than where I found the bodies, the house is fairly undisturbed."

"Who are the victims?"

Baker pulled out his notepad and flipped it open. "Mike and Stephanie Cramer, and their son Michael, aged twelve. Dad works at an auto body shop, mom's a receptionist at a law firm. Lived here fifteen years. Quiet. Neighbors never heard any arguments or saw any signs of trouble."

Twelve? "What can you tell me about the homicides? Who survived?"

Please let it be the kid.

"Stephanie, the mother, is on the way to the hospital, gunshot wound to the head. The other two are deceased. The boy, looks like a gunshot wound to the head. The father, Mike, it's unclear exactly how he died. It's probably better you see for yourself."

Someone had tried to kill an entire family? A child? Why? "Did the neighbor tell you anything else?"

"No."

"We'll need to talk to them again."

Baker nodded. "Understood."

Glancing around at the vehicles surrounding the home, I couldn't see the forensics team van. "What's the ETA on the CSI team?"

"Should be here any minute."

"Who's been inside?"

Baker said, "Just myself and the paramedics. I have to warn you, it's bad." The look on his face told me how bad it was.

We had worked two cases together now, and neither had been great—pretty awful actually. His warning meant this was either just as bad or a different kind of bad. "Anything else we should know before we go in?" I asked.

With a nod, he said, "Brace yourself."

The sheriff said, "Val, Brady. Any resources you need, they're yours."

"Great." Turning to Brady, I said, "Let's go in," before adding, "you too, Baker. I'd like you to talk us through everything you observed from the time you arrived." Considering the paramedics had been there, the scene may have been disturbed by any measures they'd taken to try to save the victim.

Baker said, "Okay. I took pictures while I waited for the paramedics to arrive."

"Well done." We suited up and followed Baker to the porch. He said, "When I got here, the front door was slightly ajar, not completely wide open. No sign of forced entry."

Studying the lock and door frame, I agreed with his assessment.

He stepped inside and I followed. He continued, "The hallway was undisturbed." Studying the floor and walls, I couldn't help but feel a pang in my heart. The walls were adorned with several family photos taken throughout the years. In one, the boy was grinning wildly with two front teeth missing. Each picture told me they'd been a happy family with their natural smiles and a shine in their eyes. Trying to not think of how that family had been destroyed, I focused on the floors and wall for any signs of a struggle. There weren't any spots or marks that would indicate blood splatter or a fight.

We continued down the hall and arrived at the open-plan kitchen, dining room and living room.

"This is the kitchen."

I peered in before I walked around the island. It was clean except for the pots and pans on the stove, still with food inside. Like someone had just prepared dinner. There were no dishes in the sink. If there had been a struggle, it hadn't happened in the kitchen area.

Baker stood waiting, and when I emerged, he led me to the

dining area. "This hasn't been touched by any of us or the paramedics."

Dinner plates with food were on the table, mostly untouched. Chicken, rice, and broccoli. A bouquet of colorful daisies adorned the center of the table. Someone had interrupted their dinner. Likely an unexpected visitor.

So far, no sign of a crime. Eyeing me, Baker said, "Now, brace yourself."

Baker walked over to the living room. Two sofas, a coffee table, TV, and game console. On one sofa, the boy, laying face up, head turned to the side. His skin had turned a pale gray. A small wound in his head indicated a gunshot. Close range. It was odd; he was lying so peacefully, his arms by his side as if posed, or maybe he'd been asleep and his killer positioned him afterwards. How could someone do something like this to a child? I had to look away, as I kept thinking of my own son and that was too much to process. I needed to focus on the scene. I forced my thoughts back to the homicide. If they'd been eating dinner, why would the boy be asleep on the couch? Studying his hands and arms, there were no signs of defensive wounds. My stomach lurched. The child had been executed.

After a few calming breaths to ensure my dinner stayed down, I turned toward the second couch. It had a large brownish-reddish stain but no body. There were footprints marking the carpet, likely from the paramedics.

"Was this where Stephanie, the mom, was found?" I asked, trying to piece together the scene.

Baker said, "Yes. When I came in, I checked for a pulse on the boy, but he was already cold to the touch. Then I went over to the mother. She was warm, with a faint pulse. She looked a lot like the boy—as if sleeping. I called it in before searching the rest of the house."

No sign of the father. Perhaps a family annihilator? The

father drugged his family during dinner, murdered them and then turned the gun on himself? It was sick, but not unheard of.

"Walk me through your next steps."

Baker took a breath and headed down the hall. I noted what looked like blood drops on the carpet. He stopped at the first room on the right but didn't go inside. "I've seen all I need to see in there. I checked for a pulse but I knew he was gone."

Baker stepped back and we entered the room in silence. What I saw was not what I was expecting. Not a family annihilator.

Michael Cramer sat on an office chair with his hands tied behind his back and his ankles tied to the legs of the chair with zip ties. His face was blue and swollen, his neck slashed, his chest and legs appeared as though they had been stabbed. His jeans and T-shirt had multiple entry points and there was a lot of blood. I glanced around at the walls and the surrounding furniture—the desk, the chair, and the bookshelf—was adorned with blood splatter, with a pool underneath Michael Cramer.

I leaned forward to get a better look at his face.

Whoever had done this was angry, brutal, unforgiving. My preliminary assessment, based on the status of the wife and child and how they had been assaulted, suggested that this man was the target of someone's rage. I straightened up and turned toward the door, relieved to see a man standing next to Baker. It was Swanson, head of the CSI team.

"Hey, Swanson. We need *everything* cataloged from the scene."

"Yes, ma'am. I'll tell the team." He headed out.

Turning back to Brady, I said, "What do you think?"

With horror in his eyes, he said, "Somebody wanted this man dead, and in their mind, they had a really good reason to kill him the way they did."

My assessment as well. To Baker, I said, "Did you go through the rest of the house?"

"Just to check for assailants. There was nobody else in the house."

"How many more rooms?"

"Two, the primary and the boy's room."

"Let's go there next."

Baker's original statement was spot on. It was *bad*. Gruesome. Savage. We would need to find out every single detail about the Cramer family.

SIX

VAL

Outside the house, I removed my gloves and booties, taking a deep breath of fresh air. I had been warned that the scene was bad. Beyond the tragedy of a deceased child—which was never easy to see—the brutality inflicted on the father, Michael Cramer, was appalling. It seemed the perpetrators were either trying to extract information or they were seeking revenge, or perhaps a bit of both. We needed to learn more about him and his family to try to work out why anybody would do something like this.

Turning to Brady, I said, "Let's go back over to the neighbor's house, notify them of what's happened, and see what we can learn about the family."

"Do you need me?" Baker asked.

"Brady and I can handle it."

Kingston, the sheriff, said, "Baker was at the end of his shift."

Not only had Baker put in a full day's work, but he was also in need of a break. What he'd discovered at the Cramer residence was likely the worst thing he'd ever seen.

"All right, Baker, if you can give us the neighbor's details, we'll see you later."

He nodded, his expression a bit withdrawn but clearly glad to be leaving the scene. Once he'd provided all the details, we bid him goodnight.

I said to the sheriff, "How did Baker react to the scene?"

"He was sick. Physically. He may need to take a few days off."

"Understandable." It didn't surprise me. Despite everything I'd seen in my career, to say this scene was brutal was an understatement. The violence inflicted was vicious. With a nod and a wave, Brady and I headed across the expansive property toward a two-story home with a wraparound porch. The property lines were clearly marked by the surrounding redwood trees and tall shrubs.

Brady knocked on the door.

A woman, around fifty, appeared, with a man of about the same age standing behind her.

"Hello," Brady said. "I'm Deputy Tanner, and this is Valerie Costa, a consultant with the sheriff's department. Are you Joy Davis?"

"Yes. And this is my husband, Todd."

"Nice to meet you. We'd like to ask you a few questions about your neighbors."

"Are they okay?" she asked, concerned.

Brady replied, "I'm afraid not."

"What happened? Where are they?"

"We're not entirely sure what happened, but I'm sorry to have to tell you this—Michael and Mike are deceased, and Stephanie is on her way to the hospital with life-threatening injuries," I explained.

Mrs. Davis gripped her husband's hand. "Who did this?" she asked, her voice trembling.

"We're not sure, ma'am," I responded gently.

Mrs. Davis teared up, and I added, "We'd like to ask you a few questions about the Cramers. Do you mind if we come inside?"

She turned around, and I could hear the TV in the background. "The kids are inside. Maybe it's better we talk outside."

Todd nodded. "I'll tell the kids that we're just right out front," he said, before hurrying inside.

Mrs. Davis led us to a table and chairs outside. Mr. Davis joined us shortly after.

"Thank you for speaking to us. How long have you lived here?" I asked.

"We've been here about ten years, moved in from a few towns over," she explained.

"And during this time, the Cramers were your neighbors?"

"It's my understanding they've been here for fifteen years. They were here when we moved in," she confirmed.

"Were you friends with the Cramers? Did you see them socially?" I asked.

"We had block parties, but we weren't real close friends. There's a bit of an age difference between us, and they both worked full-time, so we didn't see them much. When we did, they were very friendly," Mrs. Davis responded.

"Were you aware of any disturbances at the house, or if they had a lot of visitors?"

"Honestly, I didn't really notice. I mean, as you can tell, we have big lots, and if there were any arguments, we wouldn't hear it over here." Glancing back at the Cramer property, I could see how that was likely. But I think they would have heard gunshots.

"Did you see the Cramers outside of the neighborhood? Maybe at the pizza parlor or at the diner in town?" Both popular spots for the residents of Rosedale.

They shook their heads.

"No. They were nice enough, though. We'd wave when we

saw them around the neighborhood. Sometimes they would go for walks, especially Steph."

"Did they ever give you reason to think they were into something illegal?"

"No, never. They were good neighbors," she said, a little surprised by the question.

"Anything else you can tell us about them?"

"No, just like I told the other officer. I have a friend whose older child is on the same karate team as Michael, and so they called me to go check on them because they hadn't shown up for the tournament, which was really unusual. They're a close-knit family and Mike and Stephanie are always there to support Michael Junior."

"Have you been home all day?" I asked.

Mrs. Davis said, "No. I was at work, and the kids were at my sister's house. I picked them up after I got off work and met Todd for dinner at the Chinese restaurant. We all got home around 7:30 p.m."

"Where do you work?"

"I work at The Chic Boutique in downtown Rosedale. Saturday is our busiest day, and I didn't leave until 5:30 p.m."

Mr. Davis said, "I work at the pharmacy. I left work at around six and met them at the restaurant right after."

"What time did you both leave the house this morning?" I asked.

Mrs. Davis said, "About eight."

"I left at seven," Mr. Davis said.

"Did you see or hear anything out of the ordinary when you got home this evening?"

"No. My friend Nancy called a few minutes after we got home to ask if I could check on the Cramers."

Which meant the Cramers had been attacked before 7:30 p.m.

"Do you know what time the Cramers were supposed to be at the tournament?"

"Nancy said six o'clock and Michael was about to miss his match."

"Did the Cramers ever give you a list of emergency numbers when they went out of town, or do you know any of their friends and family?"

Joy shook her head. "Sorry. No. They never asked us to look after the house."

"Did you witness anything out of the ordinary in the neighborhood in the past few days or weeks? Maybe someone who didn't look familiar or seemed out of place?"

"No. I wish I had. How 'bout you?" she asked her husband.

Todd replied, "No."

"This has been really helpful, thank you. If there's anything else you can think of, please give us a call." Brady handed him his business card, and we thanked them for their time, then headed back out to the street.

"What do you think of that?" Brady asked as we walked.

"We have to consider that it could be a random event or maybe financially motivated, although the house seemed pretty clean apart from where the victims were attacked. We need to learn everything about this family."

"You're hesitating," he observed.

"It's just an unusual scene. The way the mother and son were positioned and shot is such a contrast to what happened to the father. If it was a robbery, you'd think that they all would've been put together unless there was some sort of hidden treasure or money somewhere, and they tried to get information out of the father. But I don't know. It's too soon. All I know is that they had some reason for doing what they did to the father, and that's what we have to figure out." With a nod of understanding from Brady, I said, "Let's finish interviewing the rest of the neighbors to see if they heard or saw anything."

. . .

An hour later, we were empty-handed. None of the other neighbors had seen or heard anything out of the ordinary. Most of them had only positive things to say about the Cramers. Friendly but mostly kept to themselves. The only thing that caught my attention was that one neighbor said Mike was a little rough around the edges, and that made me wonder where Mike was from and what we'd find in his background. It wasn't much to go on, but if nobody heard a gunshot, it was either because the neighbors completely missed the two shots or the killer used a silencer. A professional?

Brady stopped in front of the Cramer home, still surrounded by flashing lights and Red Rose County vehicles. "Are you ready to head back to the station?"

"Let's quickly check in with CSI and then head back to the station and map out our strategy for finding out what happened to the Cramers and why." We had to find out who had murdered the little boy and his father in cold blood. Because whoever had done this was a monster and had to be stopped. I, for one, wouldn't rest until I'd done just that.

SEVEN

BRADY

Back at the station, Val demanded we set up a war room, a dedicated room with a murder board and a place where the team could meet to work on the case, just like we had for the Nelson case. There was something about Val. I couldn't shake the way she took charge, her confidence. Truth be told, I always had a thing for her back in school. I knew she didn't see me that way; she was competitive with me and said I was like a brother —there's nothing more crushing than being told by the girl you had fantasized about since you were ten years old that you were *like a brother*.

Through the years, I met other women, dated, and married a woman I thought I'd spend the rest of my life with. When my marriage broke down, I felt like my world had ended. But even during my marriage, as much as I loved my wife and believed she loved me, Val was always in the back of my mind. My first, albeit secret, love. They say you never forget your first love.

With old feelings creeping back since the moment I saw her back in Red Rose County, I knew I was in for it. She had given me no indication she would ever see me as anything other than a brother, even though recently I got the impression she looked at me a little differently. But I didn't want to make any assumptions. I couldn't cross that line, lose a friend or risk our professional relationship. Could I? I never invited her to dinner or lunch unless it was obviously platonic. And she hadn't invited me, so I suppose that was my answer.

Even just as friends, I wished she would take a job at the sheriff's department. Kingston was more than happy to hire her; he said he would find the budget if she'd agree. But she said she needed to take care of her mom and was still figuring out what she wanted to do with the rest of her life.

I shouldn't be glad there was a double homicide and an attempted murder, and of course I wasn't, but the fact that I was about to spend most of my time working with Val had lifted my spirits. Could she tell?

"Brady, let's get Allan, Baker, if he didn't go home, and Lucy, the old Nelson investigation gang, back for this one," Val suggested.

"Kingston's in his office. We can ask who's around."

We had just returned from the crime scene, one more brutal than anything I'd ever seen before—another uncharted territory for Red Rose County.

Val said, "Let's go talk to him. If there's somebody in this county capable of doing to that family what that killer did, they need to be stopped right away. We have no idea what we are dealing with here. We need to interview coworkers, friends, family, the kid's school, everyone at the karate dojo the kid went to—all of it, let's leave no stone unturned: financials, travel records, everything. I'm not saying Mike deserved what happened to him, but somebody thought he did, or he had information that was valuable to really bad folk which most likely means he was mixed up in something criminal."

"If Mike was the target, why would they kill his wife and son too?"

Val sat down at the conference table, her demeanor pensive.

"They looked peaceful, as if they'd been drugged, strategically placed, and then shot. Perhaps the killer has some sort of code of criminal ethics. They didn't want them to suffer, but felt Mike was worthy of suffering. Or did they think he had information they needed? If it wasn't information, it could have been revenge of some kind."

"I just can't imagine what the victim could have done to deserve that. Maybe nothing. Maybe he had something the killers wanted, so they tortured him to get information on how to get that something." It made me sick to think anyone could do that to another person.

Val smirked slightly, a mixture of intrigue and determination in her expression. "Very true. At this point the motive could be anything. Let's talk to the sheriff."

"Yes, ma'am."

Val charged out of the room and I followed behind. I tried to remain professional and not let my gaze linger on her, but the more time I spent with her, the harder it became.

Arriving at the sheriff's office, we found Kingston on the phone, his face flushed with frustration. We waited in the doorway. It was clear he was talking to someone higher up—probably the mayor. He didn't look pleased, that was for sure. He hung up and waved us in.

"Hey, you two, come on in."

I took a seat across from Kingston.

"That was the mayor. He said any resources we need, consider it approved." Turning to Val, he said, "Val, Brady, what are you thinking?"

Val said, "Brady and I were discussing how we need every aspect of this man's life investigated—financials, birth, marriages, travel, residences, places of work. We need to interview everyone connected to the family. It'll take a lot of time and resources to get through them all, but we can't have whoever did this running free around Red Rose County."

Kingston nodded. "I don't have as much experience as you do with this type of crime, but I'd say that's probably pretty accurate. The mother and son, other than the gunshot wounds, weren't messed up too bad. Not that their deaths weren't bad, but you know what I'm saying."

"I do," Val replied, full of compassion.

Kingston turned to me. "You know the team well. Who should we put on this?"

"Well, Allan, and Baker, if he's up for it. They could help organize the interviews. We also need research. Lucy and anybody she can spare on her team. I know it's a small team, but we may need to go through computer records, phone records... it's painstaking work. In order to get it done quickly we'll need as many of them on board as we can. It'd be nice to have regular contact with the forensics team, to get real-time updates. Jonathan and Swanson from CSI would be my pick."

Val looked at me with a bit of sparkle in her eyes and said, "That's a great assessment. I'm inclined to agree." She gave me a slight smile, and I wondered if it was just professional courtesy or something more. I needed to stop those type of thoughts.

Kingston said, "It's settled, then. I'll send out a memo. Everybody you just requested will be assigned to your team."

"Thanks." I paused. "Any word on how Stephanie Cramer is doing?"

"No, but I know she's over at County General," he replied.

That wasn't far. And it was good news considering it had one of the best trauma centers in Northern California. All the other hospitals in the area weren't as well equipped.

Val said, "We should head there next. Find out what condition she's in. She's our only witness. If she pulls through, she could be key to identifying the shooter."

"What's the likelihood she'll make it?" I asked, trying to brace myself for the worst.

Kingston said, "I honestly don't know."

Val added, "That's why we need to talk to her doctors."

"All right, let's head to the hospital."

EIGHT

THE SECRET ADMIRER

She was luminous. Too excited to go home, I'd listened to the police scanners to better understand Deputy Brady Tanner's visit. What I learned was quite interesting and had led me to the darkened parking lot of the Red Rose County Sheriff's station. I'd been lying in wait for nearly an hour, but my patience had paid off.

There she was. My Valerie.

Oh, how I had missed watching her every day. But I had to pay the bills somehow and work had pulled me away to another city. A necessary evil to fund my extracurriculars. But I was back, and I wasn't leaving until I had my prize.

From what I'd learned, I would get to see Valerie in her full splendor once again.

A final case.

She appeared blissfully unaware of my presence.

Valerie hurried toward the SUV, the only light provided by the street lamps illuminating the parking lot. She was in a rush, and there was Deputy Tanner, dutifully following her lead.

"Where are you going, Valerie?" I whispered to myself, a chill of anticipation running down my spine.

I didn't know but I was about to find out.

I started the engine after I saw their headlights come on. I eased out of the parking lot just as she backed out of her spot. I pulled out slowly, ahead of her.

She was soon behind me, obviously in a hurry. I changed lanes to let her pass, making it seem as though I wasn't following her.

But in my heart, I wasn't just following her—I was planning her destiny.

The thought sent a thrill through me, mixing excitement with a deep desire for what would come next.

Oh, Valerie, I have the most splendid plans for us.

NINE

VAL

The emergency room at County General Hospital was cold and relatively calm, a far cry from the usual chaos of these departments. Despite the recent events, there wasn't a lot of violent crime in Red Rose County. The usual emergencies were hiking or boating accidents, which happened in the earlier hours of the day. But it was late and there were only a few people pacing the waiting room waiting to hear about loved ones, and an elderly couple sitting on hard plastic chairs. Brady and I approached the reception desk and waited for an update on Stephanie Cramer's condition. I used the break to text Lucy back. She had likely received the memo from the sheriff because she'd texted on the drive over—it was all hands on deck to solve the latest vicious crime in Red Rose County.

Lucy: *Hey. Heard there's a new case and you're the lead.*

Val: *Yep. Brady and me. We're at the hospital with the one survivor. Condition unclear.*

Lucy: *What do you want me to do first?*

It was no surprise Lucy wanted to get started as soon as possible.

Val: *Need a full background on the Cramer family. Everything.*

Lucy: *I'll head down to the station now*

Glancing at my watch, I saw it was almost 11 p.m. In any other situation I would have told her it could wait until the morning, but based on the interviews with the neighbors, it was likely that the Cramers had been attacked four to six hours earlier. Our killer could still be in Red Rose County. Nobody would be able to sleep until we had something to go on.

Val: *Thanks. We'll head over there once we get an update on Stephanie.*

Lucy responded with a thumbs-up emoji.

Putting the phone back in my jacket, I looked at Brady and said, "Lucy is working on the background."

"Good," Brady said. "This one's bad, even for you, right?"

Nodding, I said, "It is. From the cold-blooded murder of an innocent boy to the brutality of Mike's death. It's up there with some of the worst I've seen." No doubt it was the worst Brady had seen, too. "How are you holding up?"

Crime scenes were never easy to deal with, but when a child was involved it tore your heart apart. Especially if you were a parent.

He said, "I'm okay. But I have a feeling the images will haunt me for quite some time."

Same here. This crime scene was one you would never be able to erase from your memory—so brutal, so full of rage, with the exception of the mother and son. Their deaths were awful, but it was a different kind of awful.

"That means you're normal," I said, in an attempt to reassure him. I thought that if Mrs. Cramer survives I'm sure she will have nightmares about this for the rest of her life.

I've seen this sort of brutality before, but the fact that it had happened in Red Rose County didn't make any sense. I had been back for less than a year, but from what I could tell, it wasn't overrun with crime—nothing serious, anyhow. But maybe it was, and the criminals were really good at hiding it. Not that I'd been looking for it. I'd only worked two cases since I moved home. All I knew was there was major crime in all of the surrounding cities, and that Rosedale, where I lived, was insulated.

"Are there a lot of drugs in the county?" I asked Brady.

"Red Rose County has a little bit—some fentanyl, meth— but from what I understand, the biggest suppliers are a little bit further north in Shasta."

A drug-linked killing would make sense. Was it possible Mike Cramer was mixed up in drugs, perhaps a deal gone wrong? Or he'd stolen drugs from a dangerous individual.

As I pondered this, a doctor emerged wearing a white coat with a stethoscope around his neck. "Are you with the sheriff's department?" he asked.

We nodded.

"I'm Dr. French."

"I'm Deputy Tanner with the sheriff's department, and this is Val Costa who is helping with the investigation."

Handshakes ensued. "How is Stephanie Cramer?" I asked.

"I work in the ER and saw her when she first came in. She suffered a single gunshot wound to the head. She's currently in surgery right now. It's not looking good," he informed us.

My heart sank. What a travesty. "What can you tell me about her injury?" I asked.

"There wasn't a clear exit, so the bullet is likely still lodged in her brain. They're trying to remove it now. Based on the trajectory, we think it's possible she could survive if it didn't hit anything critical like the brainstem or any major blood vessels. But if she survives, it's possible she'll have some long-term disabilities."

"How long will she be in surgery?" Brady asked.

"It could be a few more hours."

This was not how I thought this day was going to go. Was I ready for an all-consuming investigation? I was going to therapy once a week and the nightmares from my captivity never really went away. Although in the past few months I had had a handful of peaceful nights. *Progress*. Overall I felt ready.

"What happened?" Dr. French asked.

With a nod, I said, "There was an attack on her family. Husband and son both killed. She's the only survivor."

"Any idea who did this?"

"Not yet. But we are going to find out."

"I hope so," he said. "You can leave your details with the charge nurse and she'll call you when Mrs. Cramer is out of surgery."

"Thank you for your time."

He nodded before hurrying away.

It sounded like we could have a triple homicide on our hands, but you never knew how something was going to turn out. Miracles happened every day, so we wouldn't allow ourselves to give up hope just yet.

TEN

VAL

Back at the sheriff's station, I found Lucy, Allan, and the sheriff in the war room. Before I could say a word, Kingston said, "How is she?"

"The doctor said it's not looking good, but she's currently in surgery. We left our details with the nurse on duty, and she'll call us as soon as Mrs. Cramer is out of surgery."

"Did they indicate whether they think she'll make it?"

"No, but they said it looks like a single gunshot wound. The bullet is still lodged in her brain. They said it's gonna depend on a few things whether or not she'll pull through." We didn't pick up the Cramers' cell phones because we wanted the crime scene techs to bag everything first, but without them we hadn't been able to notify any relatives of what had happened to the Cramers. "Have we been able to locate any of the Cramers' relatives?" I asked.

Lucy stood up and said, "Yeah, I found some family members for Stephanie, but I couldn't find any for Michael Cramer. I'll keep looking."

"We need to contact the family. Let them know that

Stephanie's in surgery. They'll likely want to be here for her. Does it say where they are?"

Lucy nodded. "Stephanie's parents are in Concord, California, San Francisco Bay Area. A few hours away."

"Siblings? Anybody else linked to her or Mike?" I asked.

"Looks like Stephanie has a sister and a brother, both married."

We needed to find them urgently. They would want to say their goodbyes if she didn't make it, and they needed to know that Mike and Michael were dead. If Stephanie survived, she was going to need all the support she could get.

"All right, give me the parents' details. I'll give them a call."

Brady said, "Val, maybe you should have one of us with official capacity call the family."

I nodded, realizing he was absolutely correct. I didn't have an official title with the sheriff's department. I was just a paid consultant who helped out with cases. Somebody like the sheriff would definitely be more suitable.

"You're right. Sheriff, would you mind calling them?"

"Yes, of course."

"Thanks."

Lucy showed the sheriff the information on her screen. He copied the details to his cell phone and smiled weakly. It wasn't a call that anyone looked forward to making.

As soon as Kingston had gone out of the room to make the call, I said, "What else can you tell me about the Cramers? Did you find out how long they've been married? Where they were from originally?"

Lucy said, "I only have the most basic information so far. They were married for fifteen years."

Basic information could still be valuable.

"Any prior known addresses?"

"They've lived in Red Rose County for fifteen years. Based on the length of time they've been here, they must've moved shortly after they got married. Before that, Mike Cramer lived in the Bay Area, Oakland, and Stephanie, maiden name, Stephanie Jamison, lived in Pleasant Hill, California, also Bay Area."

So they were Bay Area residents who had moved north to our little neck of the woods. Were they running away from something or simply wanting to raise their kids in a different environment—one with less crime and such beautiful scenery?

Lucy said, "We've requested warrants for financial records, cell phone records, and I'm still looking up employment records."

"The neighbor said Mike worked at an auto body shop, and Stephanie works as a receptionist at a law firm."

I cocked my head, thinking back to the cars in the Cramers' driveway. They were both new—one was a luxury vehicle. Their incomes could likely cover the house, but the luxury vehicle stood out. Could they afford it?

"Do they own any other properties?"

"No. Mike Cramer had a house in the Bay Area but sold it when they moved up here." Their home in Red Rose County was modest, but it stood on at least two acres.

Brady said, "What are you thinking, Val?"

"I'm just trying to assess if they were living beyond their means." Which could potentially indicate some criminal activity, outside of their regular nine-to-five jobs. But then again, if Mike sold his house to move up here, it was possible the mortgage was quite affordable, allowing for some of the finer things in life.

Lucy said, "We won't be sure until we get the financials back."

"Depending on their salaries, who knows, maybe Mike was

doing more auto body work on the side for extra cash under the table," Brady theorized.

It was possible. I shouldn't be jumping to conclusions. The sheriff walked back into the room looking distraught. Understandably so. "How did it go?"

"The parents are, as you can imagine, in a terrible state. They said they'll get to the hospital as soon as they can and that they'll notify Stephanie's brother and sister."

"Did they ask about Mike and their grandson?"

"No, they were so worried about Stephanie they likely hadn't thought to ask. I just told them she was in the hospital with a life-threatening injury. I didn't go into any details about how she sustained the injury."

That was for the best. They were about to embark on a four-hour car journey. The devastating news that their grandson as well as their son-in-law had been murdered would keep them from thinking clearly. We wanted them to arrive safe and sound as their daughter was going to need them. If she made it.

"All right. Did you get all of their cell phone numbers?"

"Yes, I told them we'd keep in touch and meet them at the hospital when they arrived."

"I'd like to find out what they think of their son-in-law or if their daughter ever mentioned anything strange going on."

"Good idea." The sheriff rubbed the back of his head. He had bags under his eyes, and although the room was filled with adrenaline, we were beginning to show signs of wear. This was going to be a complicated case.

ELEVEN

VAL

With a sip of the sheriff's department issued coffee, I could feel the shot of caffeine boost my waning energy. For an extra buzz, I picked up a donut and took a bite. It was glazed with chocolate, but it was one of those prepackaged kinds. The donut shop wasn't open yet, but it would be soon. It was nearly 3 a.m., and everyone had been working steadily and diligently to find out as much information as possible about the Cramers. We drew up a list of people and places to visit in order to trace the Cramers' whereabouts and movements in the days leading up to the attack.

Our murder board already contained a wealth of information that we'd recovered, and a large part of the wall was covered with pictures of the crime scene. It was gruesome, but we needed to keep looking at the pictures in case we'd missed a clue. They also reminded us why we were working around the clock: the killer was still at large and could strike again at any time. We had no idea who we were dealing with. If it was a random robbery, they could do the same thing to another family.

Hopefully the crime scene techs would find something

useful, and soon. The most we could hope for was for Stephanie Cramer to survive and tell us who had murdered her family. But after a follow-up call to the hospital, I learned she was still in surgery. Hopefully, that was a good sign. She was still alive. That was something.

Lucy spoke up. "Oh, I think I got something."

"What is it?"

"Well, I've got more employment records for Mike Senior, going back almost thirty years. He didn't change jobs much, which makes it a little easier. Looks like he's always worked in the auto body space. I didn't see any business licenses for either of the Cramers' names. So, he must be an employee, not an owner. But somebody with Mike's level of experience might do custom work. Maybe the shop pulls in a lot of money from custom stuff. Or he did some on the side."

So Mike didn't own the body shop, he was an employee, and his wife was a receptionist. If he was taking on extra work outside of the shop, it could help explain the fancy car. Maybe his work on the side, or even his work at the body shop had led Mike to cross paths with whoever had killed him. Maybe he had witnessed something that got him killed. It was anybody's guess at that point.

"What about Stephanie?"

"Stephanie was younger than Mike by about twelve years. Before she met him or married him, it looks like she worked a few different jobs over about a decade. She was a waitress and worked at a clothing store before she moved up to Red Rose County to be a receptionist."

We'd have to wait for the financial records to confirm whether or not the Cramers had any money problems. And considering the hour, there weren't a lot of people available for us to question. At that point, we didn't even know what angle to look at for a motive. I wished we had financials, cell phone records, DNA forensics—all the data we needed to put the case together. It could've been a random burglary. Without the evidence, we were looking for a needle in a haystack. We needed to start ruling out possibilities. Waiting was the pits.

But as soon as Stephanie's parents, Gina and Dale Jamison, arrived, we could question them and hopefully they would provide a valuable insight into the Cramers' personal lives.

The Cramers had been attacked eight to ten hours earlier. Time was of the essence. We had patrols out speaking to various gas station owners and attendants, asking if they'd seen anyone from out of town or anyone they didn't recognize. A lot of people passed through Red Rose County as they drove up and down the coast of California, but it would be good to know if anybody stood out. This line of investigation hadn't come up with anything useful yet.

I didn't want to sit in this room anymore. As I looked up at the clock on the wall, I knew I should head to the hospital soon and get there before the Jamisons did. I said, "Hey Brady, I'm thinking we give the Jamisons a call to see how close they are. We should try to get to the hospital before they do. We don't want them to arrive and have nobody there waiting for them."

"I'll call them now to see where they're at."

Packing up my things, I heard a knock on the door and glanced up. It was the head of the CSI team, Specialist Swanson. Did he have something for us? "Swanson, how's it going?"

"We're just about finished collecting evidence from the scene. Bagging and tagging anything that could help us out. We still need to catalog it all, but we did find something unusual that we thought the team would want to know about right away."

"Oh?" I asked, adrenaline spiking at the news.

"Well, I'm assuming you have already put in for warrants for cell phone records?"

Lucy said, "You betcha. Judge already signed it. We're just

waiting for the information from the cell phone companies to come through."

"How many numbers did you request?" Swanson asked.

"Three. One for Mike Senior, one for Stephanie, and the son had his own cell phone as well, Michael Junior. They're all on the same account."

"We need to add a fourth."

Swanson met my eyes and said, "We found a fourth cell phone when the team was going through the vehicles in the driveway. Based on the positioning of the front seat in the car and the registration, it was Mike's car. The cell phone looks like a burner—hidden underneath the front seat."

"A hidden phone under the front seat? Why would he have a burner there?" Did he have a mistress? It wasn't uncommon for cheating husbands or wives to have a separate cell phone they used to communicate with their secret partner.

"You have the phone with you?"

"We do, and we've already fingerprinted it. We have the others too so you can go through the numbers."

Lucy said, "We should bring in Mark. He's our new tech genius. He'll surf through the phones and find every digital footprint."

"Has he been called?"

Lucy said, "I left him a message."

He was likely asleep, like most normal folks.

Swanson lifted up four evidence bags, each containing a cell phone, and said, "It sounds like you'd definitely like these."

"Thank you so much." Could it be we had our very first lead?

A secret cell phone meant skeletons in closets. What was Mike Cramer hiding?

TWELVE

BRADY

As I paced the near empty office space of the sheriff's station, I remembered how I dreaded this part of the job. As much as I really wanted to work major crimes like homicide, I wasn't great at speaking to grieving parents or spouses. And luckily, it wasn't something I had to do very often.

When I'd got hold of Mrs. Jamison on the phone, I'd been relieved she hadn't asked too many difficult questions. I'd been about to hang up when she said, "Wait. My son Chuck wants to talk to you."

That wasn't good. Surely he was going to ask for more details about his sister's accident. "Of course," I replied.

A deep voice said, "Deputy Tanner, I'm Chuck, Stephanie's brother. What can you tell us about Stephanie's accident? Was it a car accident?"

The team had discussed how to give the family the news and decided it would be best if it was done in person.

"We think it's best we discuss what happened to Stephanie when you get here. My partner, Val Costa—a consultant and former FBI agent—is helping us with the case. We'll discuss with you what we found and what we believe happened to your sister."

"You haven't mentioned my nephew, Michael. He's okay, isn't he?"

My stomach churned as the images of Michael moved to the front of my mind. A father myself, it was difficult not to see my own son in Michael's place, and it was almost more than I could bear. "We'll give you all the information you need when you arrive. As I said, my partner and I will be there at the hospital to meet you."

"Deputy Tanner, you're worrying me."

"We'll see you when you get here."

"Okay," he said reluctantly.

I ended the call and shook my head. In thirty minutes, the Jamisons' entire world as they knew it would be shattered.

Back in the war room, I updated the team on the Jamisons' impending arrival. Swanson was leaning against the wall, holding evidence bags. Cell phones.

Val said, "Okay, good. That gives us a little time." The look in her eye meant she had a plan. And I was more than a little interested in hearing what it was.

Swanson said, "We'll see you later. I'll let you know if anything else comes up."

Anything else? After a quick goodbye, I looked over at Val. "What did they find?"

Lucy explained the burner phone and that they were about to start scrolling through the phone to see if they could find anything useful.

Lucy, bagged phone in hand, said, "Okay this is weird. There are only two numbers in the burner phone's history."

Val said, "Let's call the last one back."

Lucy dialed it from the Polycom. It rang four times and went to voicemail. No personalized greeting.

I said, "Maybe they won't answer because it's an unknown number."

Lucy said, "Good point. I'll dial from the phone and put it on speaker." She hit send. After two rings, a deep voice said, "Mike, where you been?"

"This isn't Mike. Who is this?" Val asked.

"Who is this?" he countered rather defensively, which made me wonder why. Was he somehow involved?

"My name is Val. I'm a friend of Mike's."

"Where's Mike?"

Val met my gaze. "He's had an accident."

The line went dead.

And the room was silent.

"What do you make of that?" Allan asked.

"I don't know. But we need to get all the records from this phone. Those are the only two numbers on it. If Mike called anyone else, or anyone else called him, he deleted the information. Which is odd."

I said, "Let's call the other number, from the phone."

Lucy repeated the action. It rang four times before an automated greeting sounded through the speaker. She ended the call. Why wouldn't they pick up? Was it due to the early hour? Most likely.

Val said, "We need to know who the people behind these numbers are and track them down. If Mike was involved in anything shady, these two people will know what. They could be the key."

Lucy said, "You got it."

"I can help you write up the warrants," Allan offered.

Val said, "Thanks. Brady and I need to head out to the hospital to meet the Jamisons."

My pulse was racing. It was a legitimate lead. What had Michael Cramer been hiding? Whatever it was, it had likely cost him his life and his son's.

THIRTEEN

VAL

Back at the hospital, our first stop was the nurse's station to find out if Stephanie was still in surgery. She was, which meant she was still alive. *There's always hope until there isn't.* I willed her to survive, not just for the sake of her family, but so that we could ask her what happened to her husband and son.

Brady and I stepped aside, keeping an eye on the entrance doors to be able to spot the Jamisons when they arrived. It had been such a whirlwind since Brady showed up at my house, I hadn't had time to stop and think about how the team, Brady included, had been working for the last eight hours straight. But looking at Brady now, his dark hair mussed and his five-o'clock shadow prominently displayed, I knew he was likely tired. But dang, he looked pretty darn sexy too. Ugh. I could only imagine what I looked like at this ungodly hour. I placed my hand on his arm, and said, "How are you holding up, Brady? It's been a long night." It had been a while since I'd stayed up all night, and we'd been going nonstop.

He stepped closer, and I could feel the heat of his body.

In a hushed voice he said, "Admittedly, I'm tired, but the adrenaline from trying to get to the bottom of what happened to this family keeps me going. We can't have a family killer running around Red Rose County. And honestly, I haven't pulled an all-nighter like this in quite a while." He smiled. "Actually, I think the last time was when I worked with you, Val."

I couldn't help but smile back. There was something about Brady I couldn't shake. And standing this close, even in the thick of an investigation, was making it all very clear in my mind that I no longer thought of Brady as just my friend from high school. Since being back in Rosedale, our friendship had turned into something more. Did he feel it too?

"You're welcome," I said playfully.

"I'm glad you're here and could help us out."

"I'm always here to help if you need me." And I meant it. I wanted to be there for Brady and the community. But what with recovering from my captivity, and taking care of Mom, I hadn't put myself out there as much as I could have. I needed to work on that. Even though I still felt like my life was at a cross-road and I wasn't sure which route to take. But I couldn't just stay still while I deliberated which way to go. Because I was a woman of action, it was how I was built. And the thing about homicide investigations or missing persons cases was, I, for one, didn't want what had happened to the Cramer family to happen to anybody else. I needed to stop the bad guys before they caused more damage. Sometimes, you had to put your own issues to one side if you wanted to get the job done.

"We could use you all the time."

"I'm not sure if I'm ready to sign up for that. Honestly, I don't know what I'm going to do with the rest of my life, Brady. But I decided to sell my house back in DC. It's officially on the market," I said, feeling both sad and anxious.

Brady raised his eyebrows. "You're staying in Red Rose County?"

"Looks like it." As much as I was unsure of my future, my

instinct was telling me that future was in Rosedale. Watching him, I thought if I didn't know better I'd say Brady was suppressing a smile.

"Your mom must be pretty happy."

"I think she is. I mean, I don't know how much more time I have with her, and it's nice to be home." And it was nice to be near Brady again, to work with him and work with the sheriff's department. It made me feel more like my old self.

A group of four people entered through the automatic doors, and Brady and I instinctively raised our hands to wave. They were most likely the Jamisons, although we didn't have any photographs of them. The older of the two, presumably the parents, held onto each other as they walked forward. A man in his early fifties charged toward us.

"Are you Deputy Tanner and Val Costa?" he asked.

"I'm Val. This is Brady. You must be Chuck," I replied.

He nodded. "Yes. These are my parents."

I said, "Hello, Mr. and Mrs. Jamison."

A woman in her forties said, "I'm Darla. I'm Stephanie's sister. How is she?"

"I just spoke with the nurse. She's still in surgery."

"Is that good or bad?" Mrs. Jamison asked.

"Why don't we head over to the waiting area, and I'll let the nurse know that's where we will be when they have an update on Stephanie's condition?"

They agreed reluctantly. Brady led them over to the chairs. I hurried over to the nurse's desk to let them know the family had arrived and our location. I walked back to the family, who were all standing instead of sitting.

"I think we should have a seat," I suggested.

"With all due respect, Ms. Costa, we've been sitting for four hours," Mr. Jamison replied.

Looking at their worried faces, I said, "I understand."

Chuck said, "So what happened? Was it a car accident? Where are Mike and Michael?"

Brady and I exchanged glances, and I gave a slight nod to let him know I would be the one to break the news. I took a deep breath. "This is going to be difficult for you to hear. You may want to sit down."

Not a single Jamison budged.

With a heavy heart, I explained what had happened.

Mrs. Jamison slumped down, and her husband caught her just in time before he and Chuck lowered her onto a chair. Mr. Jamison sat down next to her, and Darla took a seat on the other side of her.

The grief was thick and suffocating.

Chuck remained standing. "I don't understand. You're saying somebody killed Mike and little Michael and shot Steph?"

"Yes. We don't know why or who is responsible," I said, softly.

The four were stunned into silence. It was going to take a lifetime to come to terms with what had happed to Stephanie and her family. My heart broke for them.

Finally, Chuck said, "Was it a robbery?"

"We're still processing the crime scene. We're not sure yet."

Mrs. Jamison placed her hand on her chest as she shook her head. "Michael... little Michael too?"

Chuck sat down next to his father.

"I'm so sorry for your loss," I said. After a few minutes' silence, I added, "I know this is a very difficult time, but it would really help us to find out who did this and why, if we could ask you a few questions about Stephanie and Mike."

Chuck, obviously the cool and collected Jamison, said, "What do you want to know?"

"Anything you can tell us about them—how they met, if you know Mike's family or are in contact with them. We weren't able to find any relatives. Any problems the couple may have had or any kind of trouble they've been in. Maybe Stephanie confided in you about something unusual, or something out of the ordinary, going on in their lives."

Mr. Jamison, with tears in his eyes, said, "They were together a long time. Steph was waitressing at a local restaurant. That's where she met Mike. They were both young, but he was older, twelve years older. At first, we weren't so sure about him. He was kind of, I don't know, unrefined, but he treated her so well. Stephanie just loved him, and they seemed happy. They lived in the Bay Area for a couple of years before they got married."

"Did either of them have any problems? Any enemies?"

They all shook their heads.

"Do you know Mike's family?" I asked.

Mrs. Jamison said softly, "The first time we met Mike, I asked about his parents. He said that they had passed on and he didn't have any siblings. He didn't have any relatives except for maybe some distant cousins, but he wasn't in contact with them and didn't even know their names."

That explained why Lucy hadn't been able to find any of Mike's family. "And you said Stephanie and Mike were happy. You weren't aware of any problems in their marriage? Or any problems in their lives?"

"Do you think this was a murder-suicide? Did Mike do this?" Darla asked suddenly, her eyes wide.

Why had she jumped to that conclusion? What did she know? "We don't think so. We're trying to understand more about their relationship and their lives. It'll help us find who did this. Why do you think Mike may have done this?"

Darla shook her head, tears still flowing. "Sorry. I don't think Mike did this. I listen to a lot of true crime podcasts and a lot of the time it turns out to be the husband who kills the wife. But Mike wasn't like that. I don't think."

The surge of true crime documentaries and forensic shows on TV turned everyone into an armchair detective. It was rarely useful in an actual murder investigation.

Mrs. Jamison cried, "Who would do this to a little boy? How did they do it? How did they kill my grandbaby?"

I didn't have the answer to that question. How could anyone kill an innocent child? "He was shot once, like Stephanie."

"Mike too?" she asked.

Arms crossed, I said, "Mike's injuries were different."

"What do you mean different?" Chuck asked.

"The official cause of death hasn't been confirmed yet, but his injuries appear to be more extensive." They didn't need to hear the gory details. And they were *gory*. If I could unsee the image, I would.

"Did Mike have any close friends? Did Stephanie? Anyone that they kept in contact with after their move to Red Rose County?"

Mrs. Jamison calmly said, "Mike had friends from work. I think we met them a couple of times and at the wedding. He did auto body work, and he was good at it too, but that was it. I don't remember their names."

The questions were likely a momentary reprieve from her grief, as she had stopped crying and looked ready to answer any and all questions.

"How about Stephanie? Did she have any close friends that she kept in contact with after the move?"

Nodding, Mrs. Jamison said, "A few friends."

"If you give us their names, and if you have their numbers, that would be really useful. They might be able to help us figure out what happened."

"Okay," Mrs. Jamison said as she ruffled through her purse to get the information.

"Do you know why Mike and Stephanie decided to move up to Red Rose County?"

Mrs. Jamison stopped rummaging. "They said they wanted to start a family and they wanted to be out of the city so that their kids could grow up hiking and fishing and boating. They wanted a different life, a better life, quiet. They were both so excited about the move. Of course, I was hesitant at first. I didn't want my daughter moving so far away from me, but they visited."

"When was the last time you saw them?"

"A few months ago. It was my husband Dale's eightieth birthday."

So far, the only useful information we had to go on was why Stephanie and Mike had chosen to move to Red Rose County and the origin of their relationship. Maybe one of Stephanie's friends, if Stephanie confided in them, could tell us if there was trouble brewing in the Cramer household.

Mrs. Jamison went back to searching her purse for the information on Stephanie's friends.

"Can I get you anything? You've had a long journey. Do you have anywhere to stay tonight? We could help you with accommodation."

"We're not leaving until Stephanie is out of surgery," Mrs. Jamison said.

Chuck said, "That's appreciated. We will need a place to stay, eventually."

I glanced over at the hallway, and a doctor wearing blue scrubs, mask down, raised his hand. "It looks like Stephanie's surgeon has an update."

Everyone sprang to their feet, and we hurried over to the man with gray hair and dark skin.

"Hi, I'm Dr. Plano, Stephanie Cramer's surgeon."

"I'm Val Costa. This is Deputy Tanner—we're with the

sheriff's department—and this is Stephanie's family, her parents, brother and sister."

Nodding, he said, "Stephanie made it through the surgery."

Cries of relief from the family filled the room, but the surgeon stayed still and said, "The next twenty-four hours are critical for Stephanie. We don't know if she'll pull through. She was lucky. The brainstem wasn't hit, and we believe we stopped the bleeding. But she has sustained a major injury."

Thank goodness she'd survived.

"When can we see her?" Mrs. Jamison asked.

"She's in recovery. We can take you to her shortly."

The family huddled together.

I said, "Thank you, Doctor. May we speak with you in private?"

He nodded, and we stepped aside, out of the family's earshot.

"Can you tell us about the injury?" I asked.

"We retrieved the bullet, which I'm sure you'll want. She was lucky, all things considered. Just a millimeter to the left, and she'd be dead."

"We think she was lying down when they shot her."

"That she was still at the time of the shooting would be consistent with the wound. Maybe she was unconscious or asleep. There are contact burns from where the bullet entered her skull."

"Close range," I noted.

He nodded. "What happened?"

Brady explained and I was grateful not to have to repeat the gory details.

Dr. Plano said, "Well, if she survives, she'll have a heck of a road to recovery, and not just physically."

That was an understatement.

The doctor continued, "We'll let you know if her status changes."

"Thank you very much."

I turned to Brady and said, "We need to be here when she wakes up."

FOURTEEN

VAL

After giving my face a wash in the station bathroom, I called my mom to see how she was doing. As I suspected, she was just fine, having her morning coffee with Julie and Diane, who had spent the night with her. Both women were widows and lived alone. Part of me wondered if they should all just live together, and I could find my own place. There was enough room at Mom's for everybody. They were always there anyway, but maybe that would change when Mom got all of her strength back. After speaking to Mom, I called Harrison but he didn't pick up. It was nearing 9 a.m. on the East Coast and he was likely asleep. I tried again. My heart warmed at the sound of his groggy voice. Part of me felt bad for waking him up, but the other part of me needed to hear my son's voice. "Hi, honey."

"Hi, Mom. What's up?"

"Just calling to hear your voice."

"Are you okay?" he said, slightly alarmed.

Great. I'd worried him. "Yes, everything is okay. I'm working a tough case and just wanted to make sure you're all right. I'm sorry to wake you."

"That bad, huh?" he asked, rather intuitively.

"It is. Well, sweetheart, I'll let you get back to sleep. I love you."

"Love you too, Mom."

My boy was safe, and that would keep me going. That and one of the breakfast sandwiches Brady and I had picked up for the team. I headed into the war room. There was a new face I didn't recognize.

"Hey, team."

"Hey, Val. How's Stephanie doing?" Lucy asked.

"Doc says the next twenty-four hours will be critical, but she survived the surgery, which is good. We dropped off the bullet they removed from her brain to forensics. Hopefully, that'll tell us something. Maybe the bullet came from a gun used in a previous crime."

Lucy said, "Excellent."

I eyed the man as Brady continued to pass out sandwiches, hash browns, and juice.

Lucy said, "Val, this is Mark. Mark joined our research team after you worked the last case with us."

"Oh yes, the new hire. And tech genius, if I recall," I said with a friendly smile.

Mark blushed. He had fair skin, blue eyes, and sandy hair. Early thirties, young. We shook hands.

"Nice to meet you, Mark."

"You too, Val, I've heard a lot about you."

Brady said, "There's extras. So, if you need more don't be shy. Bon appétit."

With that I took a seat and unwrapped a sandwich. It wasn't exactly the breakfast of champions, but it was breakfast, and considering it was 6 a.m. and we'd been working through the night, nobody was about to complain, especially not me.

We ate in silence. Everyone was clearly hungry and needed the energy to keep going.

As I ate my sausage, egg, and cheese sandwich, Lucy kept eyeing me. I felt I knew her well enough to know that she had something to tell me. Something good. I took a swig of orange juice and said, "What is it?"

"I figured I'd give you a moment to eat first," she said. She grabbed another bite of her own sandwich.

"I know you've got something."

With her mouth full, her cheeks puffed out like a chipmunk. She swallowed and scarfed down the rest before saying, "We found something."

"What did you find?"

Mark answered. "Lucy was filling me in on the details of the case, and I noticed something. I know we're still waiting on cell phone records, but they should be here any minute, right?"

Lucy said, "Yeah, we put in a rush, considering there's a deranged killer out there. We were able to get it expedited."

"That's great," Mark said. "So, while Lucy was updating me on the case, we were talking about how normally in a homicide investigation, you want to retrace the victim's steps leading up to their death, find out where they've been and who they've been talking to."

"Yeah, which we're finding difficult since the interviews with the neighbors told us that the Cramers tended to keep to themselves and they didn't seem to have many visitors. We've been waiting to interview coworkers and friends of Mike and Stephanie."

"Well, we have something else too," Lucy said.

"Oh?"

"Yeah, you see, both Mike's and Stephanie's cars are equipped with GPS."

"Oh, did you find out what trips they'd entered into their navigation system?" I asked.

Mark nodded. "Yes. That wasn't super useful. But what most people don't realize with these newer models with inbuilt GPS systems is that every trip is recorded, regardless of whether the driver used the navigations system. So, we can literally retrace every single journey Mike and Stephanie made, at least in those vehicles."

I put down my sandwich and said, "So you're telling me the car I just bought is always tracking and recording everywhere I go?" Instead of transporting my car across the country, I'd opted to buy a new SUV. I wondered if I was going to regret that decision.

"Yes, the onboard computer stores all trip information, with or without the navigation system in use. The car manufacturers, or anyone with the right software, can access the data at any time. It has raised a few privacy concerns, for sure," Mark explained.

That was disturbing. Perhaps I should ditch the new car and buy an older model. I didn't like the idea that someone could track all of my movements. But it could prove helpful in the Cramer investigation.

"How do we get the data?"

"I just downloaded the software onto my laptop, so we can start looking at it once I've hooked it up to the vehicle's computer," Mark said.

Lucy's laptop pinged and she suddenly exclaimed, "Woohoo!", jumping out of her seat and raising her arms in a victory pose. "We've got cell phone data!"

"That was fast. Legit phones or the burner phone?" I asked.

"Just the legit ones. The burner phone data should be on its way, although it won't quite give us as much data as these. The legit phones will give us an insight into their everyday lives."

"But we would get the cell tower pings with the burner, right?"

"That's right. And as soon as that information is in, we'll be able to pinpoint where the phone was used and the location of the person that used it. But even without the burner phone data, we have the GPS car data and the family's smartphones, so I think we should be able to learn a lot."

I said, "Excellent. Between the car GPS and the cell data we'll be able to figure out where they were and maybe even who they met with before the attack. When can we start looking at the GPS data?"

Mark said, "I'll hook it up to the system now."

"Great, let's find out where Mike has been. It could lead us to his killer."

FIFTEEN

VAL

An hour later, Mark was able to track the movements of Mike Senior's vehicle. It was like magic. A very disturbing brand of magic. Useful but *disturbing*.

Mark had pinpointed every location Mike had visited over the last few weeks, including routes he had repeatedly taken in the middle of the night. Did Stephanie know about the nocturnal trips? Did she go with him?

"What can you tell us about the location?" I asked.

"Shasta," Allan said, through gritted teeth.

"What is it?" I asked, not understanding Allan's obvious displeasure.

Allan said, "That area is known for high levels of meth, heroin, prescription opioids."

"Really?" I certainly hadn't heard of it until now. But then again I hadn't exactly been focusing on the crime stats in the surrounding counties, until now, either.

He nodded.

Lucy tapped away on her keyboard. "I have crime stats right here. Could be Mike was involved in drugs somehow."

Meetings in the middle of the night. A violent murder. *Yes, it could be drug related.*

After reviewing the times Mike drove out to Shasta County, about twenty minutes outside Rosedale, we were able to ascertain that these were regular visits. Over the last few weeks, Mike had made the same trip every other night, at approximately midnight, returning at around 3 a.m. What was Mike doing in those three hours in the middle of the night?

"What's at the location?"

"Let's pull it up on a map," Mark said, tapping on the keyboard. A house appeared on the screen projection on the wall. He zoomed in on it.

"Who lives there?" I said.

"Could be a lover," Brady said.

True. A love triangle, perhaps?

"Let's pull up the property records."

Lucy said, "Give me a few minutes."

While she did that, I studied the house on the screen, a small, one-story home. The garden was overgrown and there were multiple vehicles parked around the property.

Brady said, "What are you thinking, Val?"

"I think we need to meet the residents of that house."

"Gabriel Moore. That's who lives there," Lucy exclaimed.

"What do we know about Gabriel Moore?"

"Give me another minute." She hummed a tune as she tapped away and then said, "Got it. Our pal, Gabriel Moore, also Mike Cramer's pal, has been busted several times for drug dealing: fentanyl, heroin, meth."

"Recently?"

"From what I can see, for all time. At least since he turned eighteen. He's got quite the record. A few arrests for possession and distribution of narcotics. He did five years in prison for dealing heroin and was released five years ago."

I glanced at Brady. "I think you and I need to have a conversation with Mr. Moore and ask him about his late-night friend, Mr. Cramer."

"Absolutely," Brady said.

Lucy added, "His record also includes a list of known associates."

"More friends to interview," Allan said.

I looked over at Mark and Lucy, the team who had been working furiously all night. "Nice work, team. This could well be drug related. Maybe some sort of retaliation, or maybe a rival dealer took him out." I was ready to go find out.

"It's a rough neighborhood, Val. You might want to bring backup, so it's not just you and Brady," Allan cautioned.

The eagerness to interview Gabriel must have shown on my face. Allan was obviously good at reading people. "How about Brady and I pay Gabriel a visit, and you and Baker meet some of his known associates. Find out if they know Mike."

Baker said, "Solid. But before we head out, I'll call over to Shasta County narcotics team and see if they'll meet with us, tell us what they know about the guy and maybe provide backup."

I was glad that Baker was on the team. He'd taken a few hours to recover from what he'd seen inside the Cramer residence and then got straight back to work. He had told me as much as the scene had sickened him, he was able to take some time and get his head straight so that he could be part of the team that was going to find the savage individual who'd destroyed a family. *I'd always liked Baker.*

"Excellent plan."

"I'll get to it," Baker said.

"All right, just another hit of caffeine and I'll be ready to go. How about you, Brady?"

With a smile, he said, "I was born ready, Val."

SIXTEEN

VAL

"Are you sure you don't want to wait for the rest of the team?" Brady asked as we drove through Gabriel Moore's neighborhood. The houses here weren't well-kept. Older vehicles and only a few yards were maintained with respect and dignity. The others had chain-link fences and overgrown gardens, indicating a more depressed part of the area. But at this hour, early Sunday morning, it was quiet. There was nobody standing on the street corners or on the stoops. We weren't likely to be met with much hostility.

Allan and Baker were questioning a few known associates of Gabriel Moore and then planned to meet with the narcotics officers in Shasta County to get some information on the drug scene and to learn if they were aware of Mike Cramer. We didn't need Allan and Baker to question Gabriel Moore; we had patrol just a few houses down if things went sideways.

Based on Gabriel Moore's criminal record, firing shots at people who knocked on his door was not a likely scenario. "We can meet up with them after. I want to talk to Gabriel Moore now. We can't waste any time. This is our first real lead into finding out the motive for the killings."

Brady was quiet; he likely didn't agree with my approach. This was a homicide investigation and every minute counted. We were still at less than twenty-four hours since the attack, but we needed to learn as much as we could as quickly as possible. Not to mention the fact that the murders were likely already front-page news in Red Rose County.

We had a lead—somebody who was part of Mike Cramer's secret life. And if the drugs were connected to the killings, Mike was likely the target. If I had to guess, the family were collateral damage. All of this was conjecture, of course, as we didn't even have all the details of the killings. We were waiting for Dr. Edison, the medical examiner, to complete the autopsies.

We parked in front of Gabriel Moore's house and stayed there for a minute until we spotted the plainclothes officers around the corner. You didn't normally need backup every time you talked to a witness, but we were being cautious since we were going in blind. I spotted our guys in the rearview mirror and told Brady, "Patrol is in place. You good to go in?" He hadn't responded to my rebuttal to his suggestion about waiting for the team.

Brady studied my face. "I'm ready." With a playful smirk, he added, "If we catch any trouble, that's what the Kevlar is for, right?"

"Yes, sir." And I knocked on my chest, confirming I was ready for whatever came at me. I liked this side of Brady. Tough. But cautious too. It was a good trait to have.

"You take the lead, Val. You seem to have a plan for what you want to say to this guy."

Was that annoyance I detected in his tone? Maybe I needed to tread a tad more carefully. *Later.* "I do. Thanks, Brady."

Exiting the vehicle, I tugged my vest into place, and we headed down the path to the front door. It was very possible that the residents of the home were not awake yet. It was early enough that if you were someone who slept in on the weekends, you would still be asleep. I knocked on the door and took a step back.

There was no response.

We waited... and waited.

I glanced at the driveway and noted two vehicles parked in the driveway. There were likely people home, but maybe they were still asleep or had no intention of opening the door to strangers.

I knocked again and stepped back. I could hear rustling on the other side of the door and then a pause before it opened up.

A man wearing boxer shorts and a white tank said, "Who are you?"

"My name is Valerie Costa, and this is Deputy Tanner with the Red Rose County Sheriff's department. Are you Gabriel Moore?"

He nodded warily.

"We'd like to ask you a few questions about Mike Cramer."

He looked us both over. "What about him?"

"How do you know him?"

"We're associates."

"Associates how?"

"He's done work on my cars. He's real good. Five-star rating," he said, with a coy smile.

From the way he was talking about Mike, it made me think he didn't know that Mike was dead. "When was the last time you saw Mike?"

"Geez, I haven't seen him in, gosh, months. I haven't needed any work done on my car."

Studying his demeanor, I countered, "Are you sure about that?"

"I mean, it's early and you woke me up and all, but yeah, I feel like it's been a while."

"Would it surprise you then to know that we have GPS data

from Mike's car showing that he was at your house two nights ago?"

Clearly taken aback, he said, "Oh, you know, maybe he did come by. Maybe I wasn't home."

Mr. Moore's evasive behavior made me think he wasn't going to be much help. "Who else lives here with you, Mr. Moore?"

"I got my lady and my mom."

"Do you think Mr. Cramer was visiting your lady or your mom?" I asked skeptically.

He shrugged.

"Mr. Moore, let me save us all some time here. We looked you up. We know you've got a record for dealing. Low-level stuff. Nothing too serious. But you see, your name is connected to a murder investigation, and we need your help."

He raised his hand in the air and shook his head. "I ain't involved in no murder. I don't got nothing to do with no murder. Like you said, you looked me up. I'm not a violent criminal," he said, raising his voice.

Brady added, "Sir, we're not accusing you of murder."

"Then how'd my name come up? I don't know nothing about no murder. Who died?"

"Mike Cramer."

Gabriel's face fell.

"So you see why it's important we confirm the last time you saw him. We're trying to find out what happened to him and his wife and his son."

"His wife and his son?" he asked, brows raised.

"His son was killed and his wife is still in the hospital. We don't know if she will make it."

He let out a deep breath and stepped outside, closing the door behind him. He wrapped his arms around his body. "Who did this? When did it happen? Mike's whole family? Even Michael? He's only twelve." He shook his head in disbelief.

"They were attacked in their home last night. We need to know how you know Mike. And we need to ask you if you have any idea who might have done this." Judging by his reaction, Gabriel was clearly in shock, and possibly also grief-stricken.

"I have no idea who could have done something like that."

Brady said calmly, "Mr. Moore, we're investigating a homicide. We don't care about your drug affiliations, but we are trying to understand more about Mike's life. What could've gotten him and his family killed? How did you know him? We need to know everything. We need to find out who might've done this. These people killed a twelve-year-old boy. We need your help."

Gabriel looked at Brady. I think Brady had said just the right thing.

"Honestly, I don't know anything."

"We're tracing every step that Mike Cramer took. He used to come to this house regularly, every other night for the last three weeks, in the middle of the night. Now, we know he was doing something that he shouldn't have been doing. We're just trying to understand how that might've gotten him killed."

"He comes by, that's true, but we're kinda just, you know, just pals. He does do some work on the cars."

"In the middle of the night, Mr. Moore?" I asked, making no attempt to hide my disbelief.

"I feel for his family. I can't believe this has happened. He was my boy, you know. I'm not just saying that. He was older, kind of wise, you know, like an uncle or something. I can't believe it." He shook his head as though trying to get rid of the idea that Mike was dead. It wouldn't help. But it did make me think he cared for Mike and his family. Likely not our killer.

"We need you to tell us what he was involved in."

"Around here, you don't talk to cops. You'll get me killed too."

Brady took out a business card and handed it to him.

"That's my number. You think of anybody who might've wanted to hurt Mike or his family, you give me a call. Like I said, we don't care about whatever business you're in. We're just trying to figure out who tried to kill an entire family, including a little boy, Mr. Moore."

Gabriel nodded. "For sure, for sure."

Brady said, "All right, then. You take care."

I wasn't sure if I was ready to end the conversation. There was obviously more he could tell us, but Brady was right. He wouldn't tell us much more, not today.

Back in the car, Brady said, "Let's head over to the Shasta County Sheriff's department, talk to the narcotics team, and figure out what this guy is really into."

"He genuinely seemed surprised Mike had been killed."

"I got that too."

"Perhaps a rival went after the Cramers?" I suggested.

"Possibly. Let's go find out from Shasta County who those rivals might have been."

"Okay. Why don't you take the lead with Shasta and the drug angle? You've been around longer than me. And they may be more responsive to you, rather than a civilian like me." I trusted Brady and thought it was better to divide and conquer as opposed to always doing everything together if it wasn't necessary. And I didn't *always* have to be in charge. Not really.

He hesitated, then said, "It's a deal."

Brady smiled, ever so slightly, and I knew it was the right approach. There was enough work to go around and I needed to learn to not always charge ahead like a lone wolf.

SEVENTEEN

THE SECRET ADMIRER

Such a flurry of activity at the sheriff's department. On a
weekend. The forensics team and the medical examiner had
rushed to the station. It must've been the call from Saturday
night. That would explain the all-hands-on-deck strategy. My
guess was Valerie was helping out the sheriff's department
again. Or had she joined the team? Clearly, I'd missed a few
things while I was away.

Oh, how I loved watching Valerie in action. She was
exquisite. Part of me thought I should give her more time before
I took her away from all of it.

With Deputy Tanner by her side, I knew I couldn't get too
close yet anyhow.

As they'd rushed through the parking lot, along with a few
other detectives, I couldn't help but wonder where they were
going and if it was too risky to find out. I was too close to the
prize to risk it all now. I could wait a little longer.

But it was time to start getting ready to implement my plan.
Stock up on supplies, make sure I had everything just right for
when Valerie came back to me and we were finally together
again. Perhaps I should let her know I'm back. Send her a

message. It didn't seem to throw her off during her last case; she could handle it. She was tough. And I wanted to let her know that I was proud of her.

I chuckled under my breath. Yes, I should definitely send Valerie a message. I didn't want her to think I'd forgotten about her.

EIGHTEEN

BRADY

We met Allan and Baker in the lobby of the Shasta County Sheriff's department.

I said, "Hey. Did you find anything useful?"

Baker replied, "We had a brief conversation with two known associates of Gabriel Moore. A guy who goes by the name of Gemini, and the other Tank. Both told us they'd never heard of Mike, never seen him. You know the drill."

"Did you tell them Mike was dead?" I asked.

"We did. They seemed surprised, despite acting like they didn't know him. They clearly did. They were low-level, from what we could tell. I don't think they were capable of carrying out the attack."

Not all violent folks looked or acted like violent folks, though. I said, "Same with Gabriel Moore. I think Mike was definitely involved in something illegal. Gabriel was really cagey about his involvement with Mike, but admitted he knew him and that Mike had worked on some of his cars."

Baker said, "Maybe he's helping to build secret compartments in the vehicle to hide drugs and drive them over the border."

"It's possible," I said.

Val said, "I agree with Brady. I don't think Gabriel's our killer, but I sure would like to know if these guys have any enemies. I'm real interested to hear what the narcotics team has to say."

"Same here," Baker added.

The automatic doors opened and two rather large men in plain clothes walked into the lobby, checking us from head to toe. One of them carried a laptop. "Are you the Red Rose County team?" one asked.

"Yes. I am Deputy Tanner," I said. "This is Detective Allan and Detective Baker. And this is Val Costa. She's a consultant helping us with the homicide investigation. She's former FBI and has helped us out with a few other cases."

"I'm Aaron, and this is Levi. We work narcotics here in Shasta County."

Both were in their mid-thirties and looked like they lifted weights at least five days a week. "We appreciate you coming in on a Sunday," I said.

Levi said, "We're interested to understand why you need us so bad. Let's get you into a conference room. Can we get you coffee, water, tea, granola bar?"

"We're fine," I said.

We followed them into a large conference room. They sat down and said, "So what's going on?"

Taking a breath, I explained everything we'd learned since the night of the crime to this morning's interviews.

"So you think the murders are related to Shasta County drugs?" Levi asked.

I said, "It's our best lead right now. And considering Gabriel Moore said Mike was like an uncle, Mike could be deep into drugs."

"Interesting," Levi said slowly as if putting the pieces together in his mind.

"I'm guessing you know Gabriel."

Levi said, "Oh yeah. Gabe is a mid-level dealer now. We suspect he's getting the drugs from Mexico and distributing to lower-level dealers throughout Shasta County. Does a little dealing on his own but mostly his lower-level folks do that kinda work. Gabe didn't like prison too much. He's been pretty careful since he's been out. But honestly, he's not a real violent guy, and nor are his cronies. I wouldn't suspect him of homicide, especially if you're saying this guy was his friend. But you never know."

"How many associates does he have? What's he running?" Allan asked.

"We suspect whatever he can get his hands on: heroin, prescription drugs, meth. Maybe ten in his crew. They're not big-time."

"Do you know of anyone Gabe's involved with that might be capable of killing the Cramers?"

Levi was about to say something when he stopped. "Give me a sec," he said. He opened his laptop and after tapping around on his keyboard, he turned it around to face us and pointed at the screen. "Is this Mike Cramer's car?"

"Yeah, that's it," Val said.

"I thought I'd heard his name before. We've seen him on surveillance. We don't know much about him, aside from the description of him and his vehicle. We don't know what he was doing with Moore, but yeah, he was definitely a frequent visitor to the house."

"How long have you been watching Gabriel Moore's house?"

"The last few months. DEA asked us to check him out. Part of an ongoing investigation into the Mexican cartel we believe Gabe gets his supply from."

DEA? "You haven't busted him?"

"No probable cause. He doesn't deal out in the open. Or at

his house. The surveillance was in the hope we'd catch one of the Mexican cartel's members."

"Did you see any?"

"Don't know. We didn't ask questions. We handed over the video to DEA."

"You never saw Mike with drugs?" I asked. A cartel was certainly capable of the kind of violence we'd witnessed at the crime scene.

"No, we never saw him with drugs. He just met up at Gabe's house. Usually parked in the garage for a few hours and then left."

Mike could have been loading his car full of drugs—out of sight.

Allan said, "We thought maybe since Mike does auto body work, that could explain it."

"How so?" Levi asked.

"Maybe Mike was helping to fit out the cars to bring drugs over the border."

Levi said, "Maybe. Not likely, though. That might pass for moving drugs within states, but border patrol has gotten pretty sophisticated. You can't just stuff drugs in the side panel of your car and get over the border these days. They've got drug-sniffing dogs and high-tech X-ray and gamma ray machines to look for drugs in secret compartments. It's not as easy to smuggle drugs as it used to be."

That was assuring. *I guess.* But drugs were still running rampant. "How are they getting the drugs here, if not driving them over the border?" I asked.

"Boats. Tunnels. Air. Commercial goods. They find a way. It's not impossible, just not as easy as it used to be."

"How do you think Gabe gets his supply?" Val asked.

Levi said, "That's what we, and the DEA, would like to know."

"Why do you think they're getting drugs from Mexico?" I asked.

"We've tested some of the product. It's consistent with a Mexican cartel operating out of Tijuana."

Tijuana was just over the San Diego border. "How often do you think they get their supply from Mexico?"

Levi said, "We suspect once every month or two."

I turned to Val. "We need to ask Mark to check the GPS car data further back."

She nodded. "Absolutely. Maybe Mike's the connection to Mexico. Maybe he double-crossed them."

Levi said, "Maybe. Or he was with the Mexican cartel."

"Why would you think that?" I asked.

"There was something about Mike that made me think he was higher up. He carried himself like he was the boss."

I said, "Gabriel Moore did say he was like an uncle to him."

Val said, "Was the DEA able to determine if Mike was with the cartel?"

"That's a good question. They didn't report back to us. We should reach out to the DEA. If Mike was connected, it would be good to know why the cartel would want to take him—and his family—out," Levi said. "Gabe didn't tell you anything that might be useful?"

Val said, "No. He said he doesn't talk to cops, but he was really sorry to hear about Mike. I was inclined to believe him."

"I'll reach out to our contact at the DEA and see if they can provide some insight. Give me a sec and I'll call him."

The room fell silent as Levi exited the conference room. Was it possible Mike Cramer was a drug trafficker or part of a cartel? From the neighbors' account of the Cramers, they were nice, quiet, kept to themselves. No red flags to indicate a criminal lived in the neighborhood.

Levi hurried back in. "My contact at the DEA didn't

answer, but I left a message. I'll let you know when he gets back to me."

As we left the station, I said, "Val, did you suspect Mike was involved in drugs?"

"I knew it was likely he'd been involved in something pretty rough to end up like that. A Mexican cartel fits."

Val was cool and collected, not even looking remotely stressed. How did she do it?

NINETEEN

VAL

Back in the war room with Lucy and Mark, I waited as they sifted through the cell phone as well as the GPS data from Mike's and Stephanie's cars. I explained that we needed to go back several months to see if Mike had visited any ports, gone to Mexico, or visited airfields—anything that could potentially link him to the Mexican drug cartel. It was nerve-racking to watch them. Nothing was coming up so far.

While I waited for news from our techies, Brady and I made a list of all the people we needed to interview, both of us sitting around like a bunch of phone operators, calling to make appointments. I was still waiting to hear back from the owner of the auto body shop Mike worked at, to learn more about the business, about Mike as an employee, and to find out the names of his coworkers so we could interview them too. It would be important to talk to them considering they were the people who spent the most time with Mike outside of his family.

I wasn't terribly surprised that Mike might be connected to drugs. The way he was killed was purposeful and targeted. I wasn't one hundred percent sure of all his injuries, but whoever killed him wanted him to feel pain. To kill, or try to kill,

Stephanie and her son was particularly unusual, even for a Mexican cartel. Usually, they kept the family out of it unless the killer was particularly vicious, someone who placed no value on human life. There were enough people like that so I shouldn't be surprised, but the scene wasn't like anything I'd seen before. Once the autopsy and catalog of Mike's injuries were complete, we'd put the details into ViCAP, the Violent Criminal Apprehension Program, to see if there were any matches to the crime. This crime was unique, and if the killer had killed before details of similar crimes would be in the database.

Mark said, "I got something."

My pulse raced. "What is it?"

"Looks like Mike took a trip all the way to the Bay Area a few months ago. He stayed there for about a week and then drove back. Maybe he was meeting with dealers?"

I deflated at the news and reviewed my notes from the Jamisons. "What were the dates?"

"January 28th to February 3rd."

As I suspected. "He was visiting his in-laws. It was Mr. Jamison's, Stephanie's father, eightieth birthday."

Mark said, "Well, I've gone back three months. There's no sign of anyone driving his vehicle to an airfield, the coast, any port, anywhere outside of Red Rose and Shasta Counties. If I had to guess, I'd say Mike wasn't going to Mexico, but I'll keep looking. The car's about nine months old. I can go back that far, but not any earlier."

"What about Stephanie's car?"

Mark said, "Hers is easy. She hasn't left Red Rose County in the past three months." That ruled out the idea Mike could have used his wife's car for drug dealing purposes.

"Thanks. Keep looking into Mike. Let me know if there's anything outside of Red Rose and Shasta Counties."

He nodded and returned to the task.

What was the connection between Mike, Gabriel Moore

and his drug dealing? I felt he was likely connected to the cartel. When Shasta County told us about the Mexican cartel I thought, this is it—a cartel member did this. It had the style of a cartel-organized crime style hit. The murder left a message. What that message was remained unclear. But I'd bet there was one. That's what was odd about the crime scene; it seemed to have left a message, but not necessarily for us. But maybe I shouldn't let my mind wander that far. We needed details from the autopsy before we could draw any conclusions.

There was still one lead that might explain everything. To the room, I said, "I'm going to go and call the hospital to see if there is any improvement in Stephanie's condition."

Silent nods from the room as everybody continued to work —Lucy and Mark sifted through data, while Allan and Baker scrolled through cell phone logs.

In the hallway, I called the hospital and found that Steph had been placed in an induced coma while her brain healed from her injuries. I dialed Mrs. Jamison's cell number.

"Hello?"

"Mrs. Jamison, this is Val Costa."

"Hi, Val."

"I just spoke with the nurse, and they told me that Steph is in an induced coma."

"She looks so frail, bandaged up. She's so pale, but I think she squeezed my hand."

If she had, it was a good sign. "Really?"

"I think so. Nobody else thought so, but I felt it. Are you a mother, Val?"

"I am, Mrs. Jamison." And I could only imagine being in Mrs. Jamison's shoes. If Harrison was lying in a hospital bed recovering from a gunshot wound to the head, I'd be a heap on the floor. Or at least feel like it. Part of me thought that if something like that ever happened, I'd be a pillar of strength and I'd be out there pounding the pavement trying to find out who hurt my child, but I knew in my heart that's not where I would be. I would be right by my son's side. To be there when he woke up and to ensure nobody could hurt him ever again.

My heart skipped a beat.

Who was protecting Stephanie?

Four family members were with her, but none of them were law enforcement or could assess a threat from what I could tell. We needed 24-hour surveillance on Stephanie's room in case the killers came back to finish what they started.

"Then you understand. A mother's intuition—she's gonna come back to us."

I did, and I hoped her intuition was right. "That's wonderful news, Mrs. Jamison. I was calling to see if there's anything I can do to help the family—you must be exhausted. There's a motel not far from the hospital, I can arrange for rooms and food. You can take it in shifts and get cleaned up or get a little rest."

"That's so kind of you, Val. I'd hate to put you out, though."

"It's no problem at all. I'll make a few calls. The sheriff's department, and the whole county, wants to ensure you're well taken care of while you're here, okay?" And I'd request a guard at Stephanie's door.

"Have you found who did this yet? Why would anyone do something like this to my beautiful Steph, my baby, and my grandbaby? I just can't process it."

"That's normal, Mrs. Jamison, and unfortunately, we don't have any answers yet. But we have some new leads that we're following. You can call me anytime you want to talk, or would like an update, okay?"

"Thank you, Val. I appreciate it."

I couldn't help but take a moment to be grateful. Stephanie's mother said she'd squeezed her hand. She probably had. An excellent response for someone who suffered a brain injury. We all had to believe she'd come through.

There was some rustling from the line, and then she said, "My son would like to talk to you. Is that okay?"

"Of course."

After a brief pause, a deep voice said, "Val, this is Chuck."

I proceeded to repeat to Chuck what I'd said to his mother about organizing food and accommodation for them.

"That's so kind of you. Different than the Bay Area, isn't it?"

"I've never lived in the Bay Area, but I lived in DC, and Red Rose County is definitely a special place. We take care of our people here. Now, what can I help you with?"

"I wanted to know if there was anything we can do to help find out what happened to my sister, my nephew, and my brother-in-law."

Chuck was in fight mode, and I appreciated it. "The best thing you can do is be there for Stephanie. I'll let you know if I need anything. I'm about to call your sister's friends to see if they might know of anything that could have led to this. We're also waiting on the financials. Do you know if Mike was doing any work in addition to working at the auto body shop?"

"Not that I know of. Do you think this has something to do with the auto body shop?"

"We're not sure yet. We're exploring all avenues right now."

"You'll let us know as the investigation progresses?"

"Yes. We're in the process of tracking the movements of both Mike and Stephanie over the last couple of days, weeks, even months, to see where they went, maybe someone they encountered."

"Could it have been a random robbery?"

"It's possible."

"But you don't think so?"

"We don't have enough evidence to say either way. But the more we can learn about their lives, the easier it'll be to work out who did this to your family. That's what we're trying to understand—who did this and why."

"Thank you, Val."

"You take care. I'm gonna make some calls and make sure your family is well taken care of."

"Thank you again."

"And please let me know if there is any change in Stephanie's condition. If she wakes up, she can tell us what happened."

"We will."

I ended the call and went back into the conference room where Mark and Lucy were discussing something with Allan.

"What did you find?" I asked.

"Unfortunately, nothing," Mark replied. "I went back and wrote a script that alerts me to any routes Mike took outside of Red Rose County and Shasta County. There were no hits. I can look through it manually too, but it doesn't look like he was meeting up with anybody outside of Shasta County or Red Rose County. Mostly he visited the pizza parlor, the kids' school, his place of work, home, restaurants around town. He didn't visit any other homes in the neighborhood, so maybe they really did keep to themselves."

I sat down. "We may have to wait for the callback from the DEA to see if Mike's known to them or the Mexican cartel they suspect supplies Gabriel Moore. In the meantime, I just spoke with the Jamisons. Stephanie is in an induced coma. Her mom thinks she squeezed her hand, which is a great sign if it happened. I said we need to get them set up with a hotel and food—the whole shebang. They need to be taken care of here. Also, I want to make sure that whoever did this isn't coming back for Steph or the family. We need 24-hour surveillance on her hospital room."

Baker said, "I'm on it. I'll get a couple of patrols over there.

We can go over in shifts. We'll make sure the Jamisons are looked after and that nobody gets to Stephanie."

"Good. The story hit the news. If the cartels are involved, they won't want any witnesses."

"I'll get right on it."

"Thanks, Baker." To the rest of the room, I said, "I have a few of Stephanie's friends' names that her mother gave me. Let's divide and conquer. Ask them about Stephanie's marriage, anything unusual going on with the Cramers. Like if something was bothering her, maybe something at work, school, karate, sports—anything involving the son or the husband. And be gentle; they're likely learning of Stephanie's condition from you."

There were more nods from around the room. I wrote out the different names, handed them to Brady and Allan, and gave a list to Lucy to match up with the cell phone data.

"All right, I'll call Taylor from one of the small offices. According to Mrs. Jamison, Taylor was Stephanie's best friend."

"Good luck."

Hopefully, one of Stephanie's friends could shed some light on whether the Cramers were having any problems. We had assumed Mike was the target of the crime, but it could just as easily have been Stephanie. Perhaps Stephanie had a few secrets of her own.

TWENTY

VAL

After a careful explanation for the call, Stephanie's best friend Taylor asked, "Is she going to make it?"

"I'm sorry to say that we don't know yet. Her parents, brother, and sister are at the hospital with her now."

Taylor's voice shook as she said, "I just can't believe it. And little Michael... I just don't understand who could've done this."

"That's what we're trying to figure out. We want to find out who did this to Stephanie and her family. I'm hoping that you'll be able to answer a few questions for me."

"Like what?"

"We're trying to learn everything we can about Stephanie and Mike. It's standard for an investigation like this to learn as much as we can about the victims' lives. It can help us piece together what could've led to the events of last night."

"Like if they had any enemies or something? Do you think that they were specifically targeted? Like it wasn't random?" Taylor couldn't hide her surprise.

"We're not sure yet. We're still trying to gather all the facts."

After a sniffle, Taylor said, "What do you want to know?"

"How often did you speak with Stephanie?"

"It's hard because I'm still in the Bay Area and she's up there, and we've got our kids and our lives. But we kept in touch about once a week. I'd call or text or she'd call or text."

"It sounds like she valued your friendship."

"We've been best friends since we were six years old. I don't know what I'll do if she doesn't make it," Taylor said, her voice breaking. "Do you think I should be there with her?"

"I can keep you updated on her condition. That's probably the easiest for you. Her family is with her. It sounds like you have a lot of responsibility yourself."

"I do. Two kids and a husband. My youngest is only five."

I briefly thought back to Harrison wearing dinosaur pajamas and roaring around the house like he was a T. rex. Five-year-olds were full of energy, and I recalled having a hard time keeping up with him. I couldn't imagine having two. "I promise I'll update you as soon as there is any change to Stephanie's condition, okay?"

"Thank you."

I wanted to tread gently, but I needed more information. "When you spoke with Stephanie or texted, did she ever mention any problems between her and Mike?"

"No. I mean, every once in a while she'd be annoyed that he was working too much, but nothing major. They were solid. He adored Steph. I can't believe he's gone," Taylor said, still in disbelief.

I noted the description of a solid marriage. "Do you know if there were any disagreements or anything unusual going on in their lives, something maybe Stephanie was worried about?"

"I don't think so. I know that Michael wasn't doing great in school, but he was able to pull his grades up a little. But no, things were going really good actually."

Actually? Perhaps things weren't always so good. "What do you mean?"

"Well, neither one of them made a whole lot of money, and

Mike was good at saving, but things were tight what with having a son to raise and inflation making everything more expensive. Mike was worried about money, but then he started taking on some work on the side and making more money. Steph said things were going great and she was relieved."

"They had more money, so they weren't stressed about that anymore?"

"Exactly," Taylor said.

"How long ago did Mike start doing extra work?"

"A few years ago, maybe five, I think. Bits and pieces here and there. First, it was just a little to help out financially, and then in the last year, it really picked up. That's why they were getting excited. They were planning a family trip to Disneyland. Steph said Michael was so excited."

My heart broke for the family. Michael would never see Disneyland or meet Mickey Mouse. He wouldn't get to do anything anymore. It wasn't fair. He should have had the opportunity to grow up. To see the world. Like Harrison had. "Did Stephanie say what kind of side work Mike was doing?"

"Auto body work. He's really good. Been doing it for years. He's great at restoring old cars. Detail work is his specialty. He's really a wizard at it."

"Restoring cars and doing bodywork was the side work he did?" It was possible, but I seriously doubted it.

"Yeah, that's what Steph said. Do you think that his side work got them killed?"

"We don't have anything to support that right now. We want to make sure we understand everything that was going on in their lives. Was there anything else new or out of the ordinary?"

"No, I don't think so." She paused. "Actually, during our last phone call a few weeks ago, I was on the phone with her when Mike got home. She greeted him and asked how he was doing. He was real short with her. She asked him what was wrong, and he said nothing. So she told me she'd call me back because it seemed like he was upset about something, and that wasn't like him. Not at all. He was usually a happy guy," Taylor said.

What had put Mike in a bad mood? Had he been worried about something before his death? "Did you ever find out from Stephanie what had been bothering Mike?"

"No, I didn't hear anything about it. I just thought he'd had a bad day at work. It happens," Taylor said, dismissing the thought.

"It does. Sounds like you knew Mike pretty well."

"When they were still in the Bay Area we spent a lot of time together. And then when they moved, they'd come back to visit and my family visits them in Rosedale. Such a beautiful area. My son is the same age as Michael, and the two get along..."

The sudden realization that she'd used the present tense must have hit and made her lose her train of thought. It was understandable.

"And everybody got along?"

After a sniffle, she said, "Yeah, Mike's a really great guy. He was really friendly and he got along well with my husband," her voice trailing off again.

"Taylor, is there anything else you could tell me that might help the investigation? Anything that would help me learn more about Mike and Stephanie?"

"I don't think so. I can't believe this. You'll let me know if there are any developments?"

"I promise I will." I thanked Taylor for her time and ended the call.

It wasn't concrete evidence, but it sounded like something had been bothering Mike, and that was useful to know. He'd been doing side work, like we thought, and if the income spiked recently, that might have something to do with his death.

I walked back over to the war room, waving to the team, which now included the sheriff. "Anything new?" I asked.

"Not from the one I spoke to," Lucy said.

"How about Stephanie's other friends?"

Allan said, "Her friend Tina said Mike and Stephanie were a good couple. Nothing of use to us."

Brady added, "Same story from Amy. No red flags. No enemies. Nothing helpful. How about the one you spoke to?"

"Taylor, best friends since they were six, said they were a great couple, and that Mike did side work. The side work, auto body-related, increased in the last year, bringing in some much-needed cash. Also that he'd been in a bad mood shortly before his death, but Taylor didn't know why."

Kingston, the sheriff, said, "Sounds like the drugs could be the extra cash."

I nodded. "We'll definitely want to explore that further. Any word on the financials?"

Lucy said, "No, but we should get them soon."

Had Mike's side work, whether actually auto body work or drug dealing, been the reason behind the brutal attack on the Cramers?

TWENTY-ONE

BRADY

We had been sifting through phone records, GPS data, and making calls to people who hadn't called us back for *hours*. Lunch hadn't helped boost my waning energy as I'd hoped. I hadn't slept in more than twenty-four hours and I was beginning to think I was too old for these all-night investigations. Plus, with no new leads, we were simply waiting. We needed something to fuel our adrenaline and keep us going. We needed a break in the case.

We knew that Mike was affiliated, or at least friends, with a known drug dealer, but all we knew was that he did side work. That could've been a cover for his wife for what he was really doing—either dealing or using drugs. Stephanie may have been completely unaware of his clandestine meetings in the middle of the night with the dealer in Shasta County. But until she woke up from the coma, we wouldn't know for sure.

Glancing around the room, I saw the team was weary and needed a break. Well, everyone but Val. She had dark circles under her eyes, but she seemed wired. Her intensity was fascinating to watch. She didn't seem to skip a beat or pause for breath. If it weren't for her eyes and wrinkled clothes, you'd think she just started her shift. She was incredible.

I was about to suggest a break, at least to go home and take a shower, when I got a call.

"This is Brady."

"Brady, this is Agent Stew from the DEA. I got your number from Shasta County."

Hopefully this would be the break we needed. "Good to hear from you," I said with a burst of energy.

Val's eyes locked onto mine. Did she know it was the DEA? Nothing seemed to get past her.

"Did you learn anything about Mike Cramer?" I asked.

"That's what I was calling about. Shasta County told me about the situation and Mike Cramer's affiliation with Gabriel Moore. We've seen them together. We believe they're associates, but we're not sure of Mike's involvement. We don't think it's with the Mexican cartel. We've never seen him outside of Shasta County with Gabriel Moore. I checked in with a couple of our undercover agents in Mexico and showed them a picture of Mike Cramer. Nobody's seen him. They're fairly certain he's not part of the cartel. And there is no word about a hit on him either."

Not exactly the news I was hoping for. "I was beginning to suspect that. We've been through all of the GPS data from his car. He didn't make any trips to Mexico or any airfields or ports."

"Sorry we couldn't be of more help, but without any kind of affiliation with the cartel, it's unlikely they would've gone after him or his family. Unless it was someone locally that Mike upset, for whatever reason."

That was an avenue to explore. "Do you know of any rival drug dealers in the area that may have wanted to take him out?"

"Not that we know of, and we think the cartel supplies all of

Shasta County, but if we hear of anything brewing, I'll let you know."

"Thanks." I hung up, and Val was by my side in a flash. "Who was that?"

"DEA."

Her rapid-fire questioning began. "Do they know Mike? Is he part of the cartel? Have they seen him associating with the cartel?"

Answering all three questions with a single "No", I then recounted what the agent had told me.

Val said, "Unless he was undermining them somehow. You don't have to have met them to do that. Stephanie's friend said that he'd had a spike in income over the last year. Maybe he was double-crossing the cartel, or even Gabriel and his crew."

"If that's true, and the DEA doesn't know about it..."

Val smirked. "Gabriel Moore might."

"We can interview him again, but I don't think he's going to talk to us. What can we do?"

"I don't know, find a reason to arrest him. Put pressure on him. I don't know. I have to think on it." Val furrowed her brow and raked her fingers through her hair, which was now sticking up in all directions. Maybe she was as tired as the rest of us. We could all use a rest to clear our minds and start fresh in the morning.

"Can I talk to you outside?" I asked Val.

Val cocked her head. "Sure."

We headed out of the conference room and a few doors down to a quiet area. I stopped and leaned against the wall.

"What is it, Brady?" There was such care and concern in her voice, I couldn't help but smile. As tough and focused as Val was during the case, there were moments like this when I felt her softer, empathetic side. And honestly, I wasn't sure which side I liked more. Maybe both equally.

"I was thinking since we're pretty much just waiting on

records and people to call us back, maybe the team should get some rest, or take shifts. I know I'm tired, and I'm pretty sure the team is too."

Val reflected for a moment, then with a nod, said, "You're right. We're just waiting. A break will do us all some good. We don't need to be waiting at the station. We have cell phones. We can call if we need to. I think in-person interviews are going to be what leads us to answers. The autopsies aren't complete yet and the labs could take until Monday or Tuesday to come back. Unless something comes up between now and tomorrow morning, let's all take a break. Monday morning, we pound the pavement."

"Sounds good. Do you want to let the team know?"

"I will."

As much as I wanted to catch the person who had murdered the Cramers, I knew a nap and a hot shower were calling my name.

TWENTY-TWO

VAL

As I packed up, I couldn't wait to get home and have a hot shower, and hopefully something home cooked. And of course, I wanted to check in on Mom and give Harrison a quick call. I still felt a bit guilty for waking him up earlier and I wanted to make sure he wasn't worried about me. He didn't know about the new case I was working, and if I explained it he'd know I wasn't in the line of fire and he'd understand my need to talk to him and find out how he was doing. We'd made a deal after my capture by the Bear that whenever I was working a case we would stay in regular contact. About to zip up my bag, I stopped when Sally, the medical examiner, poked her head around the door.

"Knock knock."

I set my bag back on the floor. "Hey, Sally. What's up?"

She'd been up for as long as the rest of us, arriving at the scene and staying overnight to get the autopsies finished and samples off to the lab for Mike and Michael. "Finished. Lab results will be in tomorrow. Jonathan is working around the clock. He's got everything set up. Samples are prepped."

I walked over to her and said, "What did you find?"

"He had some pretty gnarly injuries," Sally said. "Mike, that is."

"Oh?"

She pushed a stray strand of red hair from her eyes, and said, "Maybe I should show you what I mean, if you're up for it."

"Drinks after?" I said. Drinks weren't exactly a rest, but it was a break.

"Throw in a cheeseburger and you've got yourself a deal. Where is everyone?"

"Taking a break. We're waiting on people to call us back and more records to come in. They've been working for the last twenty-four hours."

"Smart. Fresh minds are better than weary ones," Sally said.

"It's bad, huh?"

"Let's just say I hope I never see anything like this again." Sally led the way down the hallway to the medical building, and we went to the autopsy suite. Inside, gowned up, I felt the chill of the room and the sight before me.

On one table a small body lay under a sheet. Michael. On another table, a larger figure lay under a sheet. Mike. A father and son—extinguished, just like that.

Sally led me over to the small body. She pulled back the sheet to his shoulders, and my heart nearly stopped at the sight of his face. *Michael.* The boy looked so young and innocent— because he was. If it wasn't for the grayish color, he could have been sleeping. He lay clean and motionless. In that moment, I made a silent promise to Michael that I would find the person responsible. No child should be lying under a medical examiner's sheet.

"Cause of death?" I asked.

"Single gunshot wound to the head. He died instantly."

Had he seen it coming? Was he terrified? Of course he would have been. "Any other injuries?" I asked.

"None that I could find. I checked his arms and legs for bruising, any kind of prints or marks that would show he was forcibly put into the position he died in. There were none. And no defensive wounds, either."

He'd just laid down? "Stomach contents?"

"Bits of chicken and rice."

That matched the dinner that was still on their plates on the dining table. "Toxicology?"

"Labs are still processing."

"Any signs he'd been drugged? Surely he didn't just lay down and let someone shoot him?" *Please say he was drugged and was unaware of the horror that had happened to his family.*

"Perhaps with a gun on his mother and father, he'd complied with any demands the shooter made."

How terrifying for anyone, especially a child. What kind of monster were we dealing with? "Labs will be back tomorrow?" I asked.

She nodded. "Are you ready to see Mike?"

"I am." Was I?

"You think you are, but trust me, you're gonna need that drink after."

I knew he had been brutally tortured before being murdered, but there had been so much blood at the scene it was difficult to see all of his injuries. Sally pulled back the sheet completely, exposing Mike Cramer's body. The injuries were stark and disturbing.

"Start head to toe?" she asked.

I swallowed. "Okay."

"Several blunt force traumas to the head and face, probably with something small, like the butt of a gun and maybe a fist. Or a combination of the two."

He had been severely beaten. Why?

She pointed to his wrists and ankles. "He was zip-tied to the chair, which I believe you saw at the scene. There was a lot of resistance. You can tell by the contusions."

"He's a big guy. Do you think one person could've done this?"

"I don't think so. There was a major struggle. He didn't just sit down and let them tie him to a chair."

Two killers.

Sally continued. "Most of his injuries were inflicted after they'd tied him up. See the stab wounds on his chest? None hit anything critical, likely just to cause pain. You see the slices on his arms too."

Before taking a step lower, she pointed to his groin area. "The injuries are extensive and were done perimortem. He was alive when they mutilated him."

Likely to punish or dehumanize him. Or our killers were into satanic rituals. It was unusual... and gruesome. Mike died a slow and painful death. Nobody deserved that.

"What actually killed him?"

She pointed to his neck. "His carotid was severed. He bled out. It was likely the very last cut, to end it. Although, even without the last injury he wouldn't have made it for much longer. It's clear they wanted him to suffer."

That much was obvious. But why? What had Mike done? Who had he met that would do such a thing?

"In your time with the FBI, you ever see anything like this?"

"Mutilation, yes. Combined with the death of the son, attempts on the wife—no." It was hard to get my head around.

"Are you thinking that maybe they killed his family as part of the torture?" Sally asked.

Maybe. The scene is so bizarre. "Were you able to determine the time of death for both?"

She nodded. "Michael died roughly between 5 and 6 p.m. last night. Mike Senior, I would guess, about an hour later. It's a little hard to say, but it's a pretty close window. Mike's food was digested slightly more than Michael's, making me think maybe it was about an hour. It's not exact. But I'd guess they died within an hour of each other."

My mind was trying to put together the pieces. If this was the work of a Mexican cartel, it made sense. It was a brutal crime, sending a message, maybe revenge. I will kill your family and then you, painfully and slowly. I shook my head. "My first thought when I looked at the scene was they were targeting him for some reason."

"Any leads yet?"

"We think he might have an affiliation with a drug dealer in Shasta County. We talked to the DEA. They don't think he's part of a Mexican cartel or known to them, or that the hit was placed by them. I have no idea who could've done this."

"You'll figure it out."

I appreciated the vote of confidence. "I hope so."

"You ready for that drink?"

"Absolutely."

I was keen to get out of there as fast as possible so that I could work on pushing the gruesome images of the deceased parent and child out of my head. I didn't need any new nightmares.

As we exited the suite, my thoughts drifted back to what I'd learned. Michael had been killed first. The only "good" thing about that was it meant he hadn't witnessed what they'd done to his father. Given the obvious fight Mike had put up, we were potentially dealing with two killers, not one. Two *vicious* killers. Was it the killers' first time? Or was there a pair of serial killers running around Red Rose County?

TWENTY-THREE

THE SECRET ADMIRER

From the shadowed corner of the parking lot, I watched Valerie and her redheaded friend step out of the building. The sun bathed her in a golden light, and she seemed momentarily disoriented, probably from being inside for too long. I had been biding my time, waiting for this moment, anticipating the brief instant when she would let her guard down.

She headed toward her car with Dr. Edison, chatting away before making a call. She glanced around as if sensing something amiss. My pulse quickened. It was time to leave before she noticed me. My car, parked strategically for a quick getaway, was ready. I slid in and waited for them to leave, keeping my eyes on her. The thrill of the chase filled my veins, but I had to remain calm and collected.

As soon as they left, I drove away faster than usual, needing to put some distance between us. I began to plan. My mind raced with possibilities, each more thrilling than the last. She was perfect, her routines meticulously observed, her habits so familiar to me now. But I needed to focus and not get distracted. Everything had to go flawlessly.

Once home, I locked the door and drew the curtains. My

sanctuary, filled with hundreds of detailed notes and photographs of her, awaited. I sat at my desk, spreading out the latest images. She was always so close yet always just out of reach. The time was nearing when I would change that.

Tonight, I would finalize my plans. The next step had to be precise. There could be no mistakes. I considered the places she frequented, the times she was most vulnerable. Each detail was critical. I would capture her attention, draw her into my web. She wouldn't suspect a thing until it was too late.

With my finger, I traced the outline of her face in the photographs, imagining the moment she would finally be mine. The thought of her fear, her realization, sent a shiver down my spine. It wouldn't be long now. The pieces were falling into place. Soon, she would be mine.

TWENTY-FOUR

BRADY

Showered and fed, I collapsed onto my couch at home. It was unnervingly quiet. I still hadn't gotten used to the lack of noise since my divorce. The house used to be filled with the sound of kids practicing the flute, bickering among themselves, or playing their pop music too loud. My youngest was in her last months of high school and spent most of her time with her mother, and my oldest was away at college. I missed having someone around all the time. Even when things had started to deteriorate before the divorce, at least there was someone to talk to. Even through the hard times, we were polite, at least in front of the kids. Most of our exchanges revolved around "How was your day?" or "What do you want for dinner?" Nothing deep and meaningful, but it was strangely comforting to know someone else was there.

It had been four years since I left the Bay Area, and my family had splintered. The life I had built seemed to slide away like an avalanche in my coldest winter. I didn't usually spend my time moping around or feeling sorry for myself. Perhaps it was the fatigue or the latest news that my ex was getting remarried. Maybe a combination of both. At least she wasn't marrying the guy she'd had an affair with while we were married. I don't know why that would be worse, but it seemed like it would be. Through painful marriage counseling I learned the affair wasn't about the men she'd slept with. It was the fact that our marriage hadn't been good for a while. We had fallen into a monotonous routine with conversations that didn't mean anything. We had ignored the indifference we felt toward each other by focusing on our children's activities and ensuring they had lasting family memories. Like vacations to the Grand Canyon and beach getaways to Hawaii. From the outside we'd looked like a happy family. It wasn't until I'd learned of the affairs that I realized we had actually grown apart years before.

How long does that burning, gotta-have-you love last? For my ex and me, I think it lasted five out of the twenty years we'd spent together. Since the divorce, there hadn't really been anybody I wanted to date. I had been on dating apps and gone on a few dates here and there, but it just wasn't for me. Nobody made it past two dates, and not a single person I met was even half as interesting as Val.

Would she ever see me that way? I still wasn't sure. I didn't want to ruin our friendship, but what if it was one of those situations where she only realized what she'd had right in front of her when it was too late? I wasn't a sappy romantic, but being around her, my thoughts would drift to what it would be like to kiss her. That usually led to more fantasies. My dreams were filled with her.

The desire to catch even just a glimpse of her was the real reason for the frequent trips I made to check on her mom. Not that I wasn't genuinely interested in Elizabeth's well-being and the progress she had been making since her stroke, but I couldn't resist the opportunity to see Val. We usually made small talk or discussed work, but I knew that when she asked questions she wasn't just being polite; she was interested in what I had to say. Okay, enough, I needed to stop thinking like this. And I needed to give my brain a break from cell phone records, GPS data, and thoughts of Val.

Despite my exhaustion, I found it difficult to shut my eyes and let my mind drift off. I was too wired. Maybe something on TV would lull me to sleep. I grabbed the remote, turned on the TV and clicked through the streaming service until I found something that I always fell back on: true crime documentaries. There was one on Pablo Escobar. Perhaps that would do the trick and relax me, or would it only make me think of work? I started the documentary, and then *bam*.

It hit me.

I leapt up and turned off the TV, grabbing my gun and badge on my way out.

TWENTY-FIVE

VAL

With a full belly, I hugged Sally and told her I'd see her the next day at work. She climbed into her car and headed home for a well-deserved good night's sleep. I could definitely use a shower and a rest too. I headed to my car, got inside, started the engine, and was about to back out of the parking space when I stopped. I hadn't done everything I could do tonight. *I don't go home and sleep when there's a killer, or killers, running around my home town!* I turned off the engine and called Mom.

"Hey, Val."

"Hi, Mom. How's everything there?" I asked.

"We just started a game of gin rummy."

"Sounds fun."

"How's the case going? Any leads?"

"The whole team has been working nonstop looking at the Cramers' lives. One digital record at a time. We've got a few leads to follow."

"You know, I hardly knew them at all. They must've really kept to themselves."

"That's what we're learning."

"Any suspects yet?"

"Not yet, but we have found a few unexpected things."

"Are you coming home soon, or will you be out another night?"

My mother knew me so well. "There's one thing I want to finish up at the office. I just had dinner with Sally. I plan to head back to the office for a bit, but I should be home tonight unless I get caught up."

"Okay, take care, honey. I love you."

"Love you too, Mom."

I then called Harrison. He picked up right away, "Hey, Mom."

"Hi, honey." I apologized for calling him earlier and then answered all of his questions about the case I was working.

He said, "Wow. Right there in Rosedale?"

"It's unsettling. But we'll catch whoever did this."

"I know you will."

"I'll call tomorrow. I love you."

"Love you too, Mom."

Music to my ears.

With my mother and son safe and sound, my thoughts turned back to the two bodies in the morgue and the woman fighting for her life. Speaking of which, I hadn't heard from the hospital for a while, or for that matter, Baker, who had been in charge of ensuring the family had everything they needed, and that there was security on her room. It was likely everything was in order, but I figured I would text Baker to make sure.

While I waited for him to text me back, I found myself thinking of the autopsy results. As Sally and I discussed the case over dinner, I realized there were more leads we could be following up on. I needed to input all the details from the crime scene into ViCAP, including the discoveries Sally had made. If we found any similarities, it could lead us to our suspects, and maybe even a motive. I wouldn't be able to sleep until I checked the database. If I found nothing, I'd go home and rest. Because I could use it.

A text from Baker confirmed there was still no change in Stephanie's condition, and her family was taking shifts to ensure everyone got something to eat and got some rest. Baker had taken the first shift guarding Stephanie's room. *Good. Now to find out who put Stephanie in that hospital bed.*

TWENTY-SIX

VAL

Full of confidence and determination, I strode through the sheriff's department and was about to head back to the conference room when I spotted a familiar face huddled with a few men I didn't know. Smiling, I waved and hurried to join them.

Brady said, "Couldn't sleep either?"

"Nope. There's one more thing I need to do before I can rest."

"Same. Val, this is Chris and this is Paul. They're on the narcotics team in Red Rose County."

Chris was middle-aged with sandy hair and tanned skin, likely an outdoorsman. Paul was dark-skinned with a bright smile and broad shoulders, handsome. We shook hands and exchanged the usual pleasantries. I looked back at Brady, and the penny dropped.

I said, "Why hadn't we thought of this earlier?"

"I don't know, Val. I was at home watching a Pablo Escobar documentary, and something clicked. What if Mike was dealing here in Red Rose County?"

It made perfect sense.

That was why it was so important to have a break, even if only for a few hours. Thank goodness for Brady and his level-headedness. Admittedly, I could get a little hyper-focused and lose sight of things like food and sleep, but rest was essential. We'd missed something so obvious, like actually checking in with our own narcotics team in Red Rose County.

I asked, "Have you found anything out yet?"

"No, I just got here. They met me a few minutes ago, even though they're technically off today."

"Thank you so much for coming down. Let's go into the conference room and see if we can learn anything new about our victims."

Paul smiled that megawatt smile. "Perfect."

The light in the conference room was on. Was someone else here too? We stepped inside, and I spotted a familiar face at the end of the conference table, her laptop propped open and her big glasses perched on the end of her nose. Lucy looked up.

"You're back," she said.

"We are. Didn't expect to see you here." *Kind of.* I should have known better than to think this team would all just go home for the night. Hopefully she'd at least taken a dinner break.

"Understandable. We were all supposedly taking the night off. I guess that's not the case," she said with a knowing smile.

"What brings you in?" I asked.

"I got a notification saying the burner phone cell phone data is back."

"Perfect. These are the narcotics officers."

Lucy nodded. "Oh yeah, I know Chris and Paul. Hey, guys."

"Hey, Lucy," Paul said.

"Red Rose County narcotics. Of course we should be talking to them," Lucy said.

The two officers studied the murder board.

"Gruesome," Chris said.

"Yeah, the autopsy was just completed. Sally walked me through it. It's way worse than it looks up there," I said.

Brady looked at me, likely surprised I hadn't told him about it. "That's why I came back. I want to check for similar crimes in ViCAP. Maybe our killers have done this before and it'll lead us to their identities."

"*Killers?*" Brady asked.

Nodding, I described the gory details Sally had uncovered during the autopsy and explained that based on how hard Mike had fought there had to have been at least two perpetrators.

Lucy said, "Good thinking to check ViCAP. There's no way that kind of brutality happens every day. I can see why you came back in. And thankfully the lab results will be ready tomorrow."

No doubt Lucy had received an update from Jonathan, the head of the testing lab.

"Looks like you've got a brutal homicide on your hands," Chris said.

"We do."

Brady explained what led us to Shasta County and Mike's relationship to Gabriel Moore.

Chris rubbed his chin. "I see."

Brady said, "We've also been in contact with the DEA," and went on to explain what they'd told him.

"I see," Chris said again.

We all took a seat around the conference table. Brady began, "So what we're thinking is because he has this connection with Gabriel Moore in Shasta County, maybe he's dealing here in Red Rose County. We're hoping you can give us an insight into the current state of narcotics in the county, see if Mike Cramer fits in."

"What else can you tell us about Mike Cramer?" Paul asked.

"Mike Cramer, fifty-seven, worked at an auto body shop. Apparently great at detail work and restoring old cars. We learned from a friend of his wife's that he was doing work on the side. We think maybe that side job could be drug dealing as opposed to working on cars."

Paul said, "Interesting."

These narcotics guys weren't wordy, I'd give them that. "So what can you tell us about drugs in Red Rose County?" I said, jumping in.

"In the last year or so, there seems to have been a surge in drug-related crimes. Dealing. Overdoses. We assume that means more drugs are flowing into the county. We've been able to catch a few low-level guys, but we don't know where the drugs are coming from. Nobody will talk."

"Are any of the low-level guys still in custody?"

Chris nodded. "Both are currently in county jail."

"And you don't know where the drugs are coming from?"

"There have always been drugs in Red Rose County, but in the last year or so, we've noticed a definite uptick, which made us think there could be a new player in town. Perhaps your guy, Mike Cramer."

Brady and I exchanged glances. "The friend who told us about Mike's side work told us that in the last year or so he'd been taking on even more side work and his income increased considerably."

"Okay, so you're telling us that Mike Cramer, the guy who got whacked, was friends with a drug dealer in Shasta County and started making big money over the last year, at the same time there was an uptick in drugs here? That can't be a coincidence. Cramer could be the missing link for us."

It was a strong possibility. "Have you had any communications with Shasta County about the rise in drugs here in Red

Rose County? They have samples of the drugs from Gabriel Moore, and that's how the DEA was able to connect him to the Mexican cartel. If it's the same drugs, we might have our source."

My heart was beating faster. This was a *real* lead. It's possible that Cramer was dealing in Red Rose County, and maybe somebody didn't like that and killed him and his family.

Chris said, "We haven't. But we certainly will now."

"Is it possible to talk to the people you have in custody? Find out if they know Mike Cramer and let them know he's dead so there wouldn't be any repercussions," I asked.

"Yeah, we'll get you on the visitors' list."

Chris said, "Thanks for reaching out, Brady. Looks like we could be helping each other out here."

"Anything from the burner phone data?" I asked.

"Mostly data that corroborated what we saw with Cramer's car and regular cell phone records, but there are a few phone numbers in the records that weren't stored on either of Mike's phones. A few from the burner and one from his regular cell phone," Lucy said.

"Do you know who the numbers belong to?"

She shook her head. "Not listed. I need to keep digging."

Interesting. "Are they burner phones?"

"Or virtual numbers. We may never find out the owner's identity. But I want to try calling them again. First time I called, no one answered. But now that we're talking about drug dealers in our county, if there are cell records for the two you have in custody maybe we can match them up."

Smart.

Brady said, "And once we know where they were dealing we can match the GPS data from Mike's car to see if it lines up with the stash houses, or wherever the deals went down."

Chris said, "We can definitely help with that. If we find any matches, it'll give us some leverage when we talk to the two dealers we have in custody."

I said, "All right, let's compare notes and get a meeting scheduled at County. I'm open to first thing tomorrow morning."

Chris said, "Yes, ma'am."

I smiled before looking over at Brady, who gave me a wink.

TWENTY-SEVEN

VAL

I should've known better than to expect a good night's sleep. Perhaps it was wishful thinking because I needed to be fresh and ready the next morning to interview the dealers at County lockup about the case. Instead, my dreams were plagued with images of captivity. The Bear watching me with his piercing eyes, hungry to inflict more pain. The nightmares never went away completely, but they had become less frequent. However, last night's nightmare was the worst I'd experienced in a while. I suppose it was because I was working a new case involving brutal killers. The horrific crimes brought all the trauma of my captivity to the forefront as soon as I tried to go to sleep at night. The chains that tied me to the beams burning my wrists. The vicious fist to my face. The burn of the blade that left me with the mark of the Bear. *Great.* Just when I thought I was starting to feel normal again.

It had been a while since Kieran had last updated on the Bear investigation, which meant there had been no developments regarding his whereabouts. Nobody knew where he was. It was like he had just vanished into thin air. His last known location was Nevada nine months ago when I was rescued by my team. We'd assume he'd pick another victim at random and torture them to death. He always kidnapped and killed four women before moving on to another state. It was his MO. But there hadn't been a fourth victim in Nevada. So where had he gone?

And then it hit me.

Intervals.

He didn't kill continuously; he never had. His method of four kills per state was probably to evade law enforcement. He'd only hit four states and we weren't sure if the six to nine months between the killings was a real pattern, considering the limited number of data points. But that had to be it. It had been nine months since I was rescued. He must be "on a break." But the pattern was incomplete. Had he changed his MO?

I climbed out of bed, walked over to my desk, and flipped open the Bear files Kieran had shared with me. I'd had them tacked to the wall for months, only taking them down recently when my mother's friend had caught sight of them as she'd walked past my room. It had freaked her out, so I'd taken them down.

Now, staring at the four states where we had tracked him, I started noting down timelines, beginnings, and ends. There was a lull of six to nine months between each set of four killings. Was it significant? Did it mean something? Sometimes serial killers had a cooling-off period. Maybe it was more than that. And that could be the key.

I grabbed my cell phone and called Kieran.

"Everything okay?" he said immediately.

"Hi, Kieran, yeah, everything's fine. I'm actually working on another case, a double homicide in Rosedale."

"Oh?"

I brought him up to speed on the case. Then I said, "That's not why I'm calling, Kieran. I think I might've figured out something about the Bear."

"What?"

"Last night, I had a terrible nightmare, the worst in months. In fact, the worst since nine months ago when I was still trapped in that barn. And then I realized it had been nine months, and in all that time no one's heard from him. I started to map out all of the clusters of killings he had done. Four states, and between each state and each group of killings there was an interval of six to nine months where nothing happened—a cooling-off period, if you like."

"It was something we theorized. It could explain why we haven't caught a whiff of him."

"Exactly. We had thought he likely had a seasonal job that allowed him to move from state to state. Working at a carnival or in construction. But based on the profile we have of him, he's highly intelligent. Which doesn't mean he couldn't have a job involving manual labor, but doesn't it make more sense for him to have a professional job, maybe even in law enforcement? Not a permanent employee. Like a contractor or consultant? Maybe the reason for the breaks in the murders is because he's a contract employee. Think about it."

"That would fit."

His tone implied he didn't understand the significance. "Now that I'm doing a second contract with the sheriff's department, it hit me. Maybe he's a contractor too. Maybe that's how he's able to move from state to state so easily. He works to earn money and it gives him the flexibility to travel. He could be working with law enforcement or in a lab as a temporary worker. It would explain his ability to never leave any physical evidence at the scene."

We didn't know much about the Bear so this was potentially a new line of inquiry. If we could narrow down the types of contract work that fit his profile, it could prove to be the break we needed to catch him.

"Well, it's been nine months since your captivity."

"Exactly. He could be on the hunt again, Kieran."

"You get any new notes?"

"No." And if the notes I'd received had been from the Bear all along, it would explain why I hadn't received another.

"When did you receive the last one?"

He could be too busy working somewhere to leave a note. "Seven months ago."

Kieran was silent on the other end of the line.

"It fits the theoretical timeline between his kills. Maybe the notes were from him, but they stopped because he had to take a job. Or already had one lined up."

It had been nine months; would he be coming back for me in California?

Kieran said, "It's plausible, I'll give you that."

"Can the team look into it? We should check with staffing agencies. Look for contract listing in the sciences, computers, engineering, or law enforcement. I think we need to update his profile."

"I'll update the team. We'll analyze it. I'll call you back. Nice work. We could be on to something."

"Okay." Good. Part of me wished I was with the team tracking him down, but I had a double murder to solve. And even I knew I couldn't do both.

"Take care and good luck with the case."

"Thanks, Kieran."

I ended the call and sat back in the desk chair. Was that it? Was the Bear out hunting again, or was he working somewhere? But where?

A brisk knock on the door interrupted my thoughts. "Hello?"

"Are you up? I'm about to make breakfast," Julie called out.

"Yeah, let me hop into the shower and I'll meet you downstairs."

"Okey-dokey," Julie sang out.

My mind was racing. I wanted to dig deeper into this, do my own research, but I would be too limited. I wasn't with the FBI anymore. I couldn't use the sheriff's department for my personal agenda. It would be unethical and illegal. If I wanted any kind of future with the Red Rose County Sheriff's department, I had to play by the rules. But Kieran and the team could do all the investigating. Or maybe Lucy could help me somehow. For now, I had to get to the bottom of my current case and focus on that. The Bear would have to wait. All I could do was hope he didn't already have another victim in his sights.

TWENTY-EIGHT

VAL

Brady and I stood outside the county jail waiting for Chris and Paul to arrive.

"How did you sleep?" Brady asked.

"Honestly, not great, but I think I might have had a breakthrough with the Bear."

"Are you still having nightmares?" he asked, clearly concerned.

A few times a week. More when I'm stressed or am working a case. It was difficult not to think of the Bear when I was investigating other particularly vicious crimes. At first I didn't understand why I was still having nightmares until my therapist helped me understand that when I was fighting for victims, I was relating to them since I had once been the victim of a violent crime myself. I think it was one of the reasons I hesitated to accept a full-time job with the sheriff's department.

"Just every once in a while. Anyway, I spoke with Kieran this morning, and they're going to look into a possible lead."

"That's great."

"Any epiphanies on the Cramer case?"

Brady shook his head. "Nope, not yet, but considering we

were able to match up Mike Cramer's movements with where these guys were dealing and where we think the stash house is located, hopefully they'll tell us something that might lead to whoever did this."

"How about you? Did you sleep okay?" I asked.

"Not bad. I've had a better night's sleep, but I think it's just the adrenaline from the case."

Looking into his eyes, I said, "I understand." And then added, "Hey, once this is over, how about we grab a beer? Just the two of us."

I swear there was a sparkle in his eyes, and I don't even know why I said it. Maybe it was because I did want to spend more time with him outside of homicide investigations. Why was I fighting it? Was it the fear of him not feeling the same? I wasn't usually timid but if I were being honest with myself, I think Brady was the first man since my ex with whom I thought a relationship could be something special.

He said, "Anytime."

Chris and Paul strolled up, and we greeted them before heading inside. We went through the standard security and identification procedures for questioning criminals.

We decided to divide into teams. I would go with Paul, and Brady would go with Chris. The narcotics team had a thorough knowledge of the Red Rose County drug scene, which would be useful for the interrogation.

Inside the interview room, sitting at the table, was a young man, probably not more than twenty-one, with dark hair, brown eyes, and bad skin. He looked at us curiously. I took a seat, and Paul sat next to me. Paul, 6 ft. 2 in. and muscled physique, was intimidating. He began the interview.

"How's it going, Trevor?"

"I've been better."

"This is Valerie Costa. She's an investigator with Red Rose County. She wants to ask you some questions about a case."

"You can ask, but I don't know much about anything," the young man said cockily.

"Is that right?" I said.

He shrugged. It wasn't uncommon for suspects to take a vow of silence, but the bruises on the side of his face indicated that county jail had not been kind to him.

I said, "Thank you for meeting with us. I'm investigating a double homicide and have reason to believe you knew one of the victims."

Trevor Cox looked at me with interest. From my bag, I pulled out a folder and an 8x10 photo of a smiling Mike Cramer. I slid the photo across the table.

"Do you know this guy?"

Trevor picked up the photo and then looked back at me.

I said, "He's dead."

His eyes grew wide, and he instinctively shifted his body backward. "He's dead?"

"Murdered," Paul said. "Gruesome, nasty. Wouldn't wish it on my worst enemy, truly."

"Who killed him?" he asked with surprise.

"You see, that's what we're trying to figure out. Not only did they kill Mike, but they also killed his twelve-year-old son and tried to kill his wife," I explained, trying to drive home just how heinous this crime was.

Paul added, "We're trying to find out everything we can about Mike. We have reason to believe he was dealing fentanyl before he was killed. Do you know anything about that?"

Trevor averted his gaze. "I don't know nothing about drugs."

"You knew Mike?" Paul asked.

Trevor glanced around the room, as if his enemies were listening.

I said, "Anything you say will not leave this room. This conversation is not being recorded. We're just trying to figure out who killed Mike and his son. We're still not sure if his wife will make it."

Trevor lowered his head and shook it. "He was a really nice guy. He really wasn't like a jerk or nothing. He really cared about people."

"How did you meet Mike?"

"James, my buddy at the auto shop, hooked us up. Said we should be friends."

"Mike was quite a bit older than you. I'm guessing you're about twenty. Mike was fifty-seven."

"I'm twenty-one. He was like a father figure, you know? Or like an uncle."

"Was he dealing?"

Trevor looked away again.

"We can help you if you help us."

"Homicide trumps a low-level drug dealer charge. You help us figure out who killed Mike, we'll drop your charges," Paul said.

That got Trevor's attention. "Seriously?"

Paul nodded. "We've already talked to the DA. You help us and give us something useful, and you're free to go."

And that was the plan. We'd let this kid go, follow him, and see who he met with to learn of who else may have associated with Mike Cramer. But first, we had to get Trevor to talk. We needed him to confirm that Mike was dealing.

"We need to know how you really knew Mike," I pressed.

"Okay. Like I said, my buddy at the shop hooked us up. Mike said he had a supply we could bring in to Red Rose County. The money was good. He would give us a bigger cut than we were getting from our normal supplier."

"Who were you getting your supply from before?"

"A guy named Tito. He's not a very nice guy."

I made a mental note to ask Paul how much he knew about

this Tito character. He could be our culprit. "Was Mike encroaching on Tito's territory?" I asked.

Trevor shrugged. "It was hush-hush."

"You knew what drugs he was bringing in?" Paul asked.

"I did. Fentanyl. You can't tell Tito. He's not a forgiving person."

"We won't tell him," Paul assured him. "How long was Mike supplying you?"

"About a year."

Just as we thought. "You sure Tito didn't know about Mike and his supply?"

"No, I don't think so. Tito didn't have fentanyl. Fentanyl is big, it's cheap, people spend a lot of money on it. We were making a lot of money."

"Was there anyone else Mike was taking business from?" I asked.

Trevor said, "Not that I know of."

"Do you think Tito would kill Mike and his whole family if he found out about his enterprise?"

"I don't think Tito's above taking someone out. But taking out Mike's kid, I don't know. I mean, you never know, drugs can make you crazy. And Tito liked to test his product," Trevor said quietly.

We had one dealer confirming our suspicions that Mike Cramer had been dealing drugs. There was a strong possibility that the fentanyl Mike was likely getting from Gabriel Moore was what got him and his son killed.

We wrapped up our conversation, took notes of what we'd learned from Trevor, and exited the room.

"How long before he's out?" I asked Paul.

"A few hours. He didn't have much on him when we picked him up. We knew he was low-level. It's not a big deal to let him go, to be honest," Paul replied.

"Especially if it'll get us a bigger fish," I said. "Do you know the Tito guy, Trevor's supplier?"

"We know him. You'll definitely want to talk to him."

"Do you think he's capable of the kind of violence we saw at the Cramers' house?"

"Tito's not a great guy, but that? I don't know. Unless he's having a go at being a ruthless drug lord. Maybe he's watched *Scarface* one too many times."

"When can we talk to him?"

"Let's go after we meet up with Brady and Chris. When we do talk to him, we want to be careful. I don't want anything to happen to Trevor and his associate. They're young and vulnerable. Who knows, maybe they'll turn over a new leaf."

Twenty minutes later, Brady and Chris emerged from the other interview room.

"So?" I asked.

"He rolled. Mike's been dealing fentanyl for the last year," Brady said.

"Trevor said the same thing." I filled them in on everything else Trevor had told us.

"Well, those two just got a get-out-of-jail-free card," Paul remarked.

I said, "We want to talk to Tito next." My phone buzzed and the number looked familiar. I held up a finger and answered. "This is Val Costa."

"Ms. Costa, this is Arvin, Mike Cramer's boss."

He expressed his shock at the news and said we were welcome to come down and question the staff. After thanking him, I hung up and told everyone, "That was Mike's boss. He said we can question the staff. That should include James, Trevor's friend who introduced him to Mike. We should go talk to the auto body shop people, before we talk to Tito."

Everyone agreed, and we set off to follow our first solid lead.

TWENTY-NINE

VAL

We pulled up to the auto body shop where Mike Cramer used to work. It was an establishment I'd passed a hundred times growing up. It was on the corner across from the diner where we always used to hang out. The auto shop had received a fresh coat of paint, and updates to the sign since my teenage years.

We walked into the shop and were greeted by a plump man in a dark blue shirt with the name Arvin embroidered on the pocket. After a round of introductions, he led us into his office. Seated behind his desk, he said, "I can't believe Mike's dead."

"We're sorry for your loss," I said sympathetically. "We're trying to learn more about Mike's life before he passed. What can you tell us about him? How long had he worked here? Were you aware of any problems he might have had, any enemies?"

"Mike started working for me about fifteen years ago. He was our most senior guy on the crew. Did beautiful work. I always told him I was surprised he didn't open his own shop. He said he didn't want the headache, just wanted to do the work."

"There were never any disciplinary problems with Mike? Did any customers report any problems with him?"

"No, like I said, he did great work. Everybody always asked for him so he actually always had more work than he knew what to do with."

"Did Mike ever do any work outside of the shop?"

"I think he did every once in a while, nothing big though, just a friend helping another friend. I didn't mind."

"So he worked full-time, Monday through Friday?"

Arvin nodded. "Yeah, regular hours. He said that's what he wanted. He had a son. How's he doing?"

"Michael was killed as well."

Arvin paled. "And Stephanie?"

"She was badly injured and is still in the hospital. They're not sure if she's going to make it." According to her physician, her vitals were stabilizing and it was possible she might recover or at least wake up, but she hadn't yet.

"Who would do that to them? I'm telling you, I honestly don't know anybody who had a bad word to say about any of them. I mean, honestly, Mike was a little gruff sometimes, just one of those guys who was always kind of joking around, a little rough around the edges, but he didn't offend anyone, not enough to deserve that."

"Were there any customers in particular who may have been offended by his sense of humor?"

"Not really. I mean, nobody complained to me anyways. And trust me, I get complaints from customers if they're not happy with the service or the job, and nobody has ever complained about Mike's work the whole time he was with us."

"How did Mike get along with his coworkers?"

"Pretty well. I mean, I don't think they socialized much outside of work, but they were always friendly here. Mike was pretty dedicated to his family. Didn't go out drinking all night or anything like that. Plus, a lot of my other workers are pretty young. Mike was the oldest by a good twenty years."

"He must've been a very valuable employee for you."

"Oh yeah, he brought in all kinds of business. I've been doing this a long time and I work on cars too, but Mike's gifted... was."

"Is there anybody who worked here who might have been jealous of Mike, maybe didn't like him getting all the attention?"

"No, I don't think so. I mean, I think they all looked up to him."

After a few more minutes with Arvin, we didn't learn anything new other than the fact that Mike had a crass sense of humor but was jovial in demeanor most of the time, got along with people, and was a mentor to the younger ones.

"We'd like to speak with your staff if that's okay?"

"Of course. James is on duty as well as Ralph and Blaine."

"We appreciate it."

"I'll go get them for you."

"Thank you."

As Arvin stepped out of the office, I turned to Brady and said, "What do you think?"

"It wasn't his job that got him killed, at least not his legit job."

A young man in his mid to late twenties walked in. "Hi, my name is James. I was told you wanted to talk to me."

"I'm Valerie Costa, and this is Deputy Tanner with the sheriff's department. We have a few questions about your coworker Mike."

"I heard what happened. I can't believe it. We're all devastated."

"We're sorry for your loss."

"Who did this?" James asked.

"That's what we're trying to find out. Maybe you could help us."

"Sure, anything I can do to help."

"How long have you known Mike?" I asked.

"I've been here for about five years, so five years."

"And you got along okay?" I asked.

"We did. I can't believe he's gone," he said, looking distraught.

Everyone we spoke to seemed to like Mike. It made the case all the more puzzling. "Can you think of anyone who would want to hurt him? Maybe somebody he crossed or took business away from?"

He shook his head. "No." His body stiffened. "He never had any complaints at work. He was good."

"What about outside of work? Do you know of any extracurriculars that might have caused him problems?"

He looked away. "I don't know about that."

"Do you know somebody named Trevor?"

James nodded silently.

"He told us you introduced him to Mike."

James said nothing.

"We're not trying to bust you or Trevor. We only want to know about Mike."

With resignation, he said, "Okay. Yeah. I introduced them."

"How do you know Trevor?"

"Trevor and I go way back. My little brother and him were in school together."

"Are you involved in that business?"

With conviction he said, "No, I don't do that."

I wasn't sure I believed him but I had nothing to prove he was lying. "Before Mike's death, in the last week or so, was he acting normally? Nervous? Seem concerned about anything at all?"

He shook his head, then stopped as if remembering something. "Actually, he was kind of forgetful. I don't know how to describe it. It was like his mind was somewhere else. I asked him if everything was cool, you know, like if he was worried about anything."

The unusual behavior was consistent with what Stephanie's friend had told us about Mike. "Like Tito?" I asked.

"I don't know much about that world, but I did ask him about Tito. He said he had stuff on his mind, but he said no, it wasn't Tito and to not worry. So I dropped it. I figured maybe he was having marriage problems."

"You don't think it was Tito either?"

James shook his head. "I mean, that was my first thought, but he said no."

"You haven't heard any rumblings, maybe something was brewing in Tito's world? Or that somebody was angry with Mike?"

"No, I was shocked when I heard the news. Like really shocked."

"Anything else you can tell us about Mike? Did he have any visitors at work?"

"Not that I know of."

"All right, you've been very helpful. If you can bring in the other two, that would be great."

"Okay."

After interviewing the other two coworkers, who didn't seem to know about Mike's side business like James did, Brady and I decided to grab some lunch and then go find Tito, or at least try, based on what Chris and Paul had said about his last known hangouts.

THIRTY

BRADY

Sitting across from Val at the diner, I couldn't help but notice how stunning she looked, even with the circles under her eyes. I wished I could take away her nightmares, make her feel safe. Not that there was anybody tougher than Val, but it wasn't right that someone could rob her of her security, her nights, her sleep.

"Feels like we're finally getting somewhere. Don't you think so?" she asked.

"I do. I think the crime could definitely be drug related. Somebody was mad, wanted revenge."

"That's what I think too. And considering we've confirmed that he was dealing fentanyl in Tito's territory it seems like a real possibility."

"Agreed." Except that James had asked Mike if Tito was the reason for his distraction, and he'd said no. Could another dealer have been after Mike?

"Maybe the forensic team will give us more insight into what they found at the scene. I know that Jonathan's been working around the clock, along with his team, to test the evidence that was brought in."

I said, "Nobody likes a killer running around in our town. Especially one this ruthless."

"Agreed."

After the waitress came and took our order, I said, "How's your mom doing?"

"She's doing really well. I told you that she actually took her first steps, right? Before you know it, she'll be running around again."

"That's great, Val. How's Harrison?"

"He's doing well. He's back at school. And how are Paige and Zack?"

"Well, Paige is itching to graduate, as you can imagine. She only has a few more months left of high school. And Zach is doing well at UCLA."

"Do they visit often?" she asked.

We hadn't had many personal conversations lately, and I was glad we were finally talking about something other than work. "Paige is coming up next weekend with one of her friends. It should be fun. She wants to go hiking and show her friend the nature side of her family, as she puts it."

"And she's excited about attending Boston University?"

"Super excited. We're thinking when school gets out, we'll go for a visit."

Val's eyes lit up, and I wondered if she was thinking what I was thinking. Maybe I was feeling daring because we were on a roll with the case, but I said, "You know, since Harrison is at MIT, maybe he could show us around, give Paige a feel for Boston college life."

Val smiled and said, "I bet he would love that, and I would love to visit my son. Maybe we could plan a trip when I'm out there with Harrison, and he can show us his stomping grounds."

"That would be great." I was smiling like an idiot. It felt like all those years ago when we used to sit at this diner after homecoming or after a football game.

Val read my mind. "Did you ever think we'd be sitting here all these years later, talking about having our kids show our other kids around colleges on the East Coast?" she said, chuckling.

Grinning, I said, "Not even once." Although I had often wondered what would have happened if we'd got together, I never imagined this scenario—both of us divorced, kids across the country. But I couldn't deny it, that spark was still there all these years later.

"You know, I've been meaning to reach out and do something. But with Mom and everything, I'm still slowly adjusting," Val said quietly.

I wasn't sure where that came from, but I was glad she was confiding in me. "I totally get it, and I was afraid to ask, not wanting to intrude or anything."

"You wouldn't be intruding. Are you still with your hiking club?"

"I am. We'll have to plan a hike."

With a slight smile, she said, "I'd like that."

So would I. We'd gone on a few group hikes, but none just the two of us.

The server set my burger and fries down in front of me, and Val her salad and grilled cheese sandwich. "Bon appétit," she said.

There was something about that moment that felt so natural, so right. I wondered if she felt it too. I took a bite of the burger—it was juicy, delicious, and just what I needed. I set it down when my phone buzzed. I pulled it out and looked at it. It was a text from Paige. She was asking if I had confirmed our dates for the trip to Boston yet. Her ears must be ringing.

"Is that the office?" Val asked.

"No, actually it's Paige asking if I've confirmed the dates for our trip to Boston. I told her I would check my schedule, but then Saturday night happened, and I haven't been able to get back to her."

"Oh, well, we should definitely plan some dates. I'll talk to Harrison. Let Paige know that I'll speak with him, and we'll arrange a time so that he can show her around."

I texted my daughter back, and she responded with a huge thumbs-up and "so cool, thanks, Dad."

I hated the idea that my daughter would be all the way across the country, but I knew I couldn't stop her. She was headstrong, determined, tough, and had earned it. "I told her. She seems pretty happy about the idea."

"Glad to hear it. I'll text Harrison." Val pulled out her phone, and it buzzed in her hand. Someone was calling her. She put the phone to her ear.

She said, "Great, all right, we'll be there in fifteen minutes."

"Who was that?" I asked.

"That was the hospital. Stephanie's awake."

THIRTY-ONE

VAL

Outside Stephanie's hospital room, I spoke with her brother Chuck in hushed tones. "How is she doing?" We assumed she was doing better considering the doctor had decided to reduce her sedation meds.

"The doctors said the fact that she woke up is a good sign, and she's speaking, which is another really good sign."

The relief was evident in Chuck's voice. It was good news for Stephanie and her family. And I had to admit, I was relieved too. "Does she remember anything about the shooting?"

"Not that we can tell. The doctor asked if her she knew why she was in the hospital and she shook her head. He said being disoriented so soon after coming out of the sedation is normal and could be due to the drugs she's on, but he also said that her memories could come back later... or never."

Never would be a problem for the investigation, but maybe better for Stephanie in the long run. If I had witnessed what she had, I wouldn't want any memory of it. Who would want to remember their husband and son being murdered? I shuddered at the thought. "Has anyone told her about Michael?"

"Not yet. She hasn't asked. She isn't saying much."

It was the duty of law enforcement to provide Stephanie with the death notification of her husband and child, as she was next of kin. Telling the loved ones was the worst part of working a murder investigation.

Stephanie had woken up two hours earlier. It wasn't likely she would be much help this evening, but we had to know if she remembered anything at all. Even the smallest detail could help us. Based on the autopsy results, we knew there were likely two suspects. Maybe she could tell us if it was a man, a woman, white, Hispanic—anything at all.

"You're okay with us speaking with her?"

He nodded. "If it helps us find out who did this, then yes."

"How is the family holding up? Are you able to take breaks, get food?"

"Yes, Deputy Baker and the others have been so kind. They've brought us homemade food and have taken shifts so that we can get back to the hotel and get cleaned up."

"That's great to hear."

Baker remained outside the room, standing guard. We hadn't gotten any reports of anyone trying to get near Stephanie, but it also hadn't been released to the press that she was awake. The local news had reported on the story, but as far as we knew, it hadn't gone beyond Red Rose County. If the assailants were still around, they would know that Stephanie had survived, and we didn't want to take any chances with her life.

Chuck, Brady, and I quietly entered Stephanie's hospital room. She had lucked out and had the whole room to herself. Her mother sat on one side of her bed, holding her hand, and her sister was on the other side.

Chuck said gently, "Steph, we have a couple of investigators here. This is Val Costa and Deputy Tanner. They'd like to ask you some questions about what happened to you."

She looked at us both. "Hi."

"How are you feeling, Stephanie?" I asked.

"Been better."

Her speech was slow, but clear. "We're investigating the shooting that happened at your house. Do you remember anything about Saturday night?"

"Is that when it happened?"

"Yes." The fact she didn't remember the day wouldn't bode well for the investigation. "And today is Monday. It's been two days."

"I've been here two days?" She said it as if trying to piece the information together.

"Yes."

"Where's Michael? Where's Mike?"

Nobody said a word.

Her mother sniffled and said, "I'm so sorry, Stephanie, but Mike and Michael are gone."

"Gone? What do you mean gone? Where did they go?" Stephanie asked, becoming agitated.

Mrs. Jamison, through tears, said, "Honey, they were killed. The people who shot you killed them."

We remained quiet, and although I was somewhat relieved not to have been the one to break the news, it was heartbreaking all the same.

As Stephanie struggled to come to terms with what her mother had just told her, I stood ready to answer any questions she might have.

"It can't be," she said.

After steadying my nerves, I said, "It's true. We're trying to figure out who did this to your family. Can you remember anything at all from Saturday night?" I asked.

She shook her head and began to cry. Brady and I stepped back as the family gathered around Stephanie. We gave them some time to process, but unfortunately, time was of the essence. We needed to probe Stephanie further, if she was up for it. I wouldn't push if she wasn't. This was likely the most traumatic thing she'd ever been through and as much as I wanted to find who did this, Stephanie's well-being was more important.

Brady and I stood side by side, watching the scene, wishing we were anywhere but here. It was devastating to watch. I couldn't imagine waking up in a hospital bed to be told that my family had been killed. I'd be destroyed.

It was obvious the family needed time. I turned to leave the room and speak to Deputy Baker.

"Has it been quiet around here?" I asked.

"It has been. What's going on in there?"

"Stephanie has just been informed about the murder of her husband and son."

Baker grimaced. "That's terrible."

"It is. We think the family needs some time before we can question them further. She doesn't seem to remember anything about Saturday night."

We were about to leave when Chuck came out of the room and said, "Wait, she says she remembers something."

I turned and rushed back to Stephanie's bed. "Your brother says you remember something."

"Yeah, I don't know. It doesn't make any sense, but I remember hearing another language."

"Do you know what language it was?"

"At first, I thought it was Spanish, but I don't think so. I think it was Italian or something similar. I remember thinking it was strange."

"Someone was speaking Italian to you?" *That was strange.*

She shook her head. "No, I was already drifting to sleep, I think. I think we'd been drugged. I don't know. I was lying there and could hear something about *'famiglia.'* That's why I thought it was Spanish, but then they said something else, and I didn't understand. I know a little bit of Spanish, but it wasn't Spanish. I think it was Italian."

The people who had killed them were speaking Italian? We didn't know if anyone on Tito's crew spoke the language. His file listed him as Hispanic, so I wouldn't have thought he'd be speaking Italian. But maybe there was someone on his crew who was Italian or spoke Italian. We'd have to find out when we interviewed him.

"Do you remember anything else?" I asked.

She shook her head. "No, I don't."

It was likely she'd been drugged, and so had Mike and Michael. The labs were due back any time now, so we would know one way or the other.

"Are you up for more questions, Stephanie?"

She nodded. "We have to catch these people, whoever did this."

I was shocked and in awe of Stephanie's strength and desire to talk to us. "Was there anything out of the ordinary about Mike's behavior in the past week or so?"

"Not really. He had been a little distant though. At first I thought maybe he'd met someone else. But he swore he hadn't."

"We've spoken to your friend Taylor. She said Mike took on some additional work. Do you know how Mike was making extra money?"

"He worked on cars," she said matter-of-factly. It seemed that her memory loss was centered around the actual attack. If she had been given some sort of sleep aid, that could account for it, not to mention the brain injury.

"Do you know if he was dealing drugs?"

"No, I don't think so."

"This may be difficult to hear, but we have learned that he had been. That's where the extra money was coming from, not from working on cars." I glanced over at the family, who looked shocked. "Do you remember seeing anybody lurking around the house? Anyone suspicious? Was there anybody new in Mike's life?"

She shook her head. "No. Drugs? Are you sure?"

"I'm afraid so. We have some leads into who may have done this, but anything you can remember will be a big help. Do you remember what the people who came to your house on Saturday night looked like? Were they male? Female?"

She shook her head. "All I remember, and it was so weird, is that they weren't speaking English. I wasn't sure if I was imagining it or not."

Maybe she was, maybe she wasn't. At least it was something for us to look into.

A doctor entered the room. "Hello, everyone. I'll have to ask you to leave the room for a moment, please. I need to examine Stephanie."

I looked at Stephanie and her family and as we left, said, "We'll be checking in on you. Please let us know if she remembers anything else. We'll be in touch."

Stephanie hadn't remembered much, and what she had remembered was odd, to say the least.

Back in the car, in the hospital parking garage, I said, "What do you make of that?"

Val said, "It could be something or it could be nothing, but we won't know until we find out what drugs were in her system. She could've imagined it, like she said, but in the meantime we can keep an eye out for any Italians or anyone who speaks Italian. It's unusual in Red Rose County."

Or it's a red herring. "I'll call Paul and see if he's got a location on Tito." We knew his home address and his known hangouts, but Paul and Chris said they would help interview Tito and his crew if needed. If Paul could confirm Tito's location, it would save us driving all around town.

"Good idea."

I dialed Paul's number.

"Brady, what's up?"

"We just came from the hospital. Stephanie's awake."

"Oh, that's excellent news. Did she tell you anything?"

I filled him in and then said, "We'd like to go talk to Tito. Do you have a location for him?"

"We've been interviewing a few of his pals. They said they

don't know anything, but it sounds like they were all at some party together. Tito didn't want to talk to us, but we know he's at his house. You can give it a shot. He doesn't like us much, but you two are unknowns. He may be curious enough to talk to you."

"Great. Anything we should know about this guy before we question him? Should we bring backup?"

"I don't think he'll shoot at someone he doesn't know, but be on your guard. And don't mention where you got the intel from. Just ask him if he knew Mike and if he was in the drugs game."

"All right."

He confirmed the address, and we made our way to the highway.

As we approached Tito's house, I thought it resembled more of a compound with a large home and several dwellings round the back, perhaps where he made the drugs or had family living with him. I drove up the gravel driveway and parked. Somebody was walking toward us from the porch. We got out of the car and walked up to the man dressed in a black shirt and denim.

"My name is Deputy Tanner. This is Val Costa, an investigator with Red Rose County. We're looking for Tito."

"What's your business with Tito?" he asked as he studied us from head to toe.

"We're investigating a homicide."

The man stepped back. "I don't know nothing about that."

"Are you Tito?" Val asked, with a little attitude.

"No," he said, annoyed at the question.

Val said, "We'd like to speak with Tito now, please."

"I'll see if he's available. Stay here."

Gladly. The setup was nice, pretty. Serene. It wasn't what I was expecting for a drug dealer's home. Like the wraparound porch among the forest. Who else lived there?

A minute later, a muscular man of about 5 ft. 8 in. strode toward us, presumably Tito. His forearms and neck were covered in tattoos, mostly words in old English. He didn't look like someone you'd want to mess with.

"I'm Tito. You looking for me?" he asked, slightly curious, just as Paul had suspected.

"Yes. I'm Valerie Costa, and this is Deputy Tanner. We'd like to ask you a few questions about a murder victim."

He relaxed. "All right."

"Do you know a man named Mike Cramer?"

He looked puzzled. "Doesn't sound familiar."

Val took out a recent photo of Mike from her backpack and showed it to Tito. He looked it over thoroughly and handed it back. "Don't know him."

"You've never met Mike Cramer before?" Val said, like she didn't believe him.

"Never. What's he got to do with me?"

"That's what we're trying to figure out. We have reason to believe that Mike was dealing drugs in Red Rose County," I said.

"What's he dealing?" he asked, tilting his head, like we'd got his attention.

"Fentanyl."

He shook his head, his cheeks pink. Visibly agitated.

"Did you know Mike or someone else was dealing fentanyl in Red Rose County?"

"I heard rumors."

"Look, we're not interested in busting anybody for drugs. We're trying to figure out who killed Mike and his son and tried to kill his wife."

"Other than what I've seen in the news, I don't know nothing about that."

"Where were you Saturday evening between the hours of 5 p.m. and 8 p.m.?"

Completely calm, he stated, "I was at my kid's basketball game."

"Is there anyone who can verify that?"

"Yeah, lots. And there's cameras at the school. They're everywhere these days."

He wasn't wrong. We'd have to check his alibi, but my instinct was telling me it would check out. "And you're sure you've never heard of Mike before?"

"I'm telling you, never. How long had he been dealing?"

"We think maybe a year."

He nodded like something was making sense for him. Perhaps he had suspected and had yet to find out who had been taking his business. "You know who was selling his product? Or was he selling on his own?"

He certainly wouldn't get that information from us. Tito may not have killed Mike, but he wouldn't be pleased with those working for him and that information could get them hurt. "Not sure. You hear of anyone moving in on your territory in Red Rose County?"

"I don't—"

Val cut him off. "We know you're a drug dealer. We don't care. We want to know who killed Mike."

"I heard, yeah."

"And you have no idea who it could be?" Val asked.

"I thought maybe it was coming in from Shasta."

It was. "But you're not sure who in Shasta?"

"I have my suspicions but no proof."

Got it. Tito was likely working on his own investigation. I would certainly relay the information to both Red Rose and Shasta County narcotics departments to be on the lookout for a possible turf war. "Could someone from your crew have taken out Mike—maybe jumped the gun and suspected Mike?"

He smirked. "Look, my crew, allegedly, if I had a crew, don't do nothing without my approval."

He was wrong about that, considering two of his dealers had also been working for Mike. "Who lives in the back?"

"My mom, my grandma. My auntie."

I said, "That's nice to have family so close."

"Family is important." He paused. "What other questions do you have? I'm making dinner."

A drug king pin who made dinner? "Just one more thing."

"What is it?"

"You got any friends who are Italian or speak Italian?"

He looked me up and down and said, "No. Do I look Italian to you?"

I shook my head. "Anyone on your crew? Or any friends?"

"I don't know any Italians," he said, annoyed.

Val shrugged.

"Thank you for your time. You take care, Tito."

"Good luck with your investigation," he said sarcastically.

Back in the car, Val said, "I want to know everything about Tito. Of course, we'll check that alibi."

"Do you think he knew Mike?" I asked. I was inclined to think he didn't.

"If I had to guess, I'd say he didn't. Or maybe he didn't know of him specifically. I didn't see any recognition in his eyes when he looked at the photo. Doesn't mean he didn't know someone who was dealing in his territory and had him taken out though. He doesn't necessarily need to know all the details or to have seen him before."

Seems odd that he would give the order to kill someone he didn't even know. "All right, let's go check his alibi and see if Paul and Chris found out anything useful from interviewing his crew."

Val nodded, and said, "No time like the present."

THIRTY-THREE

VAL

After a meeting with Paul and Chris from the narcotics team, we had a list of eight of Tito's crew to reinterview. Apparently Tito's crew was not fond of the narcotics officers and all they'd told them was they'd been at a party together. But there were a few people they hadn't been able to locate yet. It was getting late and it seemed like it was best to divide and conquer once again, spread out the tasks, and share what we found in the morning.

Paul said, "All right, we'll try to find the remaining three and talk to them tomorrow morning. Then we can compare notes."

"Thanks."

We headed back to the conference room to find Lucy there with Sally. Was it a social call? Another ladies' night? The girls' nights with Sally and Lucy were one of the highlights of my time back in Red Rose County.

"Hey, Brady, Val," Lucy said, with a wave.

"How's Stephanie?" Sally asked.

"The doctors are hopeful she'll make it. She's awake, she's talking, but she doesn't remember much."

Sally said, "I bet I can tell you why."

"Are the labs back?"

"They are. Michael was given Ambien before he was shot. It's common for people who take Ambien to have a twenty-to-thirty-minute period before they fall asleep where they have no recollection of anything."

"So they drugged Michael, and presumably Stephanie, laid them on the couch, and then shot them in the head. Was Mike drugged?"

Sally shook her head. "He wasn't drugged. He was alert and aware of everything that was happening to him."

Horrifying.

"Why would someone do this?" Brady asked.

That was a great question. If we knew the answer, we might be closer to finding out the truth. "If Michael and Stephanie hadn't been drugged, I would theorize they were collateral damage. Killed them and then went after Mike for whatever reason. Information. Money. Revenge. It's peculiar. But the fact the killers brought sleeping medication to the scene means the crime was premeditated. Whoever attacked the Cramers planned to subdue Michael and Stephanie, kill them and then go after Mike. This is useful. It tells us they planned for the whole family to be home." Not typical for a simple burglary, or a burglary gone drastically wrong.

"Why not just shoot them? Not to sound callous, but why go to the trouble of drugging them too?" Brady asked.

"I would think so they wouldn't suffer," Sally said.

"Then why kill them at all?" Brady asked.

"All good questions," I said. "We should see if there have been any similar crimes. I meant to search through ViCAP earlier, but then we followed the drug angle and I haven't had a chance." The last forty-eight hours had been a whirlwind of new information and leads to follow.

"You may not have searched, but I did," Lucy said with a twinkle in her eye.

"Oh?" I said, intrigued.

"I went back thirty years. Not a single crime with elements similar to the case. The only mutilation cases I found were quite different and there's no instance of drugging and shooting. This is truly a unique scene."

I said, "They wanted to make Mike suffer, not Stephanie and Michael. Think about it. If Mike was the target, killing his wife and child in front of him was likely worse than any physical cut."

Lucy nodded. "Right. If we believe the killers were after Mike, they were punishing him for something. It would definitely be the ultimate punishment to murder his family in front of him."

Lucy was right. If somebody wanted to hurt Mike, the others were simply collateral damage. But why? Perhaps we'd learn soon enough when we were able to get the alibis confirmed for Tito and his crew.

"We need to get surveillance footage from the middle school. One person of interest says he has an alibi at a basketball game."

I gave Lucy the details and she said, "I'll get right on it but honestly, it's late. The school is likely closed."

"In the morning should be fine. We could all probably use a break."

Brady said, "It's been a long day."

"It has."

Lucy said, "All right, we can check the Italian angle in the morning to see if anybody in Mike's life was Italian or if he was."

"Cramer isn't an Italian name. But maybe his mother's family was Italian." From his physical description, dark hair and eyes with olive skin, he could be. "Let's pull his birth certificate.

See if there's Italian lineage in his family. Maybe something from his past caught up with him." Perhaps he had ties to the Bay Area he'd been running from.

"Didn't Stephanie's family say Mike's family was dead?" Brady asked.

"Yes, but they also didn't know Mike was a drug dealer. We need to learn everything we can about Mike Cramer. Where he was born. Where he's lived. Where he went to school. Every single detail. If Mike was hiding the truth about his family history, we need to know why."

THIRTY-FOUR

HIM

After giving me a hug and a kiss, my wife Janis said, "I'm glad you're home. We missed you."

With a smile, I said, "I missed you too." And I did. I didn't want to have to be away from them any longer than I had to.

"How was the weather on your camping trip with Tommy?"

Before I could answer, my five-year-old came tearing down the hall, right into my arms. "Daddy, Daddy, I missed you, Daddy!" I hugged him tight and thought about what I had done.

The little boy, Michael Junior, was older than my son, but he was still just a boy. His mother and he didn't deserve what happened to them and it was eating me up inside. I set my son down.

Janis asked, "Are you hungry?"

"Yeah, I could eat." We'd eaten nothing but fast food on the trip.

"I was just about to put a lasagna in the oven."

"Sounds great. Do you like lasagna?" I asked my son.

He bobbed his head up and down. "It's my favorite," he said with all the glee of a five-year-old.

Everything I did was for my son. Had Mike done the same?

My son tugged me toward his room. "I made some things for you," he said with a lisp.

Inside his room, he sat down at his tiny table and proceeded to place drawings in front of me. "Mommy, Daddy, me, and this here, that's a dog."

"Whose dog is it?"

"It's our dog. The one we're gonna get." And he began to run through all the reasons why we should get a dog. My wife and I both had full-time jobs. Raising a rambunctious boy seemed to fill every minute, but maybe he did deserve to have a family pet. A dog could watch over my family when I couldn't. If my family had had the same kind of protection I'd had as a child maybe things would have turned out differently. Maybe I wouldn't still be having nightmares all these years later, nightmares that I could never erase. No amount of therapy or talking to my priest would make them go away. All it did was make me angry and sick to my stomach. And now I had more material for my nightmares. How had it all gone so wrong? How could I have let it?

My cell phone rang, pulling me out of my thoughts. I answered. "What's up, Tommy?"

"We have a problem."

"What do you mean?"

"She's alive."

I stood up from the table and said, "Who is?"

"We shouldn't talk about this on the phone."

"Are you sure about that?" Part of me was relieved, the other part terrified.

"I just got home and checked online for news, and it's a problem."

"Come over. Janis is making lasagna."

"I'll stop by, but just for a minute. Meet me outside. I won't come in. It's better we aren't seen talking about it."

"Okay."

I ended the call and refocused on my son. Little Ricky looked up at me with concern. "Daddy, who was that? You look sad. Are you sad, Daddy?"

I looked down at my son, his big brown eyes looking at me like I was a hero. "No, I'm not sad. Everything is great. That was Uncle Tommy. He wanted me to tell you hello."

"Uncle Tommy," he said in a silly voice. "I love Uncle Tommy."

And so did I. "Of course you do."

"Is he coming over for lasagna?"

"No, he just remembered he accidentally kept something of mine in his backpack from our trip. He's going to drop it off real quick."

"Okay. Do you want to see my dinosaur?"

"Yes, I do."

As I watched my five-year-old get his plastic dinosaur and run around the room with it roaring, I thought about her still being alive. Would she be able to identify us? If she hadn't already, there was only one way to ensure she never would. And as sick as the thought made me, I knew it had to be done.

THIRTY-FIVE

VAL

Thankfully the nightmares weren't as bad last night. I only woke up once and was able to get back to sleep and actually get a few hours' rest. The case lay heavy on my mind. Who would try to kill this entire family? I couldn't help but think about Stephanie's memory of hearing Italian. How did she know it was Italian? Personally, I would've been able to recognize it as my mother's family was of Italian heritage, and so was my father's. Mom didn't speak it, but Dad did, and every once in a while, he'd say a funny phrase in Italian. But my sister and I had never learned the language. Mom was known for her pasta sauce, her lasagna, and her *ziti*. At Christmas, she always baked *pizzelle*, my personal favorite, and my sister Maxine's favorite, the colorful and figgy *cuccidati*. Mom said she'd wished she had more time to cook, but she had been a single mom and a sheriff for most of our childhood.

Clutching my mug at the dining table, Mom asked how the case was going. I explained we hadn't gotten too far but had discovered some surprises about Mike's past. I didn't divulge what those were just yet.

"Mom, do you know any Italians in town or people who speak Italian?" I asked.

"Why, that's a funny question, Val."

"Our one surviving witness says she might've heard Italian being spoken. As far as I can remember, there weren't any Italians growing up in Rosedale. Do you know of any?"

I figured I'd ask Mom since she'd lived here for decades and knew just about everyone.

"No, I don't think so. We don't even have an Italian restaurant," she said with a smile.

Other than a pizzeria, it was true. "Maybe it was somebody from out of town," I said.

"True. San Francisco is less than a four-hour drive away and houses a large Italian population in North Beach. Maybe it was somebody from San Francisco."

It was a good point. Mike was originally from the Bay Area. Had he been involved in drugs back there, too? Maybe he'd crossed someone and that was the real reason for the move to Rosedale. It could explain why the family mostly kept to themselves, possibly fearing Mike's enemies in San Francisco would track them down. "You're right. There could very well be a connection to the Bay Area. Thanks, Mom."

"I'm glad I could help. You sure you can't tell us what you found out about his past?"

"I'd rather not say just yet."

Julie sat down and said, "You know that what happens at the dining table stays at the dining table."

I figured that telling my mother and her friends wouldn't jeopardize anything. Mom certainly wasn't going to tell the press that Mike had been a drug dealer. "Okay. If it stays at the table."

Nods from Mom and Julie.

Discussing a case outside of work felt uncomfortable even if it was with people I completely trusted. Cautiously, I told them everything we had learned so far.

"All of that going on right here in our town," Mom said with a hint of sadness.

"It is surprising." Not to mention the murders happened five minutes from our home.

"I'm guessing you'll have another busy day today?"

"I think so." But I was ready for it.

Mom said, "Well, you'd better get going, then."

I swear the only time I took orders was when I was at home with my mother. As I stood up, my phone started to buzz, indicating an incoming call. I recognized the number as Chuck, Stephanie's brother. I hope she hadn't taken a turn for the worse.

"Hi, this is Val."

"Hi, Val, this is Chuck Jamison."

"Hi, Chuck. Is everything okay?"

"Yes, Steph's getting stronger. The doctors are really hopeful that she'll make a full recovery."

"Oh, that's great news," I said, nodding at my mom and Julie with a smile.

"But she told us that she's starting to remember more about what happened."

"What did she remember?"

"She says that there were two of them. The details are fuzzy, but they were white men, and that's all she remembers. She says they made her drink something, and she doesn't really remember much after that."

Awesome. Maybe she remembers enough to sit for a sketch artist. "That's really helpful. Thank you so much for calling me. Brady and I will come down to the hospital and get a formal statement. I'm so glad to hear she's doing well."

As I ended the call, Julie said, "Good news?"

"Yes, Stephanie is doing better, and she's remembered more

about the attack. I'm going to go down there and get her full statement. It's great news."

Although we had already begun to believe two suspects had been involved, the fact they made her drink something likely laced with a sleep aid meant we were really on to something. I could feel it. I took one last sip of my coffee and then I called Brady to let him know to meet me down at the hospital to talk to Stephanie. It was time to catch these guys.

THIRTY-SIX
VAL

With Stephanie's statement on record, Brady and I headed back to the station. Stephanie was remembering more and more each day. She'd told us she remembered seeing two men, middle-aged, with dark hair. At gunpoint, they'd forced her and Michael to drink from water bottles they had brought with them. She remembered thinking it was weird and suspected the drink was laced with some kind of drug, but they'd had no choice.

After we'd explained that traces of Ambien had been found in Michael's system, she'd said that made sense. She still wasn't one hundred percent sure if it was Italian that she'd heard while drugged, but it was definitely something we needed to follow up. She said her memories were still hazy and she'd struggled to make out the features of the men, except that they looked Italian, which could be why she had dreamt or thought she'd heard the language being spoken. It was a good sign she was remembering more about the event.

Back at the sheriff's station, we met with Paul and Chris from narcotics and relayed what we'd learned from Stephanie.

"Is Tito and his gang associated with anybody from the Bay

Area? Maybe the Italian mob?" Organized crime was everywhere, even in the Bay Area. It wasn't just in New York, Chicago, and Las Vegas, like the movies portrayed. They were all over the Bay Area, hidden in plain sight. And I knew the Italians' involvement in organized crime hadn't stopped with the major takedown of the New York families in the early to mid-2010s; they'd simply gotten smarter at hiding their activities.

"Not that we know of. We're fairly certain Tito gets his supply from some bigger players in Los Angeles, but we can check their travel records, see if he's visited the Bay Area," Paul said. "It's a good angle, but Mike was originally from the Bay Area. Is it possible something from his past had come back to haunt him?"

I said, "He has no criminal history in the Bay Area or here. For some reason, he started dealing once he was here. Maybe it was simply because of Gabriel Moore."

Chris said, "Or maybe he was better at hiding it. I mean, he was under our radar for an entire year."

It was a good point. "But everything we've seen in his background says he's always worked in auto body shops."

"Well, a lot of drug dealers go to auto body shops for custom detail work on their vehicles. Maybe he crossed paths with a dealer, specifically, Gabriel Moore. Gabriel offers to cut him in, and Mike started dealing."

"True. Stephanie still says she didn't know anything about the drugs. I don't think she's lying."

Paul added, "Well, nobody suspected him, not Tito or rival dealers from what we can tell. Maybe Mike was great at keeping secrets."

And those secrets possibly got his family killed. "How about the other members of Tito's crew? Did you get anything from them?"

Paul said, "Nothing, but you may want to have a second round with Tito after you've confirmed or disproved his alibi."

"All right. I'll talk to Lucy and see if she has been able to get the surveillance footage from the school." I glanced at my watch. It wasn't even lunchtime yet, but I knew Lucy was someone who was on top of everything *at all times.*

Brady said, "We can finish up the interviews, if you need us to."

Paul nodded. "Thanks. But we only have a few more to track down. Once we've done that, we'll come to you with what we find, and Lucy and the team can help verify alibis. I'm sure they'll all say they had one."

I said, "We appreciate it."

We said our goodbyes and made our way toward the conference room. As I suspected, Lucy was staring at the screen on her laptop, with Allan sitting next to her.

"You got something?" I asked.

Lucy said, "I just received the surveillance footage from the middle school—Tito's alibi. Your guy Tito is on camera. He was at the basketball game from 5 p.m. to 7:30 p.m. He couldn't have killed the Cramers."

It didn't come as a major surprise, especially after Stephanie's description of the two men as white and middle-aged. Tito was thirty-five years old and Hispanic, covered in tattoos. She said the men didn't have any tattoos that she could see—they looked like "regular guys." Which was even more alarming—just "regular guys" had annihilated her family.

"What's next?" Lucy asked.

"Narcotics is gonna continue interviewing members of Tito's gang, see if any of them have a connection to the Bay Area or any other population of Italian-speaking dealers or associates."

"Focusing on the Italian angle?" Allan asked.

I said, "Yes, and I talked to my mom. She says there aren't

any Italians in town that she's aware of. We don't even have an Italian restaurant. Other than the pizza joint, of course."

Lucy looked at me, puzzled. I explained, "I'm Italian. Both my mother's and father's parents were from Italy."

Brady said, "That's where the name Costa comes from." He winked at me. He and our other friends used to tease me in high school, joking that I was related to the Super Mario Brothers. All out of love, of course.

I said, "Exactly."

"And boy, can your mom cook. I still dream about her *ziti*. Remember that from high school?"

Mom would cook up big batches for us to eat after school as Brady and our other friends would often hang out at our house rather than going home straight after school. "I do." And I missed Mom's cooking. She hadn't been able to cook at all since her stroke.

"Have you heard back from the lab on any of the trace testing? Anything they picked up at the scene that could lead us to who did this?"

Lucy said, "Not yet, but Jonathan said they were almost done."

As if on cue, Jonathan appeared in the doorway.

"Hey, Jonathan. Did you get something?" I asked.

"We did."

Thank goodness. Could this be our breakthrough?

THIRTY-SEVEN

VAL

Jonathan began to give us his report on the forensic testing from items collected at the scene. "We didn't get any fingerprints, not a lot of foreign particles, but we were able to recover bullet fragments from Michael and from Stephanie. We ran them through ballistics, and we believe it was a .22 that killed each of them. It's likely from the same gun."

"Has the gun been used in other crimes?" I asked.

Jonathan shook his head. "No. We know what type of gun it is, and we could compare for a match if we had the weapon in our possession, but we don't."

At least we were starting to paint a picture of what happened. Two white suspects, middle-aged, dark hair, light skin, shot Michael and Stephanie after drugging them with Ambien, using a .22 handgun before torturing and killing Mike with their fists and a knife. Absolutely no mercy had been shown.

"Well, if we recover the weapon in the future, that'll help us," I said.

Jonathan continued, "We didn't find any trace dirt or any other additional fibers except for fragments from a latex glove."

"You think the perpetrators wore gloves?" I asked.

Jonathan nodded. "It's consistent with not finding any unidentified fingerprints at the scene. Latex gloves are easy to obtain; we ran a search on the database to try to match up the brand with where the gloves might have been sold. They're pretty common, sold in stores such as Target, Walmart, and home improvement stores. So it's not going to help us narrow down where they were purchased."

"How big of a piece did you find?" I asked, wondering if they had gotten a large enough fragment to get a fingerprint or touch DNA from inside the glove.

"Not very big, a centimeter in diameter, likely torn from the glove when the perpetrator cut themselves."

"Did you get any DNA from the glove?"

"No." He paused, tucking a strand of his long honey-brown hair behind his ear. "But we did find DNA—other than that of the victims."

I turned to Lucy, and she gave me a knowing smile. She knew and hadn't told us. Maybe she didn't know the whole story. "Okay, tell me more."

Jonathan said, "From the crime scene in the office, where Mike was killed, we found Mike's DNA but we also found a second profile."

Allan jumped in. "Did you find the killer's identity?"

He certainly would have, if the DNA was in CODIS, the combined DNA Index System. Was it going to be that easy to solve the case? You'd think Jonathan would've been more excited about that.

As if reading my thoughts, he said, "No, the DNA is not in CODIS."

That doesn't help us too much, unless we had a suspect to compare it to. "Can we determine any characteristics based on the DNA? Hair color, eye color, origin?"

"I thought you'd never ask."

Having worked with Jonathan on previous cases, I was beginning to see that he had a flair for the dramatic. He was deliberate in the way he spoke, but I could tell he loved telling the story of what his team had found in the lab. I humored him.

"We did an ancestry analysis and likely characteristics based on the DNA. The origin is European. White male, dark hair, dark eyes."

That confirmed Stephanie's eyewitness testimony. "Can we get a composite of what the suspect looks like?"

"The phenotyping is pretty accurate with hair color, eye color, skin color, and ancestry, but facial features can be trickier. It's a much more complex analysis and can't necessarily predict lifestyle choices, whether somebody's overweight, has bad skin, any scars, or alterations like plastic surgery."

"So, basically, you're saying it's not as accurate," I said.

"Correct."

"Does your team do that?"

"No, we don't have that capability in-house. We'd have to send it out to another lab to complete a 3D model. Our department isn't that sophisticated."

"Do we have the budget to send it out?" I asked.

"I don't know. We'd have to check with the sheriff. Even if we secure funding for it, it'll take some time. It's not as simple as clicking a few buttons."

It sounded like it might not be fast enough to actually help us with our investigation but if we started hitting walls with nowhere else to turn to, I'd ask Kingston for the funds. It would likely be quicker to get a sketch artist and go back to Stephanie to see if she could remember any more details.

"That's good information. Is there anything else?" I asked, hoping I didn't sound greedy.

"Nope, but if you find a suspect, we can match up the DNA and tell you if it's him or not."

"Thanks. I appreciate it."

All we needed were some suspects to compare the DNA to. Then we needed to find the weapon and compare it to the bullet fragments found in the Cramers. At the very least, we could start ruling people out.

THIRTY-EIGHT

HIM

If what Tommy was saying was true, we had a problem. If the wife survived, she could identify us, tearing our whole world apart. It's not what we wanted. Sitting in my backyard with Tommy on one side, visibly nervous and not playing it cool at all, I looked at my home, my kid's swing, and the tree where I was going to build a treehouse this summer. I would lose everything. I didn't want her to suffer. I didn't. I really didn't. Had this been a mistake, or was it simply a snag that could be corrected? We hadn't gotten off easy. We had suffered our whole lives.

But Mike didn't know his wife had suffered and how she now had to live with the knowledge her son was dead. I couldn't imagine what that must be like. If I lost my son, I don't know if I'd be able to carry on. I would certainly want revenge, but revenge is what got us into this mess in the first place. I knew I should have let it go, but Tommy had pushed and thought it was the right thing to do.

Tommy said, "What do you think we should do?"

"We have to take care of it. If we lose our families, we lose everything. He doesn't deserve to take that from us too," I said. I must have hesitated because Tommy picked up on it.

"Don't give up now, not after what he did to us. Our family deserves this."

I flashed back to that day, crouched down, huddled with my little brother. I still had nightmares about it, but I'd never told my wife or anyone about what happened. I didn't want them to know how my brother and I had hid in the closet, listening. In that closet, as terrified as I was, it was then I knew I would get my revenge, and he would never do that to another family ever again. But I wasn't sure I had it in me to kill his wife. I'd barely had it in me to take care of Mike.

"I know, I know. Let me think. I just need to think about how we can do this."

Tommy said, "If she starts talking, we're done." As if I didn't know that.

"But she has no idea who we are. I mean, unless somehow they get onto us?"

I had to take a moment to think about that. Could they? Would they? It wasn't beyond the realm of possibility. Maybe part of me knew that when I'd cut myself and hadn't had time to clean up, the whole thing could blow up in our faces. Deep down, I knew that if there was even the remotest possibility of finding our DNA, they'd find it.

"What are you thinking?" Tommy asked.

"Maybe we do nothing, let it blow over." We could lay low. Or we could act. I didn't like the idea of going back. It was the nightmare of how it had gone all wrong that plagued me. Was it too late to turn back now? My mind was in turmoil.

"Blow over? It's not gonna just blow over!" Tommy was talking too loudly.

"Lower your voice, Janis might hear."

"We gotta finish this. I don't like it any more than you do, but we gotta finish this, for Dad."

That's right. We'd done this for Dad. But now it all just seemed like a terrible, terrible mistake.

"Let me think. I'll handle it." Tommy had already done enough, more than enough. So much so that I worried about his mental health and what he was capable of. Why had he done it? He didn't have to. He didn't. But he had. And the sick feeling in the pit of my stomach was growing, and I knew it was true. She was a problem.

"How?" he asked, but I wasn't sure yet.

"You don't need to do anything. I'll take care of it."

"I can't let you do it by yourself."

"If somehow she remembers us, two of us will be more conspicuous. If there's only one of us, it's better. Just sit tight and keep an eye on Janis and Little Ricky while I'm gone, okay?"

"If you're sure."

"I'm sure."

THIRTY-NINE

BRADY

It was a lucky break that one of our killers had cut themselves. And based on Stephanie's description, the two men looked alike with similar features. It was a lead we could follow. I said, "I'll talk to Paul and Chris, see if they know of any friends or associates that fit the description of the killers in Gabriel Moore's or Tito's crew."

Val nodded. "I can come with you."

"I was just gonna give them a quick call if they're not in the station."

She hesitated. I got the impression she wanted to leave the room with me. Most likely because she didn't want to miss out on any news. Perhaps it had nothing to do with me, but I was feeling optimistic that maybe it was a little bit of both. "You can come with me, we'll check to see if they're at their desks, and if not we'll give them a call."

"Okay," she responded cheerfully.

Val stood up and Lucy asked, "What do you need us to work on next?"

Val said, "We need to verify the alibis from the members of

Tito's crew that narcotics already talked to. I'll have Paul forward you the list. But also, what about those phone numbers—the ones we couldn't trace to anyone? Maybe we can try calling them again? Look at cell tower data, see where they are located?"

Lucy said, "I'm on it."

"Thanks. Once we've spoken to Paul, we may want to go talk to Gabriel Moore again. Maybe he knows of any brothers, or guys that look alike, that might have wanted to hurt Mike. And now that we have a few more answers, maybe he'll tell us how he actually met Mike Cramer."

"Good luck," Allan said.

We left the room, and I turned to Val. "That's a good idea about going back to talk to Gabriel Moore. He was pretty vague the first time we talked to him, but it will be interesting to find out how he actually met Mike Cramer. Maybe it is the car connection. Maybe he was dealing back in the Bay Area, and nobody caught onto it."

"Exactly. And the fact that we're looking for two men with dark hair, Italian-looking, should narrow down our suspects within the drug community in Northern California."

"Let's hope so."

We hurried down the hall and were walking toward narcotics when Val said, "Let's talk to the sheriff in case we need to get funding for a 3D modeling of our suspects."

"Good idea, plus we owe him an update." The sheriff likely had been in contact with other members of the team, but it wouldn't hurt to let him know what we'd found.

We took a left toward the sheriff's office, and his door was open. He glanced up as we approached.

"Brady, Val, good to see you. Come on in."

Val said, "Hi, Kingston."

"Hi."

"Do you guys have an update for me?" he asked.

"We do," and I explained the latest developments and the leads we were following.

He nodded. The DNA would be useful if we could actually identify a set of suspects. It would help with the prosecution, but not in actually understanding why the Cramers were killed.

"Good. And I hear Stephanie is awake and might make a full recovery."

"Yes. We may head over there next to see if we can get a sketch if she's starting to remember more details about the two men."

"That would be great."

Val said, "There's one more thing, Kingston."

"Oh?"

"If we don't solve this soon, we think it might be worth sending off the DNA for a 3D modeling composite of the suspect."

Kingston said, "I hear that can get expensive."

I said, "Yes, but it could be valuable if we can't get a sketch from Stephanie."

"All right, let's cross that bridge if and when we come to it. If you can't get anything out of Stephanie and we find the case growing cold, we'll see if we can find the funds."

"Thanks, Kingston."

We headed out of the sheriff's office toward the narcotics department. We were approaching Paul's cubicle when we spotted him and Chris walking toward us, chatting. They stopped when they saw us.

"What's up?" Paul asked.

"We have more details on our suspects." I told them about the DNA and the physical description of the men, including the fact that neither had any visible tattoos. "Any two men you know of fitting the description?"

"Only a few."

"Have you interviewed them yet?" Brady asked.

"We have. We've interviewed the Ramirez brothers, a couple of kids, nineteen and twenty, that do everything together. They're not Italian, but they could pass for it."

"Too young. Stephanie described the shooters as middle-aged. Likely in their forties or fifties. Any other partners in crime you can think of?"

Chris tipped his chin. "No, not off the top of my head. All of the gangs around here are pretty tatted up."

"Anybody you suspect could be involved?" I asked.

"Not really. I've got a list of alibis to be verified. Only a couple had weak alibis, so we may want to talk to them again."

"Did the Ramirez brothers have an alibi?" It was possible Stephanie was wrong about the age of the assailants. After all, she did have a serious head injury, and had been drugged.

"They did. Most said they were at a party that night. Tito went later after the basketball game, but most of the crew was there. I don't know what they were celebrating."

"You don't think they were celebrating Mike's death?" I asked.

"They said the party started at 5 p.m., so not likely."

"When you questioned the suspects, did any of them seem sketchy like they may have done the job?"

Paul said, "No. We just talked to the last one that we could think of that's connected to Tito's organization."

"Let's share our information and put together a list to give to Lucy so she can start confirming alibis."

Turning to me, Val said, "Yeah, let's get that list over to Lucy, and then you and I can go talk to Gabriel Moore. See what else he can tell us about Mike." She paused. "And we can stop by the hospital, see how Stephanie's doing and if she's remembered anything else."

There was no question Val was used to being in charge. And I had to admit, I liked it. "Yes, ma'am."

FORTY

THE SECRET ADMIRER

There she was, my Valerie. With Brady by her side as usual, but there was her friend too—the redheaded medical examiner, Dr. Sally Edison. The more I saw her, the more I was intrigued by her. She was friends with Valerie, so she must have value, must be spectacular herself, like the younger blonde with the large glasses.

Now that I was back in town, I was beginning to learn who was in Valerie's circle. I had stayed away from her house since the day I saw Deputy Tanner there. And I didn't want to bother her too much. I knew she was working on something big; it was all over the news. Somebody had tried to kill a family right here in Rosedale. Very strange. There weren't many details in the news about what exactly had happened to the family, except that there was one survivor—the mother. The fact that they hadn't released any details about the crime itself or how the father and son had died made me think it was possibly something pretty disturbing. Something they didn't want to alarm the public with, as if killing an entire family wouldn't alarm the community all by itself. Surely people were locking their doors and making sure they finally got around to installing that home security system. I sure would love to get my hands on those crime scene photos. Maybe I could help out with the case. I'm sure Valerie appreciated the last time I gave her a helping hand.

Looking at the redheaded, pixie-like medical examiner, Dr. Edison, I bet she could give me valuable details about the crime scene. And then I could help Valerie close another case, and she'd be free to join me.

It was fascinating to watch Valerie with her new community. She seemed different, happy perhaps. But I think she could be happier. Part of me wanted to put my plan on hold just a little longer. Perhaps I could have a little fun with Dr. Edison first.

Aside from Lucy, who was obviously dating the forensic scientist with the long hair (surprising they allowed that in such an establishment), Dr. Edison appeared to be single. And Deputy Tanner was likely pining over my Valerie. Well, he couldn't have her because she belonged to me.

But perhaps I needed to get to know Dr. Edison more intimately, get her to tell me about her day, about the Cramer case. Her online dating profile showed a woman looking for a serious man. *I could be very, very serious, Dr. Edison.* I have to admit I liked that she was smart. The smart are a bit more of a challenge. And oh, how I loved a challenge.

It was decided. I needed to get more acquainted with Dr. Edison, have her bring me into her world, and ultimately into Valerie's. I chuckled to myself as I watched the group spread out. Dr. Edison made her way to the sheriff's station, and Deputy Tanner and Valerie walked toward her vehicle. Yes, I would definitely get to know Dr. Edison so that I could help my darling Valerie. Why not have a little fun at the same time? A last hurrah before the main event.

FORTY-ONE

VAL

On the drive to Shasta County, I called Harrison to check in. Once I was satisfied he was safe and sound, and he was satisfied that I was too, I could return my attention to the case. I was beginning to wonder if we were spinning our wheels and getting nowhere. We had two middle-aged men who had killed Mike Cramer and his son, most likely due to his affiliation with drugs. But according to Paul and Chris they didn't match anyone in Red Rose County, so they had to be from Shasta County or maybe even outside the county. We really didn't know at this point. Considering Gabriel Moore had been closer to Mike than anybody else we'd found, he was the one we had to talk to next.

We parked in front of the home we'd been at just a few days earlier. Brady said, "Do you think he'll talk to us?"

"Now that we know more about Mike, perhaps. Maybe if he sees that we understand what's been going on, he'll be more forthcoming and give us some insight into who may have done this."

"Any chance it was random?"

"There's always a chance it was random, but I don't think

so. It was premeditated. It's pretty obvious to me Mike was the target of the attack. But what if we're looking at it from all the wrong angles? What if it was someone Mike barely knew, and it was a situation where he made the wrong guys mad. There's always the possibility we haven't even scratched the surface of who might've done this. If that's the case, we may never catch them. Unless..."

"Unless what?" Brady asked.

"There are many reasons why people kill. It could've been a robbery gone really wrong, even though nothing was taken. Something could've spooked them while they were torturing him, and they fled before taking anything. We can't rule anything out at this point, except that we know it was two men who perpetrated this crime. Two dangerous men we need to find and get off the streets."

Brady nodded. "Agreed. Let's go tell Gabriel what's what."

I stepped out of the vehicle and headed to the front door. I didn't get very far as Gabriel stepped outside and walked toward us.

"Mr. Moore," I called out.

He hurried toward us in flip-flops. "Hey. I've been hearing that you guys are talking to everybody."

I said, "That's right, and we need to talk to you again. We need you to tell us the truth."

"Look, talking to you could get me into trouble, you know what I mean? People are always watching," he said, glancing around us.

His paranoid demeanor made me wonder if he was high, or if something had spooked him. I knew the DEA had been watching, and so had the Shasta County narcotics department. But were there other people that Gabriel feared?

"Look, we just need some information. We've been piecing together what Mike was up to prior to his death. We think we understand what happened, but we don't know who else did."

"What things?"

"Well, since we spoke to you last, we've learned that Mike had been dealing drugs, fentanyl specifically, in Red Rose County."

Gabriel was fidgeting with his clothes, acting real twitchy. Something definitely had him spooked.

"We need you to tell us more about Mike. How long ago did you meet him, and how did you meet him? Those are pretty easy questions, right, Gabriel?"

"I... Look, I met Mike at the auto body shop he worked at. Okay, he did some work on my car, and then he worked on my friends' cars too. That part's true."

"How long ago was this?"

"Five years."

But Mike had only been dealing for a year. "So, you kept in touch during that time?"

"Nah."

"So what changed for him to start his side business?"

"Yes, that's the thing. You see, about his side business, I'm not gonna say anything about it. I'm just saying if he did, he came to me with some money problems, asked if there was anything I could do to help him out. Said he had experience moving product."

"He said he had experience?" I asked, surprised.

"Perhaps."

"Did he say he was dealing back in the Bay Area?"

Gabriel shook his head. "He said he didn't want to get into it, but he knew how the business worked."

How did Mike know how "the business" worked? "Can you elaborate?"

"No. I didn't ask too many questions and he wasn't offering. But I was curious. He seemed so straight, you know, but also one of the guys, you know what I mean?"

One of the guys? Like gang members? "Here's the thing: forensic tests came back. We have DNA from his killer."

Gabriel looked around nervously. "Okay."

"We need to know who you think could've done this. You don't want this kind of guy running around, do you?"

"I don't, but I can't be out here naming names. You got to know that, right?"

With a nod, I said, "Look, how about we bring you in, you tell us what you know, and then we let you go?"

"No, thanks. You asking around is already getting me some heat here in Shasta. I don't need any more."

"You're getting heat?" Brady said.

"Nobody knew about the fentanyl coming in from Shasta. Not until this investigation. Now, the crew's a little nervous."

If dealers, like Tito, in Red Rose County really didn't know about Mike dealing, they wouldn't have had a motive to kill him. Then who? Somebody within Gabriel Moore's organization?

"If they didn't know about it before, then they probably didn't take out Mike, right?"

Gabriel nodded. "They didn't find out about it until after he died and the cops started asking questions."

"Anybody here in Shasta that you think maybe didn't like Mike or didn't like what he was up to? Maybe someone he looked at wrong?"

"No, he was cool. I'm telling you, I'm not making that up. We were cool. Everyone liked Mike. It's weird. It's freaking me out."

"Look, we know about where you get your product. Anybody down south that didn't like him?"

"No, they don't even know him. I'm telling you, this crazy stuff has stirred up some trouble, and look, I gotta get going. I'm sorry, I don't know." He turned to leave.

I said, "Wait. One more thing."

He stopped and cocked his head. "What?"

"Do you know two guys, middle-aged, dark hair? No tatts. They run together."

"You think two dudes took out Mike?"

We didn't need to confirm that, not yet. "Maybe."

"Yeah, I mean, I know a couple of guys that are new to the game. Not a lot of ink. There's the Gomes brothers and the Morales boys. But I don't know why any of them would've done something like this to Mike."

"They're friends of yours?"

He shrugged. "They're friends."

"How old are they?"

"Gomes are young. Twenties. The Morales boys, I don't know, thirties, older."

It could be them. "Where can we find the Morales boys?"

"I can't be giving locations," he said. "I don't think they did this."

With that, he went back inside his house.

We needed to find the Morales boys.

FORTY-TWO

VAL

After a quick conversation with the narcotics folks in Shasta County, we were able to rule out two of the potential suspects—the Gomes brothers. Not only were they too young, but both were felons which meant that their DNA was on file. One of the men was even in jail the day of Mike's murder, so that definitely eliminated him. That left the Morales brothers. They were known to Shasta County, but neither had a felony conviction and they were in their early thirties, apparently new to the drug scene.

We parked and Brady pointed out the window. "It's here."

"Let's go."

"Yes, ma'am." He smiled, and I couldn't help but smile right back at him.

The home was relatively new, with mostly rocks in the front yard and cars in the driveway. A few succulent plants adorned the well-kept home. I knocked on the door and Brady and I stepped back. A few minutes later, a woman in her sixties with long black hair and silver roots opened the door.

"How can I help you?" she asked, instantly distrustful.

"My name is Val Costa and this is Deputy Tanner with Red

Rose County Sheriff's department. We were hoping to speak with Louis and Jose. Are they home?"

She sighed loudly before yelling out their names. Eyeing us up and down, she said, "What do you want with them? They didn't do nothing."

Not friendly. "We're not assuming they've done anything. We're investigating a crime over in Red Rose County and we think they may have known the victims."

"Victims?" She asked. "Wait, you want to question my boys about the murder of that family? They ain't got nothing to do with that."

I'm not sure how she knew that for sure. Perhaps just motherly love? "We don't think they did have anything to do with it, but we still need to speak with them. We believe they knew Mike."

Before she could protest any further, two men in sweatpants and T-shirts with dark hair and brown eyes emerged. Each had fresh tattoos on their forearms but they could easily have been covered up with a long-sleeved T-shirt.

The older looking of the two asked, "What's this about?"

"We're from the Red Rose County Sheriff's department. We want to talk to you about Mike Cramer, the guy who got killed."

"You came all the way out here for that?"

It was an odd remark, and I wondered if this man thought investigators didn't cross county lines. Maybe he wasn't too bright.

Brady said, "We'd like to speak with you."

"Fine."

"Will you step outside with us, please?" I asked.

"Sure." They both shrugged as if it was no big deal. Neither had any serious offenses on their record. Maybe they hadn't done anything, but I couldn't help notice their faces and how they matched Stephanie's description of the assailants.

"What are your names?"

"Louis Morales."

The younger one said, "And I'm Jose."

"Nice to meet you." I paused. "Where were you between 5 p.m. and 8 p.m. on Saturday?"

Louis rubbed his chin. "Between five and eight on Saturday? That was the night of the party. We were both there, together."

"Party?" I said.

Jose said, "Dave and his friends were having a party for his brother who just got out of jail. A welcome home party."

"Where was the party?"

"Right here in Shasta. Few miles from here."

"You got people who can confirm your alibi?" Probably anybody who ran with the crew would confirm his alibi, whether it was accurate or not.

Louis nodded. "Sure, and our mom could too. She dropped us off."

"She did, huh?"

Louis said, "I got a DUI, so I can't drive."

A couple of dealers without cars? "Is that how you typically get around? Your mom drives you?"

Jose said, "Usually I drive, but my car is in the shop."

"Body work?"

"Engine," Jose added, "but Mike did do some detail work on it. He was cool. Sucks what happened to him."

These two didn't seem like hardened criminals, but you could never tell.

"Well, we've been speaking with all of Mike's associates, and we'd like to get a DNA sample to eliminate you as suspects."

Their mother, who was still standing in the doorway, suddenly interrupted. "Oh no, they're not giving you DNA for nothing. My boys didn't do nothing. You're not pinning anything on them."

"Ma'am, it's completely voluntary. They're not in any trouble."

"I don't care. You shouldn't be talking to them. We want a lawyer."

"They're not under arrest, ma'am. The DNA sample is voluntary." Protective mother. I couldn't blame her. If Harrison was being questioned by the police and they asked for his DNA, I'd probably tell him not to give it either.

Jose said, "Guess you have to get a warrant for that, but like we said, we ain't done it, so that'd be a lot of work for nothing."

"You boys come in here. That's enough."

They headed back into the house. I shook my head and returned to the car.

I said to Brady, "Let's get a warrant."

"Agreed. Do you think it was them?"

"From the brief moments we had with them, I think not, but you never know. They fit the description. And they're in the drug world, so who knows? Maybe they were high that night and can't even remember."

He nodded. "You want to grab a bite to eat before stopping by the hospital?"

Brady made a great investigative partner, and things were so easy with him. I liked our working lunches. "Yes, and let's get pictures of the Morales brothers so we can show them to Stephanie. Since we don't have any DNA yet, we can at least see if she recognizes them."

"Then we serve the warrant and get those DNA samples. We'll either rule them out or slap some cuffs on them."

FORTY-THREE

VAL

Brady and I made our way to the hospital. We waved at Baker, who sat outside Stephanie's room.

"How's it going?" I asked.

"Pretty quiet around here. Seems like Stephanie is doing pretty well, all things considered."

"That's great."

"You come back to question her?"

"Yes. We have some photos of a couple of suspects that we want to show Stephanie. See if she recognizes them, or if she remembers anything else about that night."

"You think you're close to finding who did this?"

I lowered my voice and offered a brief explanation. "We're going to show pictures of a few potential suspects to Stephanie to see if it jogs her memory."

"Did you get their DNA?"

"No. They've got an overprotective mama who told them to stop talking to us and that we'd have to get a warrant if we wanted their DNA."

"So it could still be several days before you know if it's them?"

I nodded. "We've already put a call into Allan and Lucy to get the warrant going."

"Well, good luck."

We walked into the room, nodding to the family who were all diligently by her side. Stephanie was awake and looked like she had a bit more color in her face than she had just a few days ago. It was a good sign.

"Hello."

"Hi, Val. Hi, Deputy Tanner."

Brady smiled. "Please call me Brady."

Stephanie nodded.

"How are you feeling?" I asked.

"I'm doing okay. Doctors are hopeful I'll make a full recovery."

That was wonderful news.

Her mother added, "She'll need a lot of physical therapy, and we're still deciding whether or not we want to bring her back to the Bay Area with us."

"I have no doubt you'll do whatever is best for Stephanie."

"Do you have any updates on the case?" Chuck asked.

"Yes, and we also were hoping to ask Stephanie if she recalls anything more about that night." I turned to her. "Have you remembered anything else about that night or the days before?"

She frowned. "No, just the two men with the gun and then having to drink from the bottles. That was about it. And then the different language, the Italian. It felt like a dream, but it was real."

It wasn't what we were hoping for, but the photos of the suspects might jog her memory further.

"We have a couple of photographs we'd like to show you. Do you think you're up for taking a look and seeing if the men look familiar?" I asked.

She nodded.

I pulled an iPad out of my backpack, tapped a few buttons,

and showed her an image of the first Morales brother, Louis. She took the iPad in her hands and studied the photo. Brady and I looked at each other, both of us on pins and needles, hearts racing.

She shook her head.

"No, no, that's not him."

"Are you sure?"

"Yeah, he's too young. The men, they were men. This person's young. They had lines at the corner of their eyes, you know, and their skin was older. A bit of receding hairline on both. They were in their forties at least." At least she remembered the lines near the eyes and the hairline detail. It was something, and we'd take it.

Her description was consistent with men in their forties to fifties. A bit old for your typical drug dealer, especially in Red Rose and Shasta Counties.

I took the iPad and switched to the next photo: Jose, the other brother. "How about this one?" I handed the tablet back to her.

She shook her head. "No, this is definitely not them. It's not them." She seemed disappointed, and I was disappointed too. I would still get that DNA, just to be sure.

Eyewitness testimony wasn't very reliable, especially from a victim with a brain injury. My gut stirred—if these weren't the guys, then who else could it have been? All the people we'd listed as potential suspects, that both we and narcotics had interviewed, were considerably younger. No one was older than their early thirties. Were we looking in the wrong place?

"Do you remember anything else? Did they say anything else? Any other details at all?"

She furrowed her brow, as if trying to remember. She took a deep breath and then looked at the wall. "We were having dinner. I remember Michael was complaining that the food was too healthy. I told him that's what his sensei said he had to have for his karate tournament. Then there was a knock on the door. That was unusual, and Mike insisted on answering it. It was a little strange. He came back, and they had him at gunpoint."

"Do you remember what happened after that?"

"Yes." She nodded. "I think so. I asked them who they were. They told us not to ask any questions. They handed me a water bottle and one to Michael too. They told us to drink or they'd shoot Mike. But I told Michael not to worry, to just do as they said and drink it."

"Did Mike seem to know who these two men were?"

"No, he didn't." She stopped, as if trying to collect her thoughts. "He didn't know them by face. But they said they'd spoken to Mike. Mike got this strange look on his face. At that point we had swallowed the drink. I don't remember anything after that except for the Italian, which I don't know, maybe I dreamt that."

"Was Mike's family Italian?"

"Yeah, his family was. They've all passed, but his father was from Italy."

"Was it possible the two men were related to Mike?"

She shrugged. "I don't know. He didn't seem to know them, and I don't know. I just don't remember any more." She shut her eyes, and her mother hurried to her side to hold her hand.

I gave them a moment and then said, "Is there anything else you can recall? Anything leading up to that night? Anything out of the ordinary?"

She shook her head.

I said, "Okay, if you think of anything else, please call us."

"We will, Val. Brady."

To Mrs. Jamison, I said, "Did the doctors say how long Stephanie will be in the hospital?"

"They said at least another week or so. We are checking with her insurance to see if we can move her home with us and help her through it."

They didn't say it, but the implication was there: Stephanie had nothing to go back to in Rosedale.

"Do you have everything you need while you're here?"

"We're all set. Thank you so much. Everyone's been so kind."

"All right. You take care."

As we left the room, I told Baker what Stephanie had said, and he looked as disappointed as we felt. Heading back to the car, Brady said, "If it wasn't those guys, then who?"

I shook my head. "I don't know."

I felt desperate for answers. Brady said, "Maybe we can pull traffic cams. Anyone driving around the Cramer residence between 5 p.m. and 8 p.m. If they drove near or through the neighborhood, they'll show up. Picking up some tags and checking databases would mean a lot of legwork, but maybe it'll help us find what we're looking for."

"It's a good idea, Brady. Let's get that going first thing tomorrow morning."

FORTY-FOUR

VAL

Seated at the dining table, I set my morning coffee down. Julie fussed around the kitchen, frying up eggs and making toast. Nobody would let me do any chores in the house anymore. Julie, Diane, and Margie—another one of Mom's friends—were always fussing about, cleaning, cooking, and telling me I had one job: to solve the Cramer case. Mom was getting better too and was even attempting to show me how she could walk without her walker. Julie reminded her that the physical therapist had warned against that. Mom couldn't go very far, but she wanted to show me that she'd gotten to twelve whole steps, which meant she could walk across the kitchen.

"How did you sleep, Val?" Julie asked as she turned on the gas burner.

"Not too badly, thanks. I've definitely had worse nights," I said. I didn't tend to sleep well, but I hadn't in years. I always found it difficult to switch off. Last night's dreams were at least different. They weren't about the Bear, thankfully. Instead they were of dark-haired men firing shots.

My mind was actively trying to put together our next steps. Of course there was securing possible suspects' DNA and pulling traffic cam footage. But without any solid probable cause, getting warrants for Tito's and Gabriel's crews might prove difficult.

"Did I hear you speaking with Kieran earlier?" Julie asked.

"Yeah, he called. Something had occurred to me about the Bear, and the team was following up on the lead. It sounds like they're making some progress."

Mom set down the newspaper and took off her readers. "Oh?"

"I thought of an aspect of his life that could be useful in finding him. It hit me that maybe the Bear made his living as a contract employee. The team is reaching out to staffing agencies, pulling records of people who had contracts that ended around the time of the killings in each of the states."

Mom said, "Wow, sounds like the team might actually be able to narrow it down."

"Let's hope so." I didn't mention my suspicions about the Bear being on a break and potentially hunting his next prey.

Mom said, "Well, I'll be happy when he's caught after what he did to you and all those other people."

"Agreed." My phone buzzed and I saw that it was my son. I smiled.

Mom said, "Who's that?"

"Harrison. Brady and I are going to take a trip out to the East Coast so that Harrison can give Brady's daughter, Paige, a tour around Boston. She's going to be attending Boston University in the fall."

Julie set down our plates. "A trip with Brady?" she raised one eyebrow.

"Yes, we thought it would be nice for Harrison to show Paige around, and I would love to see Harrison. What's so strange about that?"

"It's not strange. It just seems like maybe you and Brady are spending a lot of time together and even going on a trip together. That's kind of a big deal, right?" Julie said.

"We're just friends."

Julie turned back toward the stove and said, "For now."

We had been spending a lot of time together, but it was mostly because of the case. Although, I did say we should get a drink afterward, and we'd been having lunches together too. I wouldn't mind a little more, to be honest. Or at least to explore what more there could be. But I had no idea how Brady felt. Maybe once the case was solved, I'd have to muster up my old courage and ask him. Or I could let things take their natural course.

Julie returned with the scrambled eggs. I buttered my piece of toast.

"Any new leads on the Cramer case?" Mom asked.

"Not really."

"Even with all the drug affiliations, you still have no suspects?" Mom asked.

Shaking my head, I said, "Nothing viable. I have to admit, it's puzzling."

"You're hesitating. What are you really thinking?"

"I've got this feeling that we're missing something. Something's off about this."

Julie joined us at the table. "I'd say so. Who would do such an awful thing to an entire family?"

"I have this feeling there's much more to Mike Cramer than meets the eye. Sure, we found out that he was dealing drugs last year, but his wife did say that his family was Italian and that she thought she heard the men speaking Italian. But I don't know, there's definitely a piece missing."

Mom said, "I'm sure you and the team will figure it out."

"I hope so." I texted Harrison back to say good morning and that I was chatting with Grandma and Julie. I smiled again.

Mom said, "Now what is Harrison saying?"

"He says he misses being around the breakfast table with us."

Julie said, "What a wonderful boy. I can see why you want to visit him."

"He really is." He told me to have a good day and sent a kiss emoji. It was so strange to think that my son was about to finish his first year at MIT. Time went by way too fast.

After breakfast, I said my goodbyes and headed toward the sheriff's station to meet up with the team. I hoped we'd find something or at least be able to get all the traffic footage. Otherwise, I had no idea where to look next.

FORTY-FIVE

VAL

Back at the station, I spotted Sally and Lucy chatting in the hallway. I walked up to them with a wave. "Hey, ladies, what's going on?"

Sally said, "We want to have a girls' night tomorrow night. You in?"

"Yes, please," I replied. Assuming there were no emergencies on the case, considering we were nearing a week out from the crime. With Stephanie safe, a guard at her door, and no other survivors, we needed to solve the case, but at this point taking breaks could only help us to see things clearer, see if there was anything obvious we had missed.

"There's a bar in town that's holding a speed dating event. Since two of us are single we could give it a shot," Sally said, breaking my train of thought.

"Speed dating event?" I asked, surprised at the idea. Did I want to speed date? I had never done that before, but maybe it would help dust off my dating cobwebs.

Lucy said, "Yep! It was my idea. I'll come along for moral support. What do you think?"

"Is Jonathan okay with that?" I asked.

"Jonathan knows he's the only one for me," she said with a goofy grin.

She was so in love. Jonathan obviously knew that and trusted her. I wondered what that was like. It had been so long since I'd been in love I couldn't remember feeling like that. "All right, I'll do it, but it's for you, Sally."

"Oh, is that right? Are you taken? Something you want to tell us?" Sally said with a sparkle in her baby blues.

"No, I'm just not sure it's for me, but I'll give it a try."

Sally smiled. "Good enough for me. And who knows, maybe you'll meet someone."

Lucy whispered, "Maybe Brady will be there."

I couldn't help but laugh. We were like a group of school-girls chatting about boys. It was so high school. We were grown women, but it was kind of fun to act like young teenagers now and again.

"Now that's settled, perhaps we should get to work," Lucy said.

"Did you find something?" I asked.

"You know how I told you there were a couple of phone numbers I wanted to check out that we couldn't trace?" Lucy asked.

"From Mike's cell phones?"

"Exactly."

"And?" I said, hoping for something concrete.

"Well, we got that warrant for the cell phone pings for the phone numbers that called Mike. I was able to find the location and movements from the callers. What I found is a bit strange."

Sally said, "Okay, I'll let you go figure out who killed the Cramers. I gotta get to work too. We'll talk later."

I waved as Sally left, and Lucy and I started walking toward the conference room. "Why is it strange?"

"One of the numbers pinged consistently from San Jose, California, and the other one, this one's really weird, is in Philadelphia."

"Philadelphia?" I echoed.

"Weird, right?"

It was weird. "So what are you thinking?"

"We call the numbers. See if they'll answer and talk to us. Maybe it's relatives or somebody who knew Mike outside of Red Rose County," Lucy suggested.

"Okay," I agreed. It was a solid lead.

Inside the conference room, we found Brady and Allan chatting.

"Hey, guys," I said.

"Morning," Brady said. "I just talked to Shasta County. They're serving the warrant for the DNA on the Morales brothers this morning. They said they'll use their lab to match up with the DNA profile."

"Great, thanks," I replied. This would either rule them out or we would be able to arrest them for the crime. My gut told me it would rule them out. They didn't seem capable of pulling off such a crime, and Stephanie was pretty adamant it wasn't them.

"What's up with you two? Looks like you found something," Allan said.

Lucy explained what she'd found.

"And you haven't been able to trace who they belong to?" Brady asked.

Lucy shook her head and sat down at the table. "Nope. When I reached out to the provider, they were able to give me the cell tower data, but they couldn't give me names, or at least they did, but they're not real names. They're both burner phones. Untraceable, except for the locations and call logs."

"Well, we know Mike was from the Bay Area. Maybe the San Jose number is an old friend?" Allan suggested.

"An old friend who uses an untraceable burner phone?" Lucy countered.

Allan nodded. "Yeah, that is strange."

Brady said, "Philadelphia is the most odd. Who did he know on the East Coast?"

"Maybe Mike had some living relatives he didn't tell Stephanie about. He did tell Stephanie and her family he was originally from Florida."

"It's possible. But if he had living relatives, why would he lie about it?" Lucy questioned.

It was a good point. It didn't make any sense. "How often did the Philadelphia number call?"

"Once a month for the last year. Maybe longer, but I only pulled the records for the last twelve months," Lucy said.

"And the San Jose number?"

"Called a few times during the month before Mike died."

"Is that from Mike's regular phone or secret burner?"

Lucy said, "The Philadelphia number called the secret burner. The San Jose number called his regular phone."

That fitted with the San Jose number being an old friend from the Bay Area.

I remembered something. "Brady, didn't Stephanie say during the interview last night that it sounded like maybe the two men and Mike had talked, but they had never met?"

Brady nodded. "Yes, she did. Perhaps the killers called from one of those numbers."

Lucy said, "Exactly. I'll call the San Jose number first from Mike's phone and put it on speaker." She dialed the San Jose number. It rang out. She tried the Philadelphia number.

"Hello?" came a male voice from the speaker.

"Hello," I said back.

"Who is this?"

"My name is Val Costa. I'm working with the Red Rose County Sheriff's department. Who is this?"

"How did you get hold of this number?" the man asked.

"It was found on one of our homicide victims. We're trying to understand who owns this number."

A brief expletive, then the line went dead.

A hush fell over the room.

"Did they just hang up?" Allan asked.

Lucy said, "Yes."

Clearly, the man didn't know Mike was dead and didn't want us to know who he was. We needed to know why.

"Based on the cell tower data, did either of the numbers venture into Red Rose County?"

"No. Over the past month, the San Jose number never left San Jose, and the Philadelphia number never left Philadelphia."

"So they can't be our killers," Allan concluded.

"Or they left the phones behind."

Lucy said, "It's possible. The Philadelphia number never left more than a mile radius within the city. Same as San Jose."

I shook my head, trying to work out how this could all fit together. Two numbers called consistently over the last year, both locations unexpected, but neither had left their cities, which in itself was strange. Who were these people?

"We could take a trip to the East Coast and San Jose and look for them?" Allan suggested.

"Maybe," I replied. I turned to Lucy and said, "Are we sure Mike was born and raised in the Bay Area before he came to Red Rose County?"

"No, we're not certain. We don't have his records from his early years. Just his adult info."

"Let's dig a little deeper. Find out where he spent his early years, where he was born, where he went to school."

"Will do," Lucy said.

My senses were tingling. I glanced at Brady, who I could feel watching me.

"I can tell you're thinking, Val."

"I am, and I have a feeling this could answer some questions for us. It's one of the few areas of Mike's life we haven't dug into. It could be the missing piece to all of this." Or at least I hoped so.

FORTY-SIX

VAL

Lucy and Jonathan left the conference room to go to lunch, and Brady asked, "Anybody up for lunch?"

Allan replied, "My wife packed me a lunch. She's putting me on a diet."

Brady chuckled. "Yeah, I've seen you eat probably far more donuts than is good for a member of law enforcement's reputation."

I laughed and said, "I could eat something."

"What do you fancy? Diner, burger, pizza," he said, running through the options.

Allan's homemade meal was starting to seem like the better choice, but I supposed the pizza place had salad and so did the burger place. They both offered healthy options but I wouldn't normally have picked them. "I vote for a burger."

"Burgers it is."

"Over lunch we can talk about our trip to Boston. I was texting Harrison earlier and he's starting to plan our itinerary," I said with pride. My son, the travel planner.

"Sounds good."

I glanced over at Allan, who raised a brow. "Paige is going to

Boston University, and my son is at MIT. The campuses are only two miles apart. We're going to visit, and Harrison will be our tour guide."

"Sounds fun," he said with a knowing look. "And have fun at lunch," he added as he gathered his things, presumably to go back to his desk to eat his healthy lunch.

"Is it weird that we're going on a trip together?" Brady asked quietly.

"I don't think so. I mean, we're friends, right?"

His face fell. Sad or disappointed?

"Of course."

There was an uncomfortable silence. Was he hoping for more? Maybe it was time to have a chat, or just maybe see what this really was. I'd be lying if I said I didn't think of him in that way. We got along so well, and I was attracted to him. I think he felt it too, and I didn't think it was just Sally and Lucy planting ideas in my head. Admittedly it would be nice to know for sure. Maybe I would have to make the first move after all. I'd looked serial killers in the eye, I could put the moves on Brady. The idea was kind of exciting. I placed my hand on his arm and said, "Let's head out."

He nodded, and we stood up.

Just then, the sheriff appeared in the doorway with a man I'd never seen before—dark-haired, dark eyes, well-built, late forties. Definitely law enforcement.

"Hi, Kingston."

"Val, Brady, there's someone I'd like you to meet."

Brady and I exchanged glances, and I said, "Come on in."

The two men entered the room and shut the door behind them.

We stood up, and Kingston made the introductions. "This is Val Costa, she is helping with the investigation into the Cramer murders. She's a consultant, former FBI. And this is Deputy

Brady Tanner, he's one of ours helping lead the case. Val, Brady. This is US Marshal Barbieri."

We shook hands, and the implications of this man's visit set in. That was it. What we were missing.

Marshal Barbieri said, "Nice to meet you both."

We all took a seat.

"Which office are you out of?" I asked.

"San Jose."

The phone number on Mike's phone that we couldn't trace. "I'm guessing you're here about the Cramers?"

"I am. I was just explaining to Sheriff Kingston that I was recently alerted to the death of Mike and his son. And the critical injuries to his wife. It's awful."

"How did you learn about the incident?" I asked, wondering if he was going to explain why he was here. Were they old friends? Or was it for another reason? My gut said it was another reason. One with heavy implications.

"When I called Mike and he didn't answer, we checked state and national databases for prison and death records. I was shocked to see he and his son had been killed."

That was vague. "How did you know Mike?"

"I was his handler. Mike Cramer was in the witness protection program."

He was in WITSEC.

The missing piece.

Mike had a past far beyond the Bay Area and Red Rose County. Had we been barking up the wrong tree all this time? Did Mike's murder have nothing to do with his drug dealing in Rosedale, but everything to do with his past?

FORTY-SEVEN

VAL

Well, that was totally unexpected. I said, "Mike was in witness protection?"

Marshal Barbieri said, "He was. For the last thirty years."

Before he met Stephanie. Before he arrived in Red Rose County. Did she know? Surely she would have told us. It could most definitely be related to the attack on her family.

Brady said, "Who was he really?"

"Mike Cramer was formerly Mike 'The Knife' Cassano. Born and raised in Philadelphia, where he lived until he was twenty-seven. He was part of the Philly mob from a young age. He only stopped his criminal activities when we arrested him on a whole slew of charges ranging from breaking and entering to capital murder."

Mike was a killer? That didn't exactly fit with his life in Red Rose County. But then again, killers could be great at fitting in with the rest of society. "Who did he kill?"

"Quite a few folks. The ones we had him for were hits sanctioned by his boss, Johnny Greco."

"You're telling us this family man was a hitman for the mob?" Brady asked, incredulous.

"Among other things. He started out running drugs, shaking down local businesses for Greco's cut, and was into theft, mostly breaking & entering. Whatever the boss wanted him to do, he did it. He gained Greco's trust and young Mikey became a made man at the tender age of twenty-three."

That explained Gabriel Moore's statement that Mike seemed to know how to run a drug business. Like dominoes, Mike's life story started to fall into place.

"How did he end up in WITSEC?"

"When we picked him up, he chose to turn on his boss and become a state witness instead of spending the rest of his life in prison. He's been in witness protection ever since."

My thoughts went back to the monthly phone calls from a number in Philadelphia. "Do you think Mike's death is connected to his ties to organized crime?"

"We're not sure. That's one of the reasons I'm here."

This was incredible. I knew there was something we'd been missing. "Did his wife, Stephanie, know about his past and his connection to the mob?" I asked.

"He said she never knew and he hadn't planned on telling her. He said he was a changed man," Barbieri replied coolly. I could tell he wasn't convinced.

Up until the last year when he started dealing fentanyl, it seemed like he had changed. His record was squeaky clean. I shook my head. "Do you have any reason to believe his death could be related to the Philly mob?"

"We're looking into that. We're hoping you can help us. Or rather we can help you."

Kingston interrupted. "Marshal Barbieri would like to partner with us on the investigation to determine whether or not the Cramer killings could be linked to organized crime, if somehow Mike's identity had been compromised. I thought we could share with Barbieri our thoughts, leads, and the evidence we've uncovered so far."

"Okay." I nodded. Although I wasn't sure how I felt about having another "partner" on the case. I preferred to lead the investigation and it wasn't always a good idea to have so many cooks in the kitchen. I supposed I'd soon learn how Barbieri felt about that.

The sheriff said, "Val, why don't you go ahead and explain to Marshal Barbieri what we've found so far?"

Had the sheriff already checked Barbieri's credentials? Barbieri must have sensed my hesitation.

With a warm smile, he pulled out his blue and gold badge along with a California driver's license from his wallet, and said, "If you want to verify I am who I say I am, I will not be offended. It's a sign of good detective work."

Kingston said, "He showed it to me earlier." But he probably didn't call it in to check his badge number. Maybe that wasn't necessary. I'd seen a few marshal badges in my day. It looked authentic and his ID was a match.

After memorizing his badge number I said, "Thank you."

Barbieri said, "No problem."

I stood up and walked over to the murder board we had constructed that listed all known associates of the Cramers, their neighbors, the timeline, photos, and possible theories. After a lengthy explanation, leading to our current look into local drug dealers due to Mike's affiliation with Gabriel Moore, Barbieri said, "It's interesting he went back to his criminal ways after staying on the straight and narrow for so long."

It was. "We believe he was having money troubles."

"I thought he'd be one of the success stories within the marshal program," Barbieri commented. "Eighty percent stay on the right side of the law. But there's that other twenty percent who can't seem to avoid a life of crime."

"How did he get involved in organized crime in the first place?" Brady asked.

"He grew up in a pretty rough neighborhood. He had two

choices, join them or be targeted by them. He chose to join the family."

Some might say Mike didn't have much of a choice. But, then again, he could have chosen not to be a killer. "You seem too young to have been part of that bust," I said.

He smiled, as he twisted a gold wedding band around his finger. "I'm flattered. But you're right, I was too young. I joined the marshals just over twenty years ago. Mike's case was assigned to me after his previous handler retired."

The sheriff said, "Since Marshal Barbieri has offered his assistance with our investigation, I'm assuming we can use his expertise with organized crime and the witness protection program to help us out."

"That would be great," I agreed. "How long are you in town?"

"Until the case is solved, or until we can clear any connections back to organized crime. Where would you like me to start?"

He recognized we were in charge, and that was good. "We were about to head out to lunch. Maybe you'd like to join us and we can discuss how best to work together."

Barbieri smiled and patted his flat stomach. "I'm starved."

"Burgers okay?" Brady asked.

"Perfect."

Could this be *the* break in the case that we so desperately needed?

FORTY-EIGHT

BRADY

On the drive over to the burger joint with Val, I couldn't stop thinking about the latest revelation in the case. Was it possible we'd been looking in the wrong place the entire time? I was starting to think if Barbieri hadn't shown up, we might have never solved the case. Especially since Val kept saying there was a missing piece. That piece just walked through our door. As usual, she was right. She was incredible. I loved how she took charge and followed her instincts—which were usually correct. Maybe I should start doing the same—with her. I could feel us getting closer and if I was reading her body language right, she felt it was more than friendship too. After the case was closed, maybe I'd finally tell her how I felt. For now, I had to keep my mind focused on the case, despite how distracting Val was. Especially since I couldn't help feeling a slight pang of jealousy.

Barbieri was a handsome man, but married. Had she been flirting with him? There had been a lot of smiles between them. But I knew Val better than to think that she would get involved with a married man.

Val said, "Boy, did this guy just open up a whole can of worms."

"Definitely... What do you think of the marshal?" I asked.

"Seems solid. Seems like he's willing to work with the team."

"That was the vibe I got too. But I did notice you didn't mention that Stephanie was awake and talking or that we had found a phone number from Philadelphia. Are you holding back from him? Do you not fully trust him?" Val's mind seemed to work differently, and I was eager to know her thoughts on how she was going to handle the new addition to our team.

"It's not that I don't trust him; I just don't want to tell him everything. I don't want it to cloud his judgment. I'd rather get his fresh perspective. Plus, I think it's better he doesn't know about Stephanie's condition because if he does, he might go talk to her and I'd rather handle that side of things. It's going to be a shock finding out about her husband's past. She knows and trusts us. I don't want to stress her out any more than necessary. She needs to rest so she can heal."

"You don't think we should just be honest with him about everything?"

"I don't think we're being dishonest."

I'm not sure how I felt about that. To me, not disclosing information could be seen as dishonest. Like when my wife cheated on me but never told me about it. That was not disclosing information and it certainly wasn't being honest. "Do you want to be the one to tell her Mike was a killer from the mob?"

"I can be. I don't think it will be pleasant. Assuming she didn't know. If we explain why we think there may be other side activities he was into, it could jog some more memories of Mike's behavior before he died. But before we talk to her, I want to know everything about Mike's background. We don't want any more surprises. And I want to be able to tell Stephanie everything if she asks. So far, we just have a summary from Barbieri.

Having the details of Mike's first twenty-seven years plus what we already know all in one place will help the investigation. Once we put it all together we can see if there's any overlap, any reason to believe it's connected to his past in Philadelphia."

She was probably right. "Do you think Barbieri would know who owns the number that was calling Mike from Philadelphia?"

"Probably not. If we couldn't figure it out, how would he know?"

True. Unless it was one of Barbieri's colleagues. "We can ask Barbieri if he knew if Mike was still in contact with anybody on the East Coast. Plus, it could still be drug-related locals who killed him."

Val hesitated before nodding. "That's true."

"You're quieter than normal. What's going on?"

"I don't know, something... I'm just seeing things differently now, I guess, knowing that he was once a cold-blooded criminal."

"Yeah, it's kinda mind-blowing. I certainly didn't suspect it. Did you?"

"No, not even for a second. His background was flawless, but that's consistent with being in the witness protection program. They don't give you flimsy records. They want to make sure that nobody could ever find you, which is unnerving if somebody had. It explains why they'd send someone from the marshal's office to investigate."

I nodded as I pulled into the burger place. "Maybe somebody found him and contacted him, and that's why he was so nervous before he died."

"Maybe."

Glancing at Val, I couldn't help wanting to open up that mind of hers to find out what she was thinking. She'd tell me in time. I parked the car, exited, and headed toward the entrance.

Barbieri met us at the door just a few moments later. "How are the fries here?"

"They're good," Val said, with a thumbs-up.

We entered the restaurant, and I spotted Dr. Edison sitting at a table with someone. I could only see the back of the person but I would surmise it was man, based on the height and broadness of the shoulders. I waved, and she did too. The man didn't turn around. Val was talking with Barbieri. She was so focused on the case, she likely hadn't noticed Dr. Edison.

We were seated by the hostess, and once the server had taken our drink and lunch orders, I said, "So, do we know if Mike has any living relatives back in Philadelphia?"

"It's possible. He had a pretty big family, not to mention tons of associates that are still around. The Philly mob wasn't as big as those families in New York, but they still run the streets."

My thoughts drifted to my upcoming trip to Boston with Val and Paige. We'd be on the East Coast should we need to conduct any interviews, not that I'd want to bring my daughter to question members of organized crime. Scratch that idea.

"Has Mike's family been notified of his death?" Val asked.

Barbieri said, "No. We don't typically notify the family after a member of witness protection dies. They usually think they're already dead, if it's part of the cover story."

"He had been out of the life of crime for thirty years. Is there even anybody alive that would want to retaliate? I mean, thirty years is a long time. You'd think that anything related to the mob or anyone associated with it would've moved on or died, right?" Val asked.

"It's most likely. We just want to make sure. Because if anybody discovered his identity, that could be a serious crack within the service."

I said, "Makes sense."

"Do you have suspects currently lined up for DNA testing against the sample that you found at the scene?" Barbieri asked.

"Yes, a set of brothers out of Shasta County. We should get the results back in a few days."

I almost divulged that we had already shown photos of the men to Stephanie and she'd said it wasn't them. But something stopped me. We couldn't assume Stephanie's memories were accurate. Eyewitness testimony was notoriously unreliable, especially if it was the victim's testimony. Unless the attacker was already known to them, it was difficult to identify or recognize anyone—unless they had any distinguishing features. But Stephanie hadn't mentioned any tattoos, or anything other than a general description of the two men.

But now that I thought about it, her description of the two men as middle-aged would be more consistent with organized crime than mid to low-level street dealers in Northern California. But even so, the ages wouldn't really align with retaliation. They would likely have been adults when Mike committed any crimes during his "Knife" days, putting them closer to fifty and sixty now.

Our burgers arrived, and Barbieri said, "This looks incredible."

"It is," I confirmed. I took a bite of the burger and glanced across the table at Val, who seemed unusually quiet. Val was one of those women that always spoke her mind, so when she was quiet, it was a bit unnerving.

"So, how's Stephanie doing?" Barbieri asked.

Val said, "They had to operate to remove the bullet from her brain. Her condition is still critical."

"Hopefully you have a security detail on her to make sure whoever did this doesn't come back to finish the job."

"Of course. Not to worry, nobody will be able to get to her."

Barbieri grabbed his burger and took a bite.

Val gave me a look across the table, before she nonchalantly picked up a fry and chewed.

Something was definitely brewing within her, but what?

FORTY-NINE

THE SECRET ADMIRER

Sitting across from the quite lovely Dr. Sally Edison, I could see why Valerie was drawn to her. If you got past the too-red hair—really, I think a nice dirty blonde would suit her better with her pixie-like features—she was quite attractive. She was intelligent and fun, and willing to let a stranger sit with her at lunch. For someone working with law enforcement, perhaps she was a bit too trusting.

She was exactly what I was hoping for, but I had to admit she was more intriguing than I had anticipated. Her fascination with her work as a medical examiner made me think we were like two sides of the same coin. Of course, her job was to figure out how a person died, and while I loved a good mystery myself, I preferred to be the one who caused the death. She was the yin to my yang.

"It's fascinating."

"Definitely keeps me on my toes," she said sweetly.

Such a sunny disposition for such a grim profession. She was young too, and seemingly all alone up in Red Rose County.

"What drew you to the field?" I asked, genuinely interested.

"When I was young, my next-door neighbor was killed. She

was a good friend of mine. It was because of the autopsy and forensic science that they were able to catch her killer. I guess it always stuck with me, you know? So when I went to college, I decided to major in biology and then I went to medical school, hoping to solve crimes to prevent another family from having to go through what my friend's family had endured."

"And where is your family from? Did this tragedy happen here in Rosedale?"

Sally sipped on her straw, seemingly enjoying her iced tea. "No, I'm originally from Utah, but it didn't really suit me. I moved out here about six years ago."

"Do you have a partner? Like a boyfriend?"

She shook her head and color rushed to her cheeks.

"No boyfriend? That's hard to believe."

"There's not a lot to pick from up here, but I've dated a little bit. How about you?" she said, twirling her straw around the glass.

"I'm new in town and I don't know very many people."

"How about work? What do you do for work?"

Now I was going to have to lie, but I didn't think she'd mind. We were sure to have fun. Surely she'd forgive this one indiscretion. "I used to be in the corporate world. But I decided to give it all up a while back to become a hiking guide."

"You just gave up everything to become a professional hiking guide?"

I nodded and smiled. "I climb as well."

"That's so incredible. What did you do before?"

"I worked in a lab, actually."

"You're kidding?"

"Nope. Perhaps that's why I was drawn to you—you're a woman of science. I could tell you were intelligent."

"Thanks," she said with a dazzling smile.

Red Rose County was going to be so much fun.

"Where are you from originally?" she asked.

"I'm originally from Washington State."

"Surely there's plenty of hiking in Washington State?" she asked.

"Yes, but nothing compares to California. It's warmer, and not as much snow. I like it."

"Me too. Since I've been here, I can't imagine ever living anywhere else."

"I completely understand."

Dr. Edison waved to someone behind me. Whoever it was hadn't come over. Perhaps that was a sign I needed to end our meeting. I didn't need to take any unnecessary risks, not when I was so close. My time with Dr. Edison was shorter than I'd like, but it would have to suffice for now. But this wasn't goodbye. She was stunning. And I was sure we could have a lot of fun together. Not to mention, she could be the link to my Valerie—a way to integrate into her life with ease. *I'd have to rewrite my plans, but oh, I do believe it's going to be worth it.*

FIFTY

VAL

Once we were back in Brady's car, he said, "What were you thinking back there?"

"What do you mean?"

"You just seemed to give me a look like maybe you don't trust Barbieri."

Had I given him a look? Perhaps I needed to work on my poker face. Or did Brady know me better than I thought? "I don't know. I can't think of anything specific that's off. I think I'm just apprehensive of new people, in general. And I tend to be cautious until I can deem them trustworthy." This was no doubt the case. I'd always been wary of strangers, even when I was younger. Throw in being held hostage by a serial killer and I was sure my trust issues would last a lifetime.

"Well, considering your line of work, I don't blame you."

"That's why I like working with you, Brady. I know you're not a secret serial killer."

Brady smiled, and I couldn't help but smile back.

"Time will tell," he teased.

"I guess so."

"So, about Boston—you said you spoke with Harrison?"

"Yeah, he gave me some dates for us to visit."

"Great. When we get back to the office we can put the details together, and I'll text Paige."

"Isn't it funny how we text everything now?" I asked.

"It is. When we were in school, we had to use the landline."

Feeling a bit old and nostalgic, I said, "I know. Everything was so detached compared to now. Everyone is now reachable by the push of a button."

"We are," Brady said. "Should we ask Barbieri about the San Jose phone number? It must have been his number, right?"

"Let's ask him to confirm." He worked out of the San Jose office, so it makes sense and it would be nice to cross it off our list of unknowns.

"You know, if we're going out to Boston anyway..." Brady stopped at a red light and said, "We don't wanna have the kids around organized crime, right?"

How did he know that's what I was thinking? "Well, if we had to go out there and the case isn't closed, Paige could stay with Harrison at least for a night. Philadelphia is not that far. We could just do a quick road trip to Philadelphia, ask a few questions, and head back. Easy peasy."

"If the case is still open, we can figure out the details closer to the time."

My thoughts drifted to the trip. What would it be like to travel with Brady? And to see him around his daughter. I knew him as a colleague and someone who checked on my mom and made sure we were okay. I hadn't seen him in his element as a father and husband, and admittedly I was looking forward to seeing him with the kids. There was something between us, but it seemed like every time we were getting close, we were also getting close to catching a murderer. We definitely needed to have a conversation once this case was closed.

"Sounds like a plan. When we get back to the office, let's ask Lucy to pull everything on Cassano and the Philadelphia organized crime scene. I want to know everything about this guy to see if there's any overlap with what's happening in Red Rose County."

"You think maybe he was involved in other things here?"

If he was once a killer and thief, why not? "Maybe." My phone buzzed, and I saw it was the hospital. I answered, "Hello, this is Val Costa."

"Hi, Val, this is Stephanie's mother."

"Is everything okay?"

"Yes, everything is great. Stephanie is doing great. The doctors think she is well enough to be transferred. I'm calling to tell you we're going to transfer Steph to another hospital back in the Bay Area to have her close to us."

"That's great, Mrs. Jamison. When do you plan to move Stephanie?"

"Hopefully tomorrow. My son and daughter need to go back to their families. They've been here a week, and it would be nice to be closer to home and start getting Stephanie settled."

"I understand you'd like to get home, but I'd feel better about you moving her if we can provide a police escort and someone from local law enforcement to watch over her until we have the shooter behind bars."

"I suppose that would be wise."

"I'll let you know as soon as it's set up."

"Okay. Thank you, Val."

"Before you go, there's been a development in the case, and I'd like to speak with Stephanie again. Is it okay if I stop by later tonight?" I hoped that what we were about to tell her wouldn't have a negative effect on her recovery. She had accepted the fact Mike had been dealing drugs without her knowledge, but to learn he'd been a ruthless killer in the mob was a different story. She seemed tough, and I hoped she would be able to handle the news.

"Of course."

"All right. Give Stephanie my best. Glad to hear she's doing better."

I told Brady what Mrs. Jamison had just told me.

"So we need to learn everything we can about Mike Cassano's life tonight?" he said.

"If we can."

What would we find?

FIFTY-ONE

VAL

Back at the station, we met up with Barbieri, who arrived at the same time as us.

"Let's start off by briefing the team with what you told us earlier, and then we'll explain our next steps," I said.

He nodded. "Do you have all the resources you need to do the backgrounds and research?"

"Believe it or not, we've got some of the best here in Red Rose County."

"That is surprising. No offense," Barbieri said.

A *little* offense taken. "We have some transplants that are quite spectacular. Lucy, our head researcher, can find just about anything. She used to work for NYPD."

"Really," he said with more surprise than I appreciated.

I had grown to respect our county and its law enforcement team. Maybe I was being a little over protective, but his tone irked me a bit. Had I had Barbieri's attitude when I first met the team? I hoped not. "Yep, and our medical examiner studied under some of the best forensic pathologists in the country."

"Sounds like y'all got lucky." he said. "Can I grab a coffee before we go in?"

Brady said, "Sure. I'll grab one with you. How about you, Val, can I get you one?"

"Yes, please. I'll meet you in the conference room."

"All right."

I knew Brady was going with him to keep an eye on him. My suspicion about Barbieri was likely just my usual distrust of strangers.

Inside the conference room, I found Lucy, Allan, and Baker. "Hi, team."

"What's up?" Allan asked.

"You have a good lunch?" Lucy asked with a smile.

"It was fine, why?" I could tell she was hinting at something.

"Allan said that you and Brady were having lunch and took a while, so we thought maybe you were just taking a *long lunch*."

"It was nothing like that. Actually, we have a big update on the case. Turns out Mike Cramer did not start out in this world as Mike Cramer. He was born Mike Cassano, a member of the witness protection program and a former enforcer for the Philadelphia mob."

Lucy gasped. Allan and Baker said, "No kidding."

Baker added, "Do you think the wife knows?"

"I don't think so, but we're going to head over there after we learn as much as we can about Mike Cassano and his affiliation with the mob. We think if she knows more about his past, it might help trigger memories of any suspicious activity from her husband before he died."

"How did you learn all of this?" Lucy asked.

At that moment, Brady and Barbieri entered the room clutching coffee cups. Brady handed one to me, and I said, "Thanks," with a smile.

To the team, I said, "And that's our next update."

I gestured toward Barbieri before introducing him to the team and explaining his role.

Lucy said, "You know, this makes so much sense."

I looked at her and said, "What do you mean?"

"Revenge. I bet if I look into how he was killed, it'll match how he killed others. He was an enforcer, like a hitman for the mob, right?"

Barbieri said, "Yes."

Lucy continued, "If someone wanted revenge, they might try to kill him exactly the way he used to kill his own victims. Maybe the wife and kid are just collateral damage, which is what we've always thought—the target was Mike."

"But you already checked ViCAP, and there were no similar crimes."

"True, but I only went back thirty years. How long has he been in witness protection?"

To Barbieri, I said, "This is Lucy, our brilliant researcher."

With a nod, he said, "He's been in witness protection for thirty years."

Lucy said, "I'll redo the search going back forty years."

I said, "Excellent. We need to see if the Cramer murders could be related to organized crime."

We sat down. "So, our new top priority is to find out everything we can about Mike Cassano, his past crimes, and who he may have still been in contact with."

"The Philadelphia phone number," Lucy said emphatically.

If I'd wanted to keep some details from Barbieri, I probably should have told the rest of the team. Lesson learned. "Exactly, and Marshal Barbieri is stationed in San Jose, California."

Lucy said, "Oh, okay, well, this is all making much more sense now."

Lucy was from New York and was probably a little more familiar with organized crime and how it impacted the area. She explained the two numbers from Mike's cell phone that we hadn't been able to trace back to a name.

"What was the number from San Jose?" Barbieri asked.

Lucy flipped open her laptop and tapped away. She rattled off the ten-digit number.

Barbieri nodded. "That's my phone number. My burner one, the one I only use for Mike. I didn't answer it because that's not how it works. I call him, he doesn't call me."

I would have assumed he'd answer it, but I didn't know the protocols of the US Marshals and how they dealt with their witnesses.

"What about this Philadelphia phone number?" Barbieri asked.

"Somebody's been calling Mike from Philadelphia. We called the number and a man answered, but he wouldn't tell us who he was. After we told him Mike was dead, he hung up. Number untraceable."

"That is concerning," Barbieri said. "It's possible Mike had been in contact with someone from his past. Maybe his death is connected to someone from that world."

Lucy nodded and said, "All right, Val. What do you want as the top priority? Because we have a whole list of things we need to do."

"All background information on Mike Cassano before he changed his name and entered the witness protection program thirty years ago. I want relatives, their addresses, their numbers. I want to know where they work and their associates. It might lead us to the phone number that's been calling him."

"And you want all this in the next few hours?" Allan asked.

Barbieri said, "Why in the next few hours?"

Allan replied, "Stephanie is being transferred to a hospital back in the Bay Area to be closer to her family, and they want to question her tonight."

I looked at Allan and could have kicked myself for not briefing the team about my intention to keep Stephanie away from Barbieri, at least for now.

"You have questioned her? She's awake?" Barbieri asked.

"She's awake, and we've questioned her, but her memories are pretty fuzzy. I wanted to go and talk to her again since it's been another twenty-four hours, and the doctor thinks she's doing pretty well. We think that she might be getting more of her memory back." I gave Allan a look, signaling not to give any more details.

"Smart. Do you know where she's being transferred to in the Bay Area?"

I said, "Not yet."

"When is she going to be transferred?"

"Tomorrow." Hopefully.

He said, "Oh, great. Once I'm home it'll be easier to follow up with her if needed, and I can ensure she's in protective custody until the case is solved."

I said, "That would be great." He obviously wanted to keep her safe. Maybe I just needed to work on my trust issues.

FIFTY-TWO

VAL

Armed with everything we could find on Mike Cassano and his past deeds, we entered Stephanie's hospital room. Her family looked refreshed and seemed a bit more upbeat. There were mostly smiles, probably because Stephanie was going to get transferred to the Bay Area and would be close to the rest of her family, not to mention her friends.

"Hi, everyone," I greeted.

"Hi, Val," Stephanie said quietly. "Hi, Brady."

"Hi, there."

She smiled. I could tell she was feeling worlds better now.

"I'm so happy to hear that you're going to be transferred home. I'm still working on the security detail. I'll let you know when we're all set."

Her parents nodded in acknowledgment.

To Stephanie, I said, "You look like you're doing a lot better."

"I am. Thank you so much for everything you've done for us here. Any updates on the case?"

"Yes. We learned some news about Mike earlier today that

makes us think he may have been involved in something other than drugs here in Rosedale."

"Like what?" she asked, a pained expression on her face.

"This may be difficult to hear."

Stephanie's face fell. "I can take it."

I glanced at her parents, brother, and sister. They looked curious but were also braced for the worst. "We were notified by the US Marshals that Mike had been in the witness protection program."

Mrs. Jamison gasped. "I don't understand."

"Thirty years ago, Mike entered the witness protection program. Before that, he was Mike 'The Knife' Cassano, an enforcer for the Philadelphia mob."

Mr. Jamison shook his head. "This can't be right. You must be thinking of a different Mike."

"I'm afraid not. Since learning of his time in witness protection, we've been working on a full background check on Mike Cassano. There's no question: Mike Cassano is Mike Cramer. Because of his criminal past, we're investigating whether that past is the reason for the attack on your family or if there's other criminal activity he was involved in here outside of drugs. Currently, we haven't been able to find a viable suspect who may have killed Mike and Michael. The reason we're telling you this is because now that we know he had lived a completely different life before he met you, we'd like to know if you knew about this."

Stephanie, stricken, let tears stream down her cheeks. "Of course I had no idea. He was an enforcer for the mob? What does that even mean?"

Mr. Jamison lowered his head.

This was a lot to take in. Stephanie was already trying to deal with the loss of her son and husband, but now she was finding out that her husband was not who she thought he was. I'd approached the subject as gently as I could, but I wasn't sure anything could soften the blow. "He was essentially a hitman for the boss of the Greco crime family and he also dabbled in drugs and theft."

Stephanie raised her hands to her face. "I just can't believe that was Mike. He was so gentle toward us, so loving."

"That may be. He was relatively young when he was involved. He was twenty-seven when he entered the witness protection program."

Mr. Jamison said, "I can't believe these mobsters came to Rosedale, killed him, killed our little Michael, and tried to kill Stephanie."

"We don't know that for sure. It's just a theory right now. Stephanie, I need you to think back now that you know this information. Is there anything you can think of that may have seemed really out of place or out of character or made Mike nervous?"

"The Italian. I must've heard Italian being spoken."

We hadn't told Barbieri that piece of information. "Yes, I recall you telling me you thought you'd heard Italian being spoken. Mike was of Italian origin and associated with a lot of Italian people back in Philadelphia."

"The mob... and he was a hitman. You're saying maybe somebody wanted revenge?" Stephanie asked.

"We always assumed that Mike was the target of the attack based on how he was killed, but that may, in fact, be the case. We have more work to do to try to figure out who may have done this. It could be a lot of people, but not everyone would've known his identity."

Stephanie said, "Before he died, before all of this, he was acting weird. I think you told me that Taylor said that to you too. He seemed on edge. It wasn't like him. Like I said, he was so warm and loving and funny, but he was kind of secretive about things too."

Possibly the phone calls from Philadelphia. They were

threatening him, maybe extorting him. That's why he needed the money. "Do you remember when Mike first mentioned having money problems? Do you know why he would have been having money problems starting a year ago?"

"He said that he wasn't making as much at the auto body shop. Business was down."

Maybe that wasn't true. Maybe somebody was blackmailing him. "Once he started making more money, which we now know was from drugs, did your financial situation improve? Were there more deposits in your bank account? Did you have brand new cars?"

"We did get new cars. I didn't notice any excessive amounts of money in our account. But we always had enough and he didn't complain about money anymore."

"Any other odd behavior over the last year that stands out to you?"

She stared at the wall as if trying to remember anything she could. "No, nothing else other than needing more money because the shop wasn't doing as well. Said Arvin cut his hours. But then everything was fine."

We would have to check with the shop owner, Arvin, to see if that was true, if there really had been a drop in business and that's why he'd needed to make more money selling drugs. He hadn't mentioned anything like that in our initial interview, but he may not have thought it was relevant.

"Do you remember anything else at all that might help? Maybe Mike had started talking about old friends or family?"

She shook her head. "No. Never, actually." It was as if she suddenly realized how odd it was that he had never discussed his family.

"Do you know which hospital you'll be transferred to?"

Mrs. Jamison said, "We'll be transferring her to Mt. Diablo Medical Center. The doctor says she'll only need about another week before she starts physical therapy. We thought it best to set her up there, and we could start moving her things into our house."

"Is there anything else we can do for you while you're here?"

Mrs. Jamison said, "No, thank you. Everyone here in Red Rose County has been so kind. Thank you so, so much."

"You take care. If you think of anything else that could help the investigation, you have my number and you have Brady's number."

I went up to Stephanie and squeezed her hand. "You're gonna get through this. I'll pray for you." I didn't know why I said that because I hadn't prayed in years.

She said, "Thank you."

Brady and I said our goodbyes and left. We spoke to the officer outside her door, and I told him, "If anybody tries to come near the room, let me know immediately."

FIFTY-THREE

VAL

Thankfully, Mike's former employer, Arvin, was willing to discuss Mike's salary without a warrant. Not that we couldn't get one. I was just hoping to get quick answers. He sat behind his desk, slowly pulling up the records from the last year.

We had assumed the Cramers were simply overstretched, what with the new vehicles and upcoming trips they had planned. But when Stephanie explained that all the purchases and plans were made after Mike had started the side work, it made me wonder what the extra money was really for.

Arvin turned his monitor toward me and said, "As you can see here, Mike actually got a pay increase at the beginning of last year."

"So his income has been steady since he's worked here?"

"Pretty much. I mean, he's gotten raises over the years. He's our highest-paid auto body specialist."

"And you didn't cut his hours?"

"No."

If that was true, the only reason I could think of for Mike needing extra money was if he was being blackmailed. A second look at their finances might reveal where the drug money was going. Although we might not find any answers since drug deals were always in cash, not traceable.

"You worked with Mike a long time. Do you have any idea why he may have needed extra money in the last year, so much so that he would go to extreme lengths to get it?"

"No. I never got the sense that he needed money for anything. He never asked for extra hours or any side work."

Strange. Maybe there was something at the Cramer residence that pointed to where the extra money was going. "Thank you very much, Arvin."

"Anything else I can help you with? Are you getting closer to figuring out who killed him?"

"We're definitely following some leads, but we haven't narrowed it down yet."

"Possibly something random?"

"Not likely."

Arvin paled. "Oh."

"Would it surprise you to learn that Mike had a criminal past?"

Arvin scratched the side of his head. "Yes and no. He didn't talk much about his younger years. You know, when people don't talk about the past, it usually means they're hiding something. I never pushed, and he was rough around the edges, so it wouldn't surprise me if he'd got into trouble when he was young. Do you think that's what got him killed?"

"We're still trying to figure that out."

As I headed out of the auto body shop, I walked toward my car. It was still early. I had a full day of work to figure out who killed Mike and why. My cell phone buzzed, and I recognized the number.

"Hello."

"Hey, Val, this is Barbieri. I just wanted to let you know that I've got an urgent matter to take care of. I might not make it in today. I'll be in touch."

"No problem. Thanks for letting me know."

"Sure thing."

It was likely par for the course for US Marshals to have a last-minute assignment that needed urgent attention. He was only helping us with our investigation and probably already had his own workload to deal with.

As I headed out of the parking lot and down the street, I started thinking of different avenues we could explore. One was going back through the residence to see if there was any paperwork to figure out where all the cash from the drug dealing went. Also, we needed to go back further with the phone records. How long had the Philadelphia number been calling him? We had only reviewed the cell phone records for the last year. If it was only the last year, that could explain why all of a sudden he needed money—perhaps blackmail or another reason—corresponding with timeline of the calls.

When I got to the office, I would definitely let Lucy know that we needed that.

Alone with my thoughts for the five-minute drive, I started thinking about the Bear. Like I ever stopped thinking about him, like he wasn't always at the back of my mind. I hadn't received any notes, not a peep from him. Could this be the calm before the storm? Possibly he was still working and wasn't back to his evil ways just yet. Or my theory was wrong. Hands-free, I called Kieran.

"Hey, Val, how's it going?"

"All right. Homicide investigation is turning into quite the case."

"Oh?"

I brought him up to date. He said, "Seriously? When I visited you, I assumed the area was quiet. But in the last nine months you've had three whoppers."

"Tell me about it." Having grown up in the area, I don't ever recall any violent crime or homicides in Red Rose County. But then again, I was young and wasn't looking for it. Mom was the sheriff, but she didn't discuss her cases with us.

"As always, if you ever need the feds for anything, you let us know."

"Thanks. Any progress on the Bear?" To be honest, it was the only reason I was calling. I knew the team was working on it, but I was feeling productive and crossing off getting updates on the Bear from my list would be satisfying. Not to mention the peace of mind it would give me, knowing that my mother and I weren't in danger. Even with the surveillance cameras and having a firearm in my nightstand, I knew it wasn't foolproof. If the Bear really wanted to get to me, I feared he could. I just needed to be ready.

"The team is still working with different staffing agencies to obtain rosters of everyone who worked and had contracts that ended in the time period during each cluster of killings. It's gonna take some time, Val, but the team is definitely working on it. We're bringing in some newer folks to help us sift through all the information. There's a ton of it, as you can imagine. I'll let you know if we find anything."

"Thanks."

"No notes or strange things you think could be related to the Bear?"

"Not a thing." Had I expected there to be? Yes. I had. The silence was unnerving. Had he been arrested for an unrelated crime? Or had something driven him away? Could he have another target in his sights? He could be anywhere.

"Well, small favors, huh? How's your mom doing?"

"She's doing great. She's starting to take steps daily now."

"That's incredible. Give her my best."

"Will do. Thanks, Kieran."

I pulled up to the sheriff's station, ready to take on the day, and was a bit surprised to see Brady standing outside speaking with the sheriff. He was likely updating the sheriff on the case, including our visit with Stephanie the night before.

I waved to them with a smile, and they both turned and waved back. I jogged over to meet them.

Brady smiled. "Hey, Val. You seem full of energy."

"It's Friday, and I'm ready to solve a case." I turned to Kingston. "Hi, Kingston."

"Hi, Val. You and me both. Brady was updating me on the case."

Nodding, I said, "I was just at the auto body shop," and told them what I'd learned.

Brady said, "So there has to be another reason why he needed money."

Kingston said, "You might be onto something with the blackmail theory."

I explained our plans for the day, and the sheriff said, "Sounds like you guys have it handled. So, I'll let you get on with it."

We headed inside.

Kingston turned off to go to his office, and Brady and I headed toward the conference room. "You seem pumped."

"I am. I can feel we're getting close." My cell phone buzzed. Glancing at the screen, my adrenaline spiked at the text. "Lucy said she's found something."

FIFTY-FOUR

VAL

Inside the conference room, not surprisingly, Lucy was laser-focused on her laptop's screen.

"Morning, Lucy."

"Good morning," she said, without looking up from her screen.

"What did you find?" I asked.

She pushed up her glasses and gazed at us. "When you told me last night about the possible angle that Mike was being blackmailed, I started reviewing the cell phone records going back three years."

Of course she did. "And?"

"The Philadelphia number has been calling Mike for the last three years. The one in San Jose only for a year."

What did it mean? "Barbieri said Mike had been transferred to him from the retired marshal who used to manage Mike's case. Maybe it was only a year ago." Come to think of it, Barbieri hadn't said how long he'd known Mike.

"What time is Barbieri coming in?"

"He said that he had some things to take care of, but he might be in later."

Lucy peered over her glasses.

"What?" I said.

"Nothing, just thinking it would be nice to be able to ask him about that."

"I can call him," I said. "Have you tried calling the Philly number again?"

"I did. No answer this time."

"All right. Well, you've already done half of what I was gonna ask you to do. Thanks. The other is to go back further in ViCAP."

I figured while Lucy did the research Brady and the rest of the team could search the Cramer house for any clues as to where Mike's drug money had gone.

"What you're saying is that I'm basically done for the day?" she said with a sneaky smile.

"What do you mean?" I asked.

"I've already done it. That's the really interesting thing I found that you're gonna want to hear."

"What did you find?" I asked, taking a seat next to Lucy.

"I did a search. Went back forty years based on how long Mike Cassano was in the Philly mob before he went into witness protection. This is why I wish Barbieri was here. He'd be able to help us out with this piece."

"Oh?" Lucy had certainly piqued my interest. I had a feeling she'd learned something crucial.

"I found all of Mike Cassano's crimes—his murders."

"And?"

"Aside from the drugging and shooting of Stephanie and Michael and them being placed peacefully on the couch, the murder of Mike is consistent with how Mike 'The Knife' Cassano killed his victims."

"The mutilation and everything?"

"Yep. His victims were tortured, brutal stuff. The mutilation was the final component of Cassano's torture. The notes say Greco dictated how certain victims were to be treated. The extra brutality was reserved for those who had disrespected him. My guess is whoever killed Mike wanted revenge and most likely..."

"His murder was connected to his past. Somebody had to have known his true identity and came here to kill him."

"And killed his wife and kid. Why them?" Brady asked.

That was a great question. "I don't know, but it's too much of a coincidence to think it wasn't a revenge kill on Mike."

I pulled out my phone and was about to call Barbieri when the sheriff showed up at the door with a man I'd never seen. It was almost like déjà vu.

"Hey, Sheriff."

"I heard the commotion. What's going on?"

"A break in the case." I glanced at the man who was standing with him.

"That's great news." His demeanor didn't exude joy. More like apprehension. Who was the man he was with? "Before we get into that, there's someone you need to meet." Kingston ushered him into the room and shut the door behind him. He turned to the man and said, "This is Val Costa, leading the investigation along with Brady Tanner, one of our deputies, and this is Lucy Kenyon, our top researcher."

Kingston turned to us and said, "This is US Marshal Black."

The room was completely silent as I studied this man with gray hair and a goatee, wrinkles likely indicating he was in his fifties. My heart began to race. I said, "Which office are you in?"

"I'm out of the Philadelphia office. After I got your call off Mike's cell phone and learned he was dead, I looked up the details in ViCAP and hopped on a plane."

My jaw dropped. *The Philadelphia phone number.*

FIFTY-FIVE

VAL

Without missing a beat, Lucy read out the unknown Philadelphia phone number we'd found on Mike's secret cell phone. "Is that your cell phone number?" she asked.

US Marshal Black said, "Yes."

"We have records showing that you called him every month for the last three years."

"Yes, this might come as a shock, but Mike Cramer was in the witness protection program. I'm his handler."

I gasped. Sheriff Kingston Phillips said, "Not Barbieri?"

"Who is Barbieri?" Marshal Black asked.

Nobody spoke.

The sheriff described the arrival of US Marshal Barbieri just the day before, and how he'd told us the same exact story.

"That's impossible. I'm his handler and have been for the last fifteen years."

I shook my head, trying to figure this out. But Barbieri's badge and ID were legit—I'd seen them! Why hadn't I called to confirm? My gut told me something wasn't right.

Marshal Black said, "Call my office. I am Mike's handler. I don't know who this Barbieri is."

I said, "I'm former FBI. I still have contacts there. I'll call the feds and pull in a favor. Stay put." I would find out the truth.

I stepped out of the office, barely able to believe what I had just heard. Why would there be two different marshals claiming to be Mike's handler? Unless... I shook my head and called Kieran.

"Twice in one day?" Kieran answered.

"Kieran, hi. Yeah, so I need your help."

"Are you okay?"

"I'm fine." Or I would be.

"What do you need?"

"You know how I told you our victim turned out to be part of the witness protection program?"

"Yeah."

Talking as fast as I could, I explained everything.

Kieran said, "That's not good. I'm guessing you want me to check out both marshals?"

"Yes, please." I pulled out my notes and rattled off the badge numbers to Kieran.

"Give me a few minutes. I'll call you right back."

Brady stepped outside, and I said, "Kieran's checking it out for us."

"One of them is lying."

"No kidding. My guess is whichever one is lying is the person who killed Mike or was at least the person who compromised Mike's identity and led the killer right to him and his family."

"Well, considering our friend Barbieri didn't show up today because he had things to take care of, I'm starting to think maybe he's not who he says he is."

It was possible. I stepped back inside the conference room and went up to Lucy and whispered, "I need you to print out a list of all of the victims' names so we can start looking into their families and associates to see who may have wanted revenge."

"I'll get onto it right away," she said, clearly worried.

To US Marshal Black and the sheriff I said, "My contact at the FBI is working on the verification."

Black nodded.

A sense of foreboding washed over me as my mind started to match up our facts with the idea Barbieri might not be who he claimed to be. The calls from San Jose started a year ago. The calls from Philadelphia at least three years ago.

Dang it.

My phone buzzed, and I stepped back out into the hallway without saying a word to anybody. I saw Brady huddled with Allan, likely filling him in. "Kieran, what did you find?"

"Barbieri works out of the San Jose office and Black works out of the Philadelphia office. They're both legit, but I called over to San Jose based on what you told me. Barbieri is not Mike's handler. Doesn't work in WITSEC, mostly apprehends fugitives. Black, on the other hand, I confirmed, is Mike Cramer's, aka Mike Cassano, handler."

I stood frozen, processing this new information.

"Val, you still there?"

"This is very bad." Why hadn't I called to ensure Barbieri really was Mike's handler? If something happened to Stephanie it was my fault.

"Does he know where the survivor is?"

"We didn't tell him which hospital she's at, but Rosedale only has one capable of handling a trauma like hers." I paused to think this through. We had a guard on her and I was still working out the security detail for her transport. "I have to go. Thanks, Kieran."

"Good luck, Val. Let us know if you need anything else."

I walked back into the conference room and lowered my

head. "Barbieri is not assigned to Mike Cassano, aka Mike Cramer."

Marshal Black said, "Now that we've got that cleared up, we need to find Barbieri. Does anybody know where he's at?"

I shook my head. "The update that we just got, Kingston and Marshal Black, is that Lucy went through all of Mike Cassano's crimes when he was a hitman for the mob. Mike was killed in the same way as his victims."

"It was a revenge killing, and from what you're telling me, it sounds like this guy used his job at the US Marshals to track down Mike Cassano's new identity and lead the killers to him, if he himself is not the killer."

My thoughts exactly.

Marshal Black said, "I'll call my colleagues over at the San Jose office to let them know what's going on."

"Okay, good."

With a nod, Marshal Black stepped away and pulled out his cell phone.

Turning to Brady, I said, "Let's talk."

FIFTY-SIX

HIM

Another call from Tommy. I told him I would take care of it, and I would. I learned everything I needed to know and stumbled upon the perfect opportunity. But I needed to be discreet. I needed to take care of the wife and not have it lead back to me.

They knew who I was and would figure out I wasn't who I'd claimed to be eventually. Typical, the one county in Northern California with an ex-FBI agent and a former NYPD researcher on the payroll.

I thought I'd nearly blown my cover when I met Val Costa and she scrutinized me. If she called my office, it would've all been over in a flash. Although I had come up with a backstory in case they had done that, it would've meant the office would have a lot of questions for me. It could compromise my job. And ruin the lives of my wife and my child. That was unacceptable.

Unfortunately it meant I needed to get rid of the one remaining witness, and the fact she was being transferred to another hospital was my perfect opportunity.

I finally answered the call from Tommy, knowing he wouldn't stop calling until I answered. "What do you want? I'm busy."

"Is it done?"

"Not yet. I'll let you know. Trust me." It wasn't something I wanted to do, but I was desperate and we'd come too far to turn back now.

"If you say so."

I ended the call, shaking my head. It hadn't taken much to realize that Stephanie was at County General. Of course, it helped that I had followed Val and Brady to the hospital the previous night when they went to question her. I could tell Val didn't trust me by the way she looked at me and that she didn't want to share all the information with me. She was smart and she was my biggest threat.

As I waited for them to transfer Stephanie into the ambulance and drive her to the Bay Area, I planned to follow the ambulance and then take it out. Make it look like an accident, and then nothing would come back to me. As long as they could never tie me to the crime or get a warrant for my DNA we'd be in the clear. I couldn't imagine the consequences if they did. What would my wife think? How would I explain to my son that I wouldn't see him grow up?

Someone was calling me on my work phone: my boss. I had taken a few days off, a long weekend, I said, to go camping. Why were they calling me? I told them I might not have reception but I answered the call nonetheless.

"Barbieri."

"Hey, Barbieri, I'm just calling to check if everything's okay."

What does he mean "if everything's okay"? "Yeah, I'm out on the trails. It's a beautiful day up in Northern California."

"Well, we got a strange phone call from the FBI."

"Oh?" Dang it. It had to be the work of Val and her contacts at the FBI.

"Someone was looking into you, asking what your job

responsibilities were here at the marshal's office. Any idea who would do that?"

"No," I said, lying through my teeth. "The feds didn't say why they were looking into me?"

"Nope, but your records were accessed. Thought it was strange. Sounds like it may be nothing."

"Yeah, maybe it's a mistake and they meant to access someone else's."

"Maybe. Well, enjoy your long weekend. We'll see you Monday."

I ended the call. Soon they would know I wasn't really Mike's handler, if they didn't already. They'd called their contacts at the FBI to check me out. But why now? It didn't make sense.

I thought I had more time. Maybe I'd said something wrong, done something to tip her off. I wasn't sure, but I had to focus and forget about it until I was done. I had one objective: make sure that Stephanie Cramer didn't make it back to the Bay Area.

But I had to be patient and wait until the ambulance crossed into the next county. A different set of law enforcement investigating the crash would buy me more time to get home and out of the area and get rid of the 1990 Toyota Camry I'd bought cheap for cash.

They may have had more intel than I wanted at this point, but I was still one step ahead. *I would get away with this.*

With adrenaline rushing through my veins, I watched as a team of law enforcement escorted a patient on a stretcher into an ambulance. *It's showtime.*

FIFTY-SEVEN

VAL

With the crime scene team on the way to the Cramer house to search for any and all financial records of what Mike had done with his drug money, and Lucy compiling a list of possible suspects based on Mike's former crimes, Brady and I headed toward the hospital. With too much adrenaline flowing, I insisted on driving knowing that I wouldn't be able to sit still in the passenger seat. Speeding down the road, I said, "Call Baker. See if they've left yet." They should have left by now.

Brady said, "Yes, ma'am."

I drove fast, probably faster than I should have. Both the car and my mind were racing. How had we not seen through Barbieri's act? I should have called in his information as soon as we'd learned Mike was in witness protection, considering the most likely suspect capable of learning his true identity was a member of the US Marshals. Maybe Barbieri wasn't entirely at fault. Maybe Barbieri and his family had been threatened and forced to give up Mike's location, leading the killers to the Cramers' doorstep. There was only one way to find out, and that was to get a hold of Barbieri and try to get him to tell us the truth.

I glanced over at Brady quickly and then focused on the road. He hung up and said, "Baker said they just left."

Right on time. "They should be on I-5 South in a few minutes. Call it in, tell them our location and we'll try to catch up."

FIFTY-EIGHT

VAL

After Brady directed the ambulance to head back to the hospital, and to park near the entrance, I pressed on the gas and sped down the highway to tail the ambulance and any rogue US Marshals that may be following it.

They weren't too far south.

Brady said, "Everyone is clear on the next steps."

"Can you call highway patrol and tell them keep an eye out for it, and not to pull me over?"

We hadn't had much time to plan, once we realized who Barbieri really was, or rather who he wasn't.

"Will do."

I turned off on the next exit and headed back toward the hospital. We needed to try to beat them there, but it wasn't likely since we also had to navigate city streets.

Hopefully, we weren't too late. I sped down the highway, heading back north. I spotted a highway patrol unit. Brady was on the phone and I wasn't sure if he'd been able to alert highway patrol yet. I didn't have time for them to pull me over for excessive speed. I should've taken Brady's police-issue vehicle, but I was too focused on the mission and he hadn't argued.

Brady said, "I called highway patrol and let them know what vehicle we are in so they don't pull us over."

"We'll get him." Assuming we were right about what Barbieri might do next.

"Yes, we will."

Like a well-orchestrated symphony, highway patrol buzzed down the highway with a wave.

Brady said, "What do we do once we get there? If we find Barbieri, we have nothing to arrest him on."

"No, we don't. Not yet. But we should be able to hold him. If he resists, we'll come up with something. Worst case, we have him followed while we take a photo of him to show Stephanie. If she confirms it was him, we can arrest him." He fit the exact description of Stephanie's attacker: dark hair, dark eyes, late forties. Why hadn't I just called the marshal's office and confirmed he was who he said he was before it was too late?

"You okay?" Brady asked.

"I should've confirmed he was there for the right reasons. I can't believe I didn't. He fits the description, Brady."

"None of us thought it was an issue. This isn't your fault."

Yes, it was. "No, but I used to be a profiler. I should've known better. The only leak that you could get, the identity of a member of witness protection, is through the marshal's office. I should've double-checked everything."

"You're being too hard on yourself. And I don't think that's true. If Mike contacted someone from his old life, word could have spread about his location. If something happens to Stephanie, it's not on you."

I shook my head. If he got to Stephanie, her death would be because of me. And my career would be over. I couldn't let someone die because of my own bad judgment.

Brady said, "Slow down."

"We're almost there," I said quickly. We were at the exit for the hospital. I took my foot off the gas and slowed as we exited the highway. I pulled back and drove past a nondescript sedan to the left on the corner of the hospital entrance. I slowed down and took a good look at it.

Brady said, "Is it Barbieri?"

"Looks like him, but let's get to the ambulance." I added, "Get the tag number as we drive past."

I sped to the entrance of the hospital. I could see the ambulance, and parking the car on the street, I jumped out and raced toward it. At the driver's window, I pulled out my ID and held it up to the glass. "I'm Val Costa, and this is Deputy Tanner."

Brady arrived a second later and flashed his badge. "I'm Deputy Tanner."

The driver rolled down the window. "All set?" I asked.

He replied, with a "Yes, ma'am."

I waved at Deputy Baker, and Deputy Smith, aka Gary, who were standing in front of one of the patrol cars behind the ambulance and hurried toward the back of the vehicle.

Baker said, "We have two deputies outside Stephanie's room. What's the latest?"

"Barbieri is parked down the street in a beige Camry."

Brady said, "I'd like you and Gary to come with me to bring Barbieri into custody."

"On what grounds?" Baker asked

Brady said, "Just for questioning."

"What if he refuses to come with us?"

I said, "Arrest him for reckless driving."

Brady eyed me. "It's something."

I shrugged.

To Baker he said, "Let's go."

As they were about to rush off, I said, "Be careful."

Brady gave me a quick nod as he jogged down the street with Baker and Smith.

The driver came over and opened up the back of the ambulance.

It was empty.

Exactly as planned.

Our trap had worked.

We were going to get this guy.

My positivity evaporated at the sound of three loud pops.

As my heart nearly beat out of my chest, all I could think was, *please Lord, let Brady be okay.*

FIFTY-NINE

VAL

I sprinted down the street in the direction of the gunfire. Thankfully the shots had stopped, but I could see Baker lying on the ground against the car. Smith was down. And to the right I could see Brady with his service weapon pointed at the man on the ground. Barbieri. Relief rushed through me. Ignoring the desire to run and place my arms around Brady to let him know how happy I was he was okay, I rushed over to Baker. "Baker, are you okay?" I looked him over. Gun shot to the upper torso. Not his heart. He'd likely make it. Thankfully, we were at a hospital.

With a grimace he said, "I need a bus. But I'll live."

"They're on the way. Keep applying pressure, like you're doing."

I rushed over to Gary. He was unconscious. Shot to the neck. I was about to pull off my shirt to stop the bleeding when I heard heavy footfall. A male voice said, "We've got it, ma'am."

Looking up, I saw four people in scrubs. They soon became two, as the others hurried past in a blur as they headed toward Baker. I stood up and made my way over to Brady. I gave him a quick smile before looking down at Barbieri. He was awake but bloody. Brady said, "Hit to the shoulder. He'll be fine. *Unless he moves.*"

Nodding, I said, "Medics are attending to Baker and Gary. When they're done, they can help our new friend." I pulled my weapon, in case Barbieri thought he still had a chance. He didn't. And there was no way we'd allow him to get away with suicide by cop. He would pay for what he did. And he would have to live with the fact his family would know what he'd done. I knew that was a far worse punishment than death.

"What happened?" I asked, as we waited for the other deputies who had stayed back to call it in.

"Baker approached. Barbieri fired before getting out of the car, and once out he fired at Gary and then I shot him, and he went down."

Brady could have been killed. Fighting back tears that were threatening to escape, I said, "The gun?"

"Kicked it over there."

I spotted it about ten feet away.

Two deputies approached. "Backup is on the way, Val."

"Thanks. The weapon is over there. Bag it."

With a nod, they walked over and one of them placed the gun in an evidence bag.

Sirens sounded in the distance.

Was it over?

It couldn't be. There were two suspects. Not one. Who else had been involved? And where were they?

SIXTY

VAL

Twenty minutes later, I made my way to Stephanie's hospital room. Mrs. Jamison looked horrified. "Is everything okay?"

Glancing down at my shirt, I realized I had Gary's blood on the front and on the sleeve from when I checked his pulse.

"There was an incident." I explained how we had set up a decoy ambulance in the event the shooter would go after Stephanie. It was very last minute but we'd pulled it off and one suspect was currently cuffed to a gurney. I'd left out the part about how two of our own had been shot. Baker would be fine, but Gary was headed for surgery.

"But there were two shooters, right, honey?" Mrs. Jamison asked Stephanie.

She nodded.

"We plan to question the suspect once his wounds have been tended to." We still didn't know if Barbieri was the shooter or just a conduit for the killings. I was about to show Stephanie the photo of Barbieri when my phone buzzed.

"Give me a second, please." I pulled out my phone and stepped outside the room.

"I just heard there was a shooting at the hospital. Is everyone okay?" Lucy asked.

After explaining the situation, I said, "We'll need positive thoughts for Gary."

"Of course. Anything else I can do?"

"Have you learned anything new?" That would be helpful.

"I compiled a list of Mike Cramer's murder victims. There weren't any with the last name of Barbieri. But one of the reports said that at one scene where a man, Ricardo Bonano, was murdered they found two boys hiding in a closet. Bonano's sons."

Had Barbieri worked with the Bonano family?

Lucy said, "So, I looked into Bonano's background. It turns out that Bonano's wife had remarried after his death. She married a man named Sal Barbieri. The couple raised her two sons: Ricardo and Thomas Barbieri. The boys had witnessed their father's brutal murder."

Knowing how Mike Cramer used to torture and kill his victims, I couldn't help but feel a pang of sympathy for the boys. I took a deep breath. "It's them. They did this." I needed proof. "Can you text me a photo of Thomas?"

"You bet. I'll send it over now."

"Okay, I'm going to put you on hold for a minute."

I hurried back into the room and pulled up a photo of Ricardo Barbieri. "Stephanie, can you look at this photo and tell me if you recognize the man?"

"Sure."

Handing her the phone, I said, "Take your time."

What if I had double-checked Barbieri's story earlier? We wouldn't be in this situation right now. Her eyes opened wide. "That's him. That's one of them."

"Are you sure?"

Nodding furiously, she said, "One hundred percent." She handed the phone back to me.

I swiped the screen and pulled up Thomas' driver's license photo. "How about him? Have you seen him before?"

She took the phone and studied the screen.

Shaking her head in disbelief. "Yes, that's the other one. Who are they? Why did they do this?"

It wasn't exactly procedure, but it was enough for me. "We're still working out the details. But we have one in custody. He can't get to you, ever."

"The other one?" Mrs. Jamison asked.

"We're working on it. Excuse me."

Stepping aside, blood pumping, I said to Lucy, "I just got a positive ID on both. Can you get someone to call down to the local PD and pick up Thomas Barbieri?"

"Yes, Thomas Barbieri, aged fifty-one, lives in San Jose, California, which is also where Ricardo Barbieri lives."

I shook my head. Would revenge destroy Barbieri's family because of his need to avenge his father's death? And Stephanie's life would be forever changed by the death of her husband and son. Even though her husband had done some terrible, terrible things in his time, it didn't make it right. I looked over at Stephanie and her mother and nodded.

"Thanks, Lucy. I'll talk to you later."

"All right. I'll let you know when they pick him up."

I ended the call and turned back to Stephanie and her mother. "That was the sheriff's department. They're calling down to the local police department in the Bay Area to pick up the man we believe is the second shooter. You're safe now. I'm not going to let anything happen to you."

SIXTY-ONE

VAL

Exhausted, I slid into the booth next to Lucy.

"What a day, huh?" she said.

"Seriously," I replied.

Sally added, "Well, if you wanted to cancel tonight, it wouldn't have been a problem."

We'd had to push back the time for our dinner due to all the activity of the day, so there was no speed dating. "No, there's no need. I need to eat, and drink. Plus, we have both brothers in custody. Thomas is in custody with the San Jose Police Department, and Ricardo, the US Marshal who found Mike Cramer, is in the hospital but will be released into police custody tomorrow morning. And I just heard that Gary is out of surgery. They think he'll make it."

Lucy said, "Good. And I'm sure once all the forensics are complete, it'll be a slam dunk case for the prosecution."

"It will." The DNA from the Barbieris was being processed. I had no doubt one of them would be a match to the second contributor we'd found at the scene. Not to mention we had Stephanie's eyewitness testimony. Once the DNA was a match there was no way they'd ever go free. I just hoped they pleaded to a deal so Stephanie didn't have to endure the trauma of a trial.

Lucy said, "Oh, and there's one more thing. *Such a crazy day.* One of our folks in the research department was able to find one of the neighbors on the same street as the Cramers who had a doorbell cam. We found one suspicious vehicle with a stolen license plate."

"A stolen car or just a stolen license plate?" I asked.

"Just a stolen license plate. We believe the vehicle, based on some of the markings, is likely a rental."

"Did you see if Barbieri had any rental vehicles?"

"I'm so glad you asked," Lucy said in a sing-song voice as the server approached.

The server said, "Hi, ladies, what can I get you?"

"Red wine, anything you've got," I said with a smile.

"You got it. And for you, miss?"

Lucy said, "I'll have a gin and tonic."

"And I will also have a glass of red wine," Sally added.

"Coming right up." As the server hurried away, Lucy said, "Barbieri rented a car the day before the shooting, and then returned it the day after the shooting to the San Jose airport."

Sally said, "Excellent. I'd say the case is just about closed. Both of the bad guys are in custody. Now we celebrate!"

"Yeah..." Lucy said hesitantly.

"Why the hesitation?" Sally asked.

"Because I read the file. What those boys witnessed would mess anybody up for life. Mike was a serious monster. The photos..."

The Barbieri brothers' lives could have been completely different if Mike hadn't killed their father. For one, they likely wouldn't have gone on to become killers themselves. And if I were being honest, I didn't feel too bad for Mike and what he got. But his wife and son didn't deserve it, and what they did to them was unforgivable. "I guess that's true, but they could've chosen not to kill an innocent child and try to kill its mother too. They destroyed Stephanie's family. And that's not right."

Lucy said, "You're right. It's just so sad, you know? If Cramer hadn't murdered their father, they probably wouldn't have murdered Stephanie's family. The cycle of violence and heartbreak—for what?"

"I wonder if they think it was worth it." We would be interviewing them both once Thomas was transferred to Red Rose County. I couldn't help but wonder if Barbieri joined the marshals only to get revenge against his father's killer. If he had, I could only surmise he'd lived a tortured existence.

"At least Stephanie and her family are safe back in the Bay Area," Sally said.

I said, "That is the one silver-ish lining. Stephanie survived, although with the trauma she's been through, I wonder if she wishes she hadn't. If I'd witnessed the murder of my son, and my husband—a man I loved—taken away from me violently... I don't know how I'd go on. My mom went through it when my father died, but she still had us. If her entire family had been murdered, who knows. I don't know how anyone can go on after a tragedy like that." My thoughts drifted back to seeing Brady after the shooting. My reaction to him being safe and sound was intense. Had I already fallen for him? How had I missed that?

Our drinks were set on the table. The three of us raised our glasses.

I said, "To justice."

"Another win for the good guys," Sally said.

"And the good gals too," Lucy added with a smile, and we all took a sip of our drinks.

I was tired, but part of me knew that being out with Sally and Lucy was exactly what I needed.

Sally set down her wine and said, "So... I have some news."

"News?" I asked. Of the romantic kind?

Lucy said, "Did you meet a guy? I want every single detail."

I couldn't help but think how nice it was to turn off the horror of the day and spend some time with my girlfriends.

Sally said, "It is. I met someone. It's so new—it was just yesterday, actually. I was sitting at the restaurant having lunch by myself, just a quick salad, you know, and a man came up to me and asked if he could join me. I said sure, why not. He was really good-looking. Tall, muscular—not too much, but you know, you can tell he works out. Beautiful blue eyes, sandy blond hair. Anyways, we had lunch together. He's just moved here. He used to be a lab scientist. I guess he worked in a lab doing analytical chemistry, and he decided that he was tired of the corporate world and gave it all up to become a hiking guide."

Just moved to town? Beautiful blue eyes? "Where is he from?" I asked.

"Washington State."

"Why did he come to Red Rose County?" I asked, sounding a little more accusatory than I'd intended.

"He said it was beautiful, and the weather is better than Washington State," Sally said with a smile.

"Are we gonna run a full background on him?" Lucy asked.

I smiled and patted Lucy on the arm. "I'm glad I'm not the only one who thinks that way."

Sally chuckled. "Oh no, he's harmless," she said. "And we're going out again this weekend."

"I hope it all works out for you. But be careful. You never know. Maybe we should look into him before you see him again."

"Oh, don't be silly. I can handle myself."

Lucy and I exchanged glances. We would most definitely conspire to learn all about this guy because my gut was screaming, *Caution!*

Sally obviously noticed. She said, "Seriously. I can handle myself. I can shoot." That made me feel a little better.

"Speaking of..." Lucy said. "What's up with you and Brady?"

What was she referring to? "Why do you ask?"

Sally gave me a little side eye. "C'mon. You two are taking a trip together soon. And the sparks have been flying."

Lucy smiled. "Like it's the Fourth of July!"

"What do you mean?" I asked, surprised by their interpretation.

Lucy said, "You seriously don't know?"

Dumbfounded, I was silent.

Lucy continued. "The little glances. The small smiles. Sitting and standing close together. Touching his arm. Planning a trip together. If I didn't know you, I'd be certain the two of you were an item."

Sally nodded emphatically.

Was all of that true? Thinking back... *Yes, it was.* And everyone had noticed. My cheeks warmed. "Nothing has happened. But, I admit, I nearly had a heart attack when I heard the shots fired. All I could think was, please let Brady be okay."

Lucy said, "I think you like him. *A lot.*"

I sighed. "I think I do."

"Finally! You've actually said what we've all known for months. Took you long enough," she said with a laugh. "Now that's something to celebrate."

A grin spread across my face as I raised my glass and thought I was definitely going to need a second round.

SIXTY-TWO

VAL

Sunday afternoon, I strolled into the sheriff's station. We had gotten news from the crime scene recovery team that they had figured out where Mike's drug money had gone, and we had both Ricardo and his brother Thomas Barbieri in custody.

We were about to learn the truth, although we had already pieced together a picture of what we believed had happened and why. From my conversations with Stephanie and her mother, Stephanie needed to know the details for her to be able to move on. She was recovering well in the Bay Area, but she wanted to understand why this had happened to her family, and I couldn't blame her.

Brady and I planned to do a road trip to the Bay Area to talk to her once everything had been wrapped up. As devastating as the news would be to Stephanie and her family, sometimes the "why" didn't make it any better, but at least they'd have answers.

I waved at CSI Specialist Swanson.

He said, "Did you hear?"

"I did. Sounds like Mike was stashing money in offshore accounts. My guess is that after Barbieri called him the first time, Mike was planning to go on the run to keep his family safe."

"That would be my guess too. Nothing else makes sense."

"Thanks for working on this so quickly."

"Anytime. I hope to see you around."

I waved and continued down the hall. I spotted Brady, and my body warmed. Trying to play it cool, I said, "How are they doing?"

"Thomas seems to be the most on edge, doesn't wanna talk. Ricardo, on the other hand, I think he knows his goose is cooked."

"Hopefully he'll tell us exactly what happened. Maybe we can even cut a deal so we don't have to prolong this any further and not put Stephanie through a trial. That would be cruel."

"We're going to try everything we can to make sure they don't go to trial."

"Is the DA here?"

"He said he'd come down if they're willing to make a deal. No matter what, they'll go to prison, and likely won't be eligible for parole. From what I know of Ricardo, he won't want to put his own family through a trial. As it is, the news is spreading fast."

"Let's hope they plead out."

With a nod, we continued to the interview room. Ricardo's door was guarded by Deputy Baker. He opened the door, and I stepped inside.

"Barbieri," I said, taking the seat in front of him.

He sat silently.

When he was arrested he'd been read his rights, and he had yet to ask for a lawyer. That was good news for us. It meant we could go at him and hopefully get him to confess.

I said, "Your brother, Thomas, is next door. Santa Clara County Sheriff's department picked him up Friday night and brought him to us. It's over."

He eyed me. "How did you know it was me? Did you check with my office? My boss called me and told me somebody was looking into my file. I assumed it was you. You were always suspicious of me."

That must have been why he had been suddenly pulled away and couldn't meet us at the station. When we'd thought he was honest, I had assumed he had urgent marshal business to attend to and didn't think much of it. "True. But Mike's actual handler, a marshal from Philadelphia, was also suspicious."

He shook his head like he had been defeated. He had been.

Brady said, "We're here to get your official statement, as well as present terms for a plea from our district attorney. If you agree, he'll come down and provide the paperwork, and we can go our separate ways. I believe Stephanie deserves to know why her husband and child were murdered. And she doesn't deserve having to endure a trial."

"He butchered my father!" Barbieri screamed.

Brady and I exchanged glances. I said, "I understand, and I can imagine wanting revenge myself. We read the file; we know that you witnessed your father's murder."

"Then you understand why I did what I did. He deserved it ten times over. Everyone thinks the mob is so glamorous. You see it in movies and on TV. Kids think it's cool to be in the mob. It's not. They're thugs with a superiority complex that rob innocent people of their lives."

Steely-eyed, I said, "I won't argue with you about that. Like I said, we've seen the files. We know what he did when he was part of the Philly mob. We know that you witnessed it. No child should ever have to see that. But you *killed* a child. An *innocent* child. There is no excuse for that."

Barbieri was red-faced, tears forming in his eyes. Shaking his head, he said, "My dad wasn't even connected. Do you know why he tortured and killed my father? Do you?" He swallowed. "Because he wouldn't pay the Greco tax! My father was a legitimate businessman just trying to provide for his family. I hope Mike rots in hell!"

Ricardo's pain was deep, and I could feel it. And if he hadn't killed Michael Junior and tried to kill Stephanie I would have felt sorry for him and hoped his deal had a reduced sentence. But he and his brother had killed an innocent child. There were no free passes or reduced sentences for that. Nor was there any sympathy.

Brady said, "What Mike did is unforgivable. I'm sorry that happened to you and your family. But that's not why we're here."

Although from what we'd read in Mike's file, the torture and mutilation was an order from Greco. Maybe Mike hadn't always been a villain, rather he'd been made into one. Perhaps he'd been relived when he was caught and cut a deal? We'd never know.

I glanced at Brady and was touched by his empathy.

Barbieri fidgeted and said, "So what now? I know you have evidence."

I said, "Yes, we do have evidence. As you know, because we disclosed everything we had about the case when you presented yourself as Mike's handler. We have DNA from the scene matching your brother's DNA. We have Stephanie's eyewitness testimony that you were there. You had motive, you had the means, and you had the opportunity. We even have your rental car on videotape near the Cramer house. You rented the car the day before you left for Red Rose County and returned it to San Jose Mineta airport the day after the murders. Ballistics match the gun that you used to shoot Deputy Baker and Deputy Smith with. There's no way out of this."

He nodded. "What's the deal?"

"Not so fast," Brady said.

"Stephanie doesn't know what happened to her husband. She assumed he was shot just like she and her twelve-year-old son had been. We want to understand, in your own words, why you did this. You've been planning it since you were a child. She's gonna have a hundred questions, and I think you owe her answers, as somebody like yourself who has witnessed such a tragedy. Don't you think she deserves answers?"

He closed his eyes, and pulled at his thick, dark hair, and then looked up. "It wasn't supposed to turn out like that. We wanted to find him, but unfortunately, by the time we did, he was married with a child. They weren't supposed to die."

Michael and Stephanie weren't supposed to die? "Why did you join the US Marshals?"

"I wanted to see criminals go to jail."

Was he not seeing the obvious fact that he had become one of them?

"Not to find Mike?"

"That was part of it. I knew he'd made a deal and was in witness protection. I looked it up when I got older."

"How did you find him?"

"After I had enough seniority, I got a few people to talk to me. Thinking I was just talking old mob stories and learned how the ones put into Witsec were given new identities. They don't change birthdays in Witsec. So, I searched and found Mike. He even had the same initials, which is common in the program. And when I was fairly sure it was him, I called him to make sure."

"You called him for a year? Why?"

"To make sure it was him."

That took a year? No. "You taunted him for a year."

"He deserved to be nervous. I told him what I was going to do to him, a few weeks beforehand. I don't think he believed me."

"So what about Stephanie and little Michael? Did you have to hurt them?"

His face reddened. "They weren't supposed to die."

Glaring at him, I said, "A gunshot to the head would do it. I assume you know that."

He shook his head. "We drugged them. I didn't want them to see what we'd seen. But..."

"But what?" I said.

He hesitated.

I said, "No matter what you say, both you and your brother are going away for life."

Resigned, he sighed and said, "Tommy got nervous that the boy and his wife would ID us. I told him they had no idea who we were. I should've known."

"What should you have known?"

"Tommy couldn't let it go. He's never been able to move past it. Tommy said he'd go and kill him all by himself. I knew he'd get caught. So I agreed to go after Mike, drug his family, and then tie him up. While he was restrained in the other room, we were going to make it seem like we'd killed them before turning the gun on Mike. But I underestimated Tommy's rage. He thought a single gunshot was too kind." He paused. "Well, you know what happened to Mike."

"That was all Tommy's handiwork?"

He looked away and nodded.

That explained why we'd only picked up Tommy's DNA at the scene.

Brady glanced at me. "Tommy shot Stephanie and Michael too?"

He nodded again.

Still a little skeptical, considering he was basically pinning the murders on his brother, I said, "You didn't want Stephanie and Michael to get hurt. If that's true, why did you go after Stephanie again?"

"Because I was in too deep. I didn't want my family to know. They're going to be devastated."

"Pretty sure they are upset. It's already hit the news."

"You know I have a son. He used to look up to me." He shook his head. "Whatever the deal is, it's fine. I don't want to put my family, or Stephanie, through any more pain. From what I could tell, she was innocent." I didn't believe his empathy for Stephanie but I did believe his desire to protect his family from further pain. It was something, I guess.

"Do you regret it?" Brady asked.

"I do now. I regret Stephanie and her child being hurt. I don't regret what happened to Mike. I wasn't sure if I'd be able to go through with it but when it was happening, I was right back in that closet. He'd shown no mercy for my father. How does someone like that get to go free and have a wife and a child of their own? It's not right. And I've looked at his file. Do you know how many people Mike butchered?"

I did. "The theory is seventeen."

"That's right. He butchered seventeen people. And he got to live a life of freedom for thirty years. All to get the boss of the Greco crime family behind bars? That's not justice! As soon as the boss was in prison, another boss sprung up right after him. Mike went free and started a happy little family and life in Northern California. It's not right. Would you be able to live with that if he had butchered your father, Agent Costa?"

I wasn't sure that I could. "I don't know, but I wouldn't have done what you did. I don't hurt the innocent, and those who are guilty go to jail. They get locked up. You don't fight the monsters by becoming one of them."

"But what if they'd made you a monster and there was nothing you could do about it?" he persisted.

"There's always something you can do. You didn't have to do this. You had a choice."

"But I did have to do this." He lowered his head and said, "I'm done."

Without another word, Brady and I stood up and left the

interview room. Brady said, "This case certainly didn't end up as I expected."

"No, it didn't. Let's try and get a statement from Tommy and then go get that beer."

A smile appeared on his face, and a flutter swam through me.

SIXTY-THREE

VAL

After my second glass of wine, I was feeling pretty tingly and loose. We had closed a huge case and put away some seriously disturbed people. Both brothers had agreed to a deal, and there would be no trial. Now all Brady and I had left to do was to tell Stephanie why her family had been attacked and murdered. It wasn't going to be easy for her to hear. Her husband had done terrible things, and I understood the Barbieri brothers' need for revenge by killing Mike. But what they had failed to factor into their plan was that the people who suffered the most were those left behind. Thankfully, nobody else was hurt, and now here I was with Brady, having some alone time. I had to admit I was enjoying myself quite a bit—the easy conversation, his smile, familiar but new.

"So what's next for you, Val?" Brady asked, leaning back in his chair.

"Well, technically, my time with the sheriff's department is over once again."

"The sheriff would hire you in a heartbeat if you wanted a full-time job."

"I'm not totally sure I'm ready for that yet, but if anybody else gets murdered or needs my help, you've got it."

"That's good to know. And if I wanted to see you not just when there is a murder to solve, would that be okay too?"

"It would." I could feel my face warm and a smile spreading across my face.

He said, "I think I'm going to miss seeing you every day."

We'd only been working the case for a little over a week, but I had to admit I thought I'd miss him too. Even though most of our time had been focused on the case, there was still that discussion about our children and our upcoming trip to Boston, plus the trip to see Stephanie and her family. There was no doubt we made a great team.

"I guess I wouldn't mind seeing you more often," I said coyly.

"You sure know how to give a guy a bit of confidence."

I laughed, and the server came by and asked if there was anything else we needed. We both shook our heads.

"Going home to see your mom and her group of ladies?" Brady asked.

"Yep, they want a full report like they always do."

"I'm glad to hear your mom's doing so much better. Hopefully, you'll stick around, even though she is getting back to her old self."

"I'm not planning on going anywhere. This feels right for me."

"Really?" he said with a huge grin.

"Yeah, and I think Red Rose County is probably big enough for the both of us."

Brady paid the check despite my protest that I had invited him out for a beer, that had turned into wine for me, beer for him and dinner for the both of us. He shook his head and said, "Don't be silly."

As we left the restaurant, it took a moment or two before I

realized he was holding my hand. It felt so natural, and welcome. He turned and faced me.

"This was fun," he said.

"It was," I replied as my whole body tingled.

He leaned in and gave me a gentle kiss that lingered. Electricity shot all the way down my body. It was exciting, and I wanted to see what would happen next.

As we headed toward the parking lot, he said, "Since you've got the week off, would you like to come over tomorrow night and I'll cook you dinner? I've got some skills in the kitchen."

Absolutely. "I would love that," I said with a stupid grin on my face. Maybe I was finally ready. Ready for what this was and what it could be.

As we approached my car, I froze.

"What is it?" he asked.

I let go of his hand and pointed at my windshield. A white envelope was tucked underneath the blade. I glanced at him, and his face fell. I hurried over and pulled out the envelope with my name in block letters: VALERIE COSTA.

I should've known he wasn't done with me. I pulled out the now familiar note card.

Valerie,
Excellent job on solving the case. I expected nothing less. S

Brady said, "I'm calling it in, or do you need to call Kieran?"

Fuming, I muttered, "I'll call Kieran."

He had been here while I was with Brady. He knew my car. He had been about a hundred feet from me. I was done ignoring what my gut was telling me. It was the Bear. And I knew he would reveal himself in time; psychopaths like him always did. One thing was certain—when he did, I would be ready for him.

A LETTER FROM H.K. CHRISTIE

Dear reader,

Thank you for reading *Hidden in the Dark*. I hope you enjoyed reading it as much as I loved writing it. If you did enjoy it, and want to keep up to date with all my latest releases, you can sign up to my author mailing list, where you'll be the first to hear about upcoming novels and other author news. Your email address will never be shared and you can unsubscribe at any time.

www.bookouture.com/h-k-christie

If you're interested in exploring more of my books, or you'd simply like to say, "hello", visit my website and drop me a message. I love to hear from readers! You can also sign up for my H.K. Christie Reader Club where you'll be the first to hear about upcoming novels, new releases, giveaways, promotions, and a free eBook of *Crashing Down*, the prequel to the Martina Monroe crime thriller series. You can also follow and reach out on social media here:

Thank you,

H.K. Christie

KEEP IN TOUCH WITH H.K. CHRISTIE

www.authorhkchristie.com

 facebook.com/AuthorHKChristie

instagram.com/authorhkchristie

ACKNOWLEDGMENTS

Many thanks to the wonderful women in my life that have inspired Val and her group of girlfriends. As much as I adore my husband, I don't think life would be quite as rich without my close female friendships, many of whom have been with me through thick and thin, *for decades*. I have always wanted to honor those friendships in one of my stories, but writing thrillers isn't always conducive to such topics. Needless to say, I absolutely love writing the Val, Lucy, and Sally scenes.

I'd like to extend my deepest gratitude to the team at Bookouture for helping bring this story to life.

And of course, a big thank you to my emotional support team. For Charlie, my little Yorkie Poo for always being by my side. *Always*. And to all of my friends, family, and husband for the endless support over the years.

Last but not least, I'd like to thank all of my readers. It's because of you I'm able to continue writing stories.

PUBLISHING TEAM

Turning a manuscript into a book requires the efforts of many people. The publishing team at Bookouture would like to acknowledge everyone who contributed to this publication.

Audio
Alba Proko
Sinead O'Connor
Melissa Tran

Commercial
Lauren Morrissette
Hannah Richmond
Imogen Allport

Cover design
The Brewster Project

Data and analysis
Mark Alder
Mohamed Bussuri

Editorial
Billi-Dee Jones
Helen Jenner
Ria Clare